PENGUIN

THE WHITE HOTEL

D. M. Thomas was born in Cornwall in 1935. He was educated there, in Australia and at New College, Oxford, where he gained a first in English. He has been a teacher and lecturer, and is now a full-time writer. His other novels are *The Flute-Player*, which won the Gollancz Pan/Picador Fantasy Award, *Birthstone* (Penguin, 1982), *Ararat* (1983), *Swallow* (1984), *Sphinx* (1986) and *Summit* (1987). He has published five volumes of verse including *The Honeymoon Voyage* and *Dreaming in Bronze*, and is also well-known for his translations of Russian poetry, including *The Bronze Horseman and Other Poems* by Alexander Pushkin (Penguin, 1982). *The White Hotel* received the 1981 Cheltenham Prize and The PEN Silver Pen Award. He has also won a Cholmondeley Award for Poetry, an Arts Council Award for Literature and the *Los Angeles Times* Fiction Prize. He has three children and lives in Hereford.

D. M. THOMAS

___

THE WHITE HOTEL

We had fed the heart on fantasies,
The Heart's grown brutal from the fare;
More substance in our enmities
Than in our love . . .

W.B.Yeats,
Meditations in Time of Civil War

PENGUIN BOOKS

PENGUIN BOOKS

Published by the Penguin Group
27 Wrights Lane, London W8 5TZ, England
Viking Penguin Inc., 40 West 23rd Street, New York, New York 10010, USA
Penguin Books Australia Ltd, Ringwood, Victoria, Australia
Penguin Books Canada Ltd, 2801 John Street, Markham, Ontario, Canada L3R 1B4
Penguin Books (NZ) Ltd, 182–190 Wairau Road, Auckland 10, New Zealand

Penguin Books Ltd, Registered Offices: Harmondsworth, Middlesex, England

First published by Victor Gollancz 1981
Published in Penguin Books 1981
Reprinted 1982 nine times, 1983 three times, 1984 twice, 1985 1987, 1988

Made and printed in Great Britain by
Richard Clay Ltd, Bungay, Suffolk
Set in Baskerville

Contents

Author's Note

One could not travel far in the landscape of hysteria — the 'terrain' of this novel — without meeting the majestic figure of Sigmund Freud. Freud becomes one of the dramatis personae, in fact, as discoverer of the great and beautiful modern myth of psychoanalysis. By myth, I mean a poetic, dramatic expression of a hidden truth; and in placing this emphasis, I do not intend to put into question the scientific validity of psychoanalysis.

The role played by Freud in this narrative is entirely fictional. My imagined Freud does, however, abide by the generally known facts of the real Freud's life, and I have sometimes quoted from his works and letters, *passim*. The letters of the Prologue, and all the passages relating to psychoanalysis (including Part III, which takes the literary form of a Freudian case history), have no factual basis. Readers not familiar with the genuine case histories — which are masterly works of literature, apart from everything else — are referred to volumes 3, 8 and 9 of the Pelican Freud Library (Penguin Books, 1974–9).

D.M.T.

Prologue

Dearest Gisela,

I give you a warm bear-hug from the new world! What with the journey, the hospitality, the lectures, the honours (mostly to Freud naturally and, to a lesser extent, Jung), there has hardly been time to blow one's nose, and my mind is in a whirl. But it's already more than clear that America is eager to receive our movement. Brill and Hall are excellent fellows, and everyone at Clark University has overwhelmed us with kindness and compliments. Freud astonished even me with his masterly skill, by delivering five lectures without any notes — composing them during a half-hour's walk beforehand in my company. I need hardly add that he made a deep impression. Jung also gave two fine lectures, about his own work, without once mentioning Freud's name! Though on the whole the three of us have got on splendidly together, in rather trying circumstances (including, I may say, attacks of diarrhoea in New York. . . !), there *has* been a little tension between Jung and Freud. Of that, more in a moment.

But you will want to hear about the voyage. It was fine — but we saw almost nothing! A great midsummer mist descended almost at once. Actually it was not unimpressive. Jung especially was gripped by the conception of this "prehistoric monster" wallowing through the daylight-darkness towards its objective, and felt we were slipping back into the primeval past. Freud teased him for being a Christian, and therefore mystical (a fate he regards the Jews as having escaped!), but confessed to feeling some sympathy for the idea as he gazed at the blank cabin window and listened to what he called "the mating cry of the foghorns"! New York was all the more impressive and unbelievable, rising out of this darkness. Brill met us, and showed us many fine things — but none finer than a moving picture, a 'movie'! Despite my wretched stomach I found it highly diverting; it consisted mainly of comical policemen pursuing even more comical villains through the streets. Not much of a plot, but the people actually do *move* in a very convincing and lifelike way. Freud, I think, was not greatly impressed!

Yes, I must tell you of the rather extraordinary occurrence in Bremen, on the eve of our departure. We were heartily thankful to have made a successful rendezvous, and naturally excited by the adventure lying ahead of us. Freud was host at a luncheon in a very luxurious hotel, and we persuaded Jung to abandon his customary abstemiousness and join us in drinking wine. Probably because he was not used to drinking he became unusually talkative and high-spirited. He turned the conversation to some "peat-bog corpses" that apparently have been found in northern Germany. They are said to be the bodies of prehistoric men, mummified by the effect of the humic acid in the bog water. Apparently the men had drowned in the marshes or been buried there. Well, it was mildly interesting; or would have been had not Jung talked on and on about it. Finally Freud burst out several times: "Why are you so concerned with these corpses?" Jung continued to be carried away by his fascination with the story, and Freud slipped off his chair in a faint.

Jung, poor fellow, was most upset by this turn of events — as was I — and couldn't understand what he'd done wrong. When he came round, Freud accused him of wanting him out of the way. Jung, of course, denied this in the strongest terms. And he is really a kind, lively companion, much more pleasant than those gold-rimmed glasses and that close-cropped head suggests.

Another brief disagreement occurred on the ship. We were entertaining ourselves (in the fog!) by interpreting each other's dreams. Jung was greatly taken by one of Freud's, in which his sister-in-law (Minna) was having to toss bundles of corn at harvest time, like a peasant, while his wife looked idly on. Jung, somewhat tactlessly, kept pressing him for further information. He made it clear that he thought the dream had to do with Freud's warmth of feeling for his wife's younger sister. I was staggered that he had so much knowledge of Freud's domestic affairs. Freud was naturally very put out, and refused to "risk his authority", as he put it, by revealing anything more personal. Jung said to me later that at that moment Freud had *lost* his authority, as far as he was concerned. However, I think I managed to smooth over the matter, and they are on good terms again. But for a while I felt like a referee in a wrestling contest! All very difficult. Keep this under your hat.

My own dream (the only one I could remember) was about some trivial childhood disappointment. Freud of course had absolutely no trouble in guessing that it related to you, my dear. He saw straight to the point: that I fear your decision not to divorce your husband until your daughters are married is a self-deception on your part, and that you do not wish to consummate our long relationship by such a profound tie as marriage. Well, you know my anxieties, and you have done your best to dissipate them; but I could not avoid *dreaming* of them, you see, during our parting (and probably affected by the depressing sea mist). Freud helped a good deal, as always. Tell Elma he was touched by her good wishes, and says he is deeply moved that she found her analysis with him so helpful. He also sends *you* his respects, and said good-humouredly that if the mother equals the daughter in charm and intelligence (I assure him you do!) I am an enviable man. . . I know that! Warmly embrace and kiss Elma from me, and pass on my respects to your husband.

Next week we are to visit Niagara Falls, which Freud regards as the great event of the whole trip; and we sail on the *Kaiser Wilhelm* less than two weeks from now. So I shall be home in Budapest almost before you receive my letter; and I cannot tell you how I long for your welcoming embrace. Meanwhile I kiss you (and heavens! much worse! much better!) in my dreams.

Forever your
SANDOR FERENCZI

19 Berggasse,
Vienna
9 February 1920

Dear Ferenczi,

Thank you for your letter of condolence. I do not know what more there is to say. For years I was prepared for the loss of my sons; now comes that of my daughter. Since I am profoundly irreligious there is no one I can accuse, and I know there is nowhere to which my complaint could be addressed. "The unvarying circle of a soldier's duties" and the "sweet habit of existence" will see to it that things go on as before. Blind necessity, mute submission. Quite deep down I can trace the feeling of a deep narcissistic hurt that is not to be healed. My wife and Annerl are terribly shaken in a more human way.

Do not be concerned about me. I am just the same but for a little more tiredness. *La séance continue.* Today I have had to spend more time than I can spare at the Vienna General Hospital, as part of the Commission investigating the allegations of ill-treatment of war neurotics. It more than ever astonishes me how anyone could think that the administration of electric current to so-called malingerers would turn them into heroes. Inevitably, on returning to the battlefield, they shed their fear of the current in face of the immediate threat: hence, they were subjected to still more severe electric shocks — and so on, pointlessly. I am inclined to give Wagner-Jauregg the benefit of the doubt, but I should not like to vouch for others in his staff. It has never been denied that in German hospitals there were cases of death during the treatment and suicides as the result of it. It is too early to say whether the Vienna Clinics gave way to the characteristically German inclination to achieve their aims quite ruthlessly. I shall have to submit a Memorandum by the end of the month.

I have also found myself drawn back to my essay *Beyond the Pleasure Principle*, which had been hanging fire, with a strengthened conviction that I am on the right lines in positing a death instinct, as powerful in its own way (though more hidden) than the libido. One of my patients, a young woman suffering from a severe hysteria, has just 'given birth' to some writings which seem to lend support to my theory: an extreme of libidinous phantasy combined with an extreme of morbidity. It is as if Venus looked in her mirror and saw the face of Medusa. It may be that we have studied the sexual impulses too exclusively, and that we are in the position of a mariner, whose gaze is so concentrated on the lighthouse that he runs on to the rocks in the engulfing darkness.

Perhaps I may have a paper on some aspect of this theme to present to the Congress in September. I am sure the reunion will hearten us all, after these terrible and dispiriting years. I have heard that Abraham intends to read a paper on the Female Castration Complex. Your suggestions on the development of an Active Therapy in Psychoanalysis seem admirable as a subject for discussion. I remain to be convinced that "one could effect far more with one's patients if one gave them enough of the love which they had longed for as children", but I shall attend to your arguments with great interest.

My wife joins me in thanking you for your kind thoughts.

Yours,
FREUD

19 Berggasse,
Vienna
4 March 1920

Dear Sachs,

Greatly though your colleagues will miss you in Switzerland, I think you are absolutely right to go to Berlin. Berlin will become the centre of our movement in a few years, of that I have no doubts. Your intelligence, buoyant optimism, geniality and breadth of culture, make you an ideal person to undertake the training of future analysts, despite your anxiety over your lack of clinical experience. I have the greatest confidence in you.

I take the liberty of sending you, as a 'parting gift' — though I trust the parting will not be for long — a somewhat extraordinary 'journal' which one of my patients, a young woman of most respectable character, has 'given birth' to, after taking the waters at Gastein. She left Vienna thin, and returned plump; and straightway delivered her writings to me. A genuine *pseudocyesis*! She was in the company of her aunt on holiday; and I need hardly add that she has never met any of my sons, though I may have mentioned to her that Martin was a prisoner of war. I shall not bore you with the details of her case; but if anything strikes the *artist* in you, I shall be grateful for your observations. The young woman has had a promising musical career interrupted, and actually wrote the 'verses' between the staves of a score of *Don Giovanni*. . . . This is, of course, a copy of the whole manuscript (the rest was originally in a child's exercise book), which she has been only too pleased to make for me. The copy is, you might say, the afterbirth, and you do not need to send it back.

If you can look beyond the gross expressions which her illness has dredged up from this normally shy and prudish girl, you may find passages to enjoy. I speak as one who knows your Rabelaisian temperament. Don't worry, my friend; it does not offend me! I shall miss your Jewish jokes — they are a terribly sober crowd here in Vienna, as you know.

I shall hope to see you at The Hague in September, if not before. Abraham promises a paper on the Female Castration Complex. Doubtless he will wield a very blunt knife. Still, he is sound and decent. Ferenczi will be trying to justify his new-found enthusiasm for kissing his patients.

Our house still feels empty without our 'Sunday child', even though we had seen little of her since her marriage. But enough of that.

With cordial greetings,
Yours,
FREUD

From the Berlin Polyclinic
14 March 1920

Dear and esteemed Professor,

Forgive the postcard: I thought it appropriate in the light of your young patient's "white hotel", for which gift please accept my thanks! It passed the train journey (again most apt!) speedily and interestingly. My thoughts on it are, I fear, elementary; her phantasy strikes me as like Eden before the Fall — not that love and death did not happen there, but there was no *time* in which they could have a meaning. The new clinic is splendid; not, alas, flowing in milk and honey like the *white hotel*, but considerably more durable, I hope! Letter follows when I have sorted myself out.

Cordially yours,
SACHS

19 Berggasse,
Vienna
18 May 1931

To the Secretary
Goethe Centenary Committee
The City Council
Frankfurt

Dear Herr Kuhn,

   I am sorry to have been so long in replying to your kind letter. I have not, however, been inactive in the meantime, when the state of my health has allowed, and the paper is finished. My former patient has no objection to your publishing her compositions along with it, and so these too are enclosed. I hope you will not be alarmed by the obscene expressions scattered through her poor verses, nor by the somewhat less offensive, but still pornographic, material in the expansion of her phantasy. It should be borne in mind that (a) their author was suffering from a severe sexual hysteria, and (b) the compositions belong to the realm of science, where the principle of *nihil humanum* is universally accepted and applied; and not least by the poet who advised his readers not to fear or turn away from "what, unknown or neglected by men, walks in the night through the labyrinth of the heart".

Yours very sincerely,
SIGMUND FREUD

I

Don Giovanni

1

I dreamt of falling trees in a wild storm
I was between them as a desolate shore
came to meet me and I ran, scared stiff,
there was a trap door but I could not lift
it, I have started an affair
with your son, on a train somewhere
in a dark tunnel, his hand was underneath
my dress between my thighs I could not breathe
he took me to a white lakeside hotel
somewhere high up, the lake was emerald
I could not stop myself I was in flames
from the first spreading of my thighs, no shame
could make me push my dress down, thrust his hand
away, the two, then three, fingers he jammed
into me though the guard brushed the glass,
stopped for a moment, staring in, then passed
down the long train, his thrumming fingers filled
me with a great gape of wanting wanting till
he half supported me up the wide steps
into the vestibule where the concierge slept
so took the keys and ran up, up, my dress
above my hips not stopping to undress,
juices ran down my thighs, the sky was blue
but towards night a white wind blew
off the snowcapped mountain above the trees,

we stayed there, I don't know, a week at least
and never left the bed, I was split open
by your son, Professor, and now come back, a broken
woman, perhaps more broken, can
you do anything for me can you understand.

I think it was the second night, the wind
came rushing through the larches, hard as flint,
the summer-house pagoda roof came down,
billows were whipped up, and some people drowned,
we heard some waiters running and some guests
but your son kept his hand upon my breast
then plunged his mouth to it, the nipple swelled,
there were shouts and there were crashes in the hotel
we thought we were in a liner out to sea
a white liner, he kept sucking sucking me,
I wanted to cry, my nipples were so drawn
out by his lips, and tender, your son moved on
from one nipple to another, both were swollen,
I think some windowpanes were broken
then he rammed in again you can't conceive
how pure the stars are, large as maple leaves
up in the mountains, they kept falling falling
into the lake, we heard some people calling,
we think the falling stars were Leonids,
and for a time one of his fingers slid
beside his prick in me there was such room,
set up a crosswise flutter, in the gloom
bodies were being brought to shore, we heard
a sound of weeping, his finger hurt
me jammed right up my arsehole my nail began
caressing where his prick so fat it didn't
belong to him any more was hidden
away in my cunt, came a lightning flash
a white zig-zag that went so fast
it was gone before the thunder cracked

over the hotel, then it was black
again with just a few lights on the lake,
I think the billiard room was flooded, we ached
he couldn't bring himself to let it gush
it was so beautiful, it makes me blush
now to be telling you, Professor, I
wasn't ashamed then, although I cried,
after about an hour he came inside,
we heard doors banging they were bringing in
the bodies from the lake, the wind
was very high still, we kept
our hands still on each other as we slept.

One evening they rescued a cat, its black fur
had been almost lost against the dark-green fir,
we stood naked by the window as a hand
searched among the foliage, it scratched,
it had been up there two days since the flood,
that was the night I felt a trickle of blood,
he was showing me some photographs, I said
Do you mind if the trees are turning red?
I don't mean that we literally never left
the bed, after the cat was taken down, we dressed
and went downstairs to eat, between the tables
there was a space to dance, I was unstable,
I had the dress I stood up in, no more,
I felt air on my flesh, the dress was short,
weakly I tried to push away his hand,
he said, I can't stop touching you, I can't,
please, you must let me, please,
couples were smiling at us indulgently,
he licked his glistening fingers as we sat,
I watched his red hand cut away the fat,
we ran down to the larches, I felt a cool
breeze blow on my skin and it was beautiful,
we couldn't hear the band in the hotel

though now and then some gypsy music swelled,
that night he almost burst my cunt apart
being tighter from my flow of blood, the stars
were huge over the lake, there was no room
for a moon, but the stars fell in our room,
and lit up the summer-house's fallen roof
pagoda-like, and sometimes the white cap
of the mountain was lit by a lightning flash.

2

One whole day, the servants made our bed.
Rising at dawn, we left the white hotel
to set sail in a yacht on the wide lake.
From dawn until the day began to fade
we sailed in our three-masted white-sailed craft.
Beneath our rug your son's right hand was jammed
up to the wrist inside me, laced in skin.
The sky was blue without a cloudy hint.
The white hotel merged into trees. The trees
merged into the horizon of green sea.
I said, Please fuck me, please. Am I too blunt?
I'm not ashamed. It was the murderous sun.
But there was nowhere in the ship to lie,
for everywhere there were people drinking wine
and gnawing chicken breasts. They gazed at us
two invalids who never left our rug.
I went into a kind of fever, so
besotted by your son's unresting stroke,
Professor, driving like a piston in
and out, hour after hour. It wasn't till
the sun drew in, that their gaze turned away,
not to the crimson sunset but the blaze
coming from our hotel, again in sight

between the tall pines. It outblazed the sky
— one wing was burning, and the people rushed
to the ship's prow to stare at it in horror.
So, pulling me upon him without warning,
your son impaled me, it was so sweet I screamed
but no one heard me for the other screams
as body after body fell or leapt
from upper storeys of the white hotel.
I jerked and jerked until his prick released
its cool soft flood. Charred bodies hung from trees,
he grew erect again, again I lunged,
oh I can't tell you how our rapture gushed,
the wing was gutted, you could see the beds,
we don't know how it started, someone said
it might have been the unaccustomed sun
driving through our opened curtains, kindling
our still-warm sheets, or (smoking was forbidden)
the maids, tired out, lighting up and drowsing,
or the strong burning-glass, the melting mountain.

I couldn't sleep that night, I was so sore,
I think something inside me had been torn,
your son was tender to me, deep in me
all night, but without moving. Women keened
out on the terrace where the bodies lay,
I don't know if you know the scarlet pain
of women, but I felt the shivers spread
hour after hour as the calm lake sent
dark ripples to the shores. By dawn, we had
not moved apart or slept. Asleep at last
I was the *Magdalen*, a figure-head,
plunging in deep seas. I was impaled
upon a swordfish and I drank the gale,
my wooden skin carved up by time, the wind
of icebergs where the northern lights begin.
The ice was soft at first, a whale who moaned

a lullaby to my corset, the thin bones,
I couldn't tell the wind from the lament
of whales, the hump of white bergs without end.
Then gradually it was the ice itself
cut into me, for we were an ice-breaker,
a breast was sheared away, I felt forsaken,
I gave birth to a wooden embryo
its gaping lips were sucking at the snow
as it was whirled away into the storm,
now turning inside-out the blizzard tore
my womb clean out, I saw it spin into
the whiteness have you seen a flying womb.

You can't imagine the relief it was
to wake and find the sun, already hot,
stroking the furniture with a serene
light, and your son watching me tenderly.
I was so happy both my breasts were there
I leapt out to the balcony. The air
was balmy with a scent of leaves and pines,
I leaned upon the rail, he came behind
and rammed up into me, he got so far
up into me, my still half-wintry heart
burst into sudden flower, I couldn't tell
which hole it was, I felt the white hotel
and even the mountains start to shake, black forks
sprang into sight where all was white before.

3

We made dear friends who died while we were there.
One was a woman, a corsetière,
who was as plump and jolly as her trade,
but the deep nights were ours alone. Stars rained

continuously and slowly like huge roses,
and once, a fragrant orange grove came floating
down past our window as we lay in awe,
our hearts were speechless as we saw them fall
extinguished with a hiss in the black lake,
a thousand lanterns hidden under drapes.
Don't imagine there were never times
of listening gently to the night's
tremendous silence, side by side, untouching,
or at least only his hand softly brushing
the mount he said reminded him of ferns
he hid and romped in as a boy. I learned
a lot about you from his whispers then,
you and his mother stood beside the bed.
Sunsets — the pink and drifting cloud-flowers, churning
off snowy peaks, the white hotel was turning,
my breasts were spinning into dusk, his tongue
churned every sunset in my barking cunt
and my throat drank his juice, it turned to milk,
or milk came into being for his lips,
for by the second night my breasts were bursting,
love in the afternoon had made us thirsty,
he drained a glass of wine and stretched across,
I opened up my dress, and my ache shot
a gush out even before his mouth had closed
upon my nipple, and I let the old
kind priest who dined with us take out the other,
the guests were gazing with a kind of wonder,
but smilingly, as if to say, you must,
for nothing in the white hotel but love
is offered at a price we can afford,
the chef stood beaming in the open door.
The milk was too much for two men, the chef
came through and held a glass under my breast,
draining it off he said that it was good,
we complimented him, the food was cooked

as tenderly as it had ever been,
more glasses came, the guests demanded cream,
and the hot thirsty band, the falling light
spread butter suddenly on the trees outside
the great french windows, butter on the lake,
the old kind priest kept sucking me, he craved
his mother who was dying in a slum,
my other breast fed other lips, your son's,
I felt his fingers underneath the table
stroking my thighs, my thighs were open, shaking.

We had to rush upstairs. His prick was up
me and my cunt began to flood
even before we reached the top, the priest
had left to lead the mourners through the trees
to the cold mountainside, we heard the chants
receding down the shore, he took my hand
and slid my fingers up beside him there,
our other friend the plump corsetière
slid hers in too, it was incredible,
so much in me, yet still I was not full,
they bore the bodies from the flood and fire
on carts, we heard them rumbling through the pines
and fade to silence, I pulled up her skirts
for she was so gripped by her belt, it hurt,
and let him finish it in her, it seemed
no different, for love ran without a seam
from lake to sky to mountain to our room,
we saw the line of mourners in the gloom
of the peak's shadow, standing by the trench,
a breeze brought in a memory of the scent
of orange groves and roses falling through
this universe of secrets, mothers swooned
crumpling into the muddy earth, a bell
tolled from the church behind the white hotel,
above it rather, half-way up the slope

to the observatory, words of hope
came floating from the priest, a lonely man
stood on the lake beside the nets, his hat
held to his breast, we heard a thunderclap,
the peak, held up a moment by their chants,
hung in mid-air, then fell, an avalanche
burying the mourners and the dead.
The echo died away, I shan't forget
the silence as it fell, a cataract
of darkness, for that night the white lake drank
the sunlight swiftly and there was no moon,
I think he penetrated to her womb
she screamed a joyful scream, and her teeth bit
my breast so hard it flowered beads of milk.

4

One evening when the lake was a red sheet,
we dressed, and climbed up to the mountain peak
behind the white hotel, up the rough path
zig-zagging between larches, pines, his hand
helped me in the climb, but also swayed
inside me, seeking me. When we had gained
the yew trees by the church we rested there;
grazing short grass, a tethered donkey stared,
an old nun with a basket of soiled clothes
came, as he glided in, and said, The cold
spring here will take away all sin,
don't stop. It was the spring that fed the lake
the sun drew up to fall again as rain.
She washed the clothes. We scrambled up the slope
into the region of eternal cold
above the trees. The sun dropped, just in time,
we entered the observatory, blind.

I don't know if you know how much your son
admires the stars, the stars are in his blood,
but when we gazed up through the glass there were
no stars at all, the stars had gone to earth;
I didn't know till then the stars, in flakes
of snow, come down to fuck the earth, the lake.
It was too dark to reach the white hotel
that night, and so we fucked again, and slept.
I felt the ghostly images of him
cascading, and I heard the mountains sing,
for mountains when they meet sing songs like whales.

The whole night sky came down that night, in flakes,
we lay in such high silence that we heard
the joyful sighs of when the universe
began to come, so many years ago,
at dawn when we crunched stars to drink the snow
everything was white, the lake as well,
the white hotel was lost, until he turned
the glass down towards the lake and saw the words
I'd written on our window with my breath.
He moved the glass and we saw edelweiss
rippling in a distant mountain's ice,
he pointed where some parachutists fell
between two peaks, we saw the sunlight flash
in the now heavenly blue, a corset clasp,
it was our friend, there was the lilac bruise
his thumb had printed in her thigh, the sight
excited him I think, my light
head felt him burst up through, the cable car
hung on a strand, swung in the wind, my heart
was fluttering madly and I screamed, the guests
fell through the sky, his tongue drummed at my breast,
I've never known my nipples grow so quickly,
the women fell more slowly, almost drifting,
because their petticoats and skirts were galing,

the men fell through them, my heart was breaking,
the women seemed to rise not fall, a dance
in which the men were lifting in light hands
light ballerinas high above their heads,
the men were first to come to ground, and then
the women fell into the lake or trees,
silently followed by a few bright skis.

On our way down we rested by the spring.
Strangely from so high we saw the fish
clearly in the lucid lake, a million
gliding darting fins of gold or silver
reminding me of the sperm seeking my womb.
Some of the fish were nuzzling guests for food.
Am I too sexual? I sometimes think
I am obsessed by it, it's not as if
God fills the waters with mad spawning shapes
or loads the vine with grapes, the palm with dates,
or makes the bull dilate to take the peach
or the plum tremble at the ox's reek
or the sun cover the pale moon. Your son
crashed through my modesty, a stag in rut.
The staff were wonderful. I've never known
such service as they gave, the telephones
were never still, nor the reception bell,
honeymoon couples, begging for a bed,
had to be turned away, as guests moved out
a dozen more moved in, they found
a corner for a couple we heard weeping
at being turned away, we heard her screaming
somewhere the next night, the birth beginning,
waiters and maids were running with warm linen.
The burnt-out wing was built again in days,
the staff all helped, one morning when my face
lay buried in the pillow, and my rump
taking his thrusts was coming in a flood

we heard a scraping, at the window was
the jolly chef, his face was beaming, hot,
he gave the wood a fresh white coat, and winked,
I didn't mind which one of them was in,
the steaks he cooked were rare and beautiful,
the juice was natural, and it was good
to feel a part of me was someone else,
no one was selfish in the white hotel
where waters of the lake could lap the screes
of mountains that the wild swans soared between,
their down so snowy-white the peaks seemed grey,
or glided down between them to the lake.

II

The Gastein Journal

SHE STUMBLED OVER a root, picked herself up and ran on blindly. There was nowhere to run, but she went on running. The crash of foliage grew louder behind her, for they were men, and could run faster. Even if she reached the end of the wood there would be more soldiers waiting to shoot her, but these few extra moments of life were precious. Only they were not enough. There was no escape except to become one of the trees. She would gladly give up her body, her rich life, to become a tree, frozen in humble existence, the home of spiders and ants. So that the soldiers would rest their rifles against the tree, and feel in their pockets for cigarettes. They would shrug away their mild disappointment, saying, One did not matter, and they would go home; but she, a tree, would be filled with joy, and her leaves would sing her gratitude to God as the sun set through the trees around her.

At last she collapsed in the bitter earth. Her hand touched something hard and cold; when she cleared away the leaves she found the iron ring of a trap door. She pushed herself up on to her knees, and tore at the ring. For some time there had been silence, as though the soldiers had lost her; but now again she heard them crashing through the undergrowth, close behind her. She tugged at the ring with all her strength but it would not give. A shadow fell across the fallen leaves. She closed her eyes, expecting everything to explode inside her head. Then she looked up into the frightened face of a small boy. He was naked like her, and blood poured from a hundred gashes and scratches. "Don't be frightened, lady," he said. "I'm alive too."

"Be quiet!" she told him. The iron ring would not budge, and she told the boy to crawl after her through the undergrowth. Perhaps the soldiers would mistake the blood on their backs for the crimson stain of the leaves. But as she crawled she felt bullets pumping into her right shoulder, quite gently.

The ticket collector was shaking her, and, apologizing, she fumbled with the clasp of her handbag. She felt stupid because, like the iron ring, the clasp would not give. Then it opened, she found her ticket, and gave it to him. He punched a hole in it and gave it back. When he had closed the door of the compartment she brushed down her black-and-white striped dress, and moved herself into a more comfortable and seemly position. She glanced at the soldier opposite who had joined her in the compartment while she slept; felt herself blush as she met his stare, and started tidying the contents of her handbag. She noticed that the young man with whom she had slept (in a manner of speaking) had placid green eyes. She took up her book and began reading again. Occasionally she looked out of the window, and smiled.

It was very peaceful: the rattle of the rails, the turn of a leaf, the rustle of her companion's newspaper.

The young man wondered how anyone could smile while looking out at the monotonous ochre plain. It did not seem a smile of happy memory or expectation, but simply of pleasure at the scene outside the window. The smile transformed her pleasant, dull features. She carried rather too much weight, but her figure was well proportioned.

One of her smiles turned into a yawn, which she stifled quickly. "A nice sleep," he said to her boldly, folding his paper in his lap and giving her a friendly smile. Her cheeks reddened. She nodded, glancing again out of the window; "Yes," she said, "or dead, rather than asleep." He found her reply disconcerting. "It's the lack of rain," she went on. "Yes, indeed!" said the young man. Still he could think of nothing more to say, and she returned to her book. She lost herself in her reading, for a few pages; then again her eyes slipped to the dry plain, behind flying telegraph poles, and her smile returned.

"Interesting?" he asked, nodding at her lap. She offered him the open book and stayed leaning forward. He was puzzled for a moment by the black and white dots which jumped about on the page to the train's rhythm, like the stripes on her dress. Thinking to find a light novel, he found it hard to adjust to the strange language, and at first he thought — for some reason — that the book was in Tamil, or some other outlandish tongue. He was on the point of saying, "So you're a linguist?" Then he realized it was music. There were words in Italian between the staves, and when he glanced at the book's stiff cover (the binding crackled in his hands) he saw the name Verdi. He returned the book to her, saying that he could not read music.

"It's beautiful," she said, running her fingers over the cover. She explained that she was taking this opportunity to learn a new role. Only it was frustrating not being able to let her voice ring out, since the part was so tuneful. He told her to go right ahead and sing — it would relieve the boredom of this damnable plain! That was not, she said, smiling, what she had meant; her voice was tired and she had to rest it. She had been forced to cut short her tour and go home a month early. The only consolation was that she would see her little boy again. Her mother was looking after him; but although he liked his grandmother it was not much fun for him being cooped up all the time with an elderly woman. He would be overjoyed to see her come back early. She had not wired to let them know she was coming, as she wanted it to be a surprise.

The young man kept nodding sympathetically during her dull explanation. "Where is his father?" he inquired. "Ah! who knows?" She dropped her gaze to the operatic score. "I am widowed." He murmured a regret, and took out a cigarette case. She declined, but said she enjoyed the smell of smoke, and it would not bother her throat. She would not be singing for some time to come.

Closing her score, she looked out of the window sadly. He thought she was remembering her husband, and tactfully kept silent as he smoked. He saw the attractive bosom of her black-and-white striped dress rising and falling in agitation. Her long straight black hair framed a somewhat heavy face. The pleasantly curved lips did not altogether compensate for the large nose. She had a darkish, greasy complexion, which he enjoyed, because he had spent three years on a very inadequate diet.

The young woman was thinking of the smoke of the train being carried away behind them. Also she saw this friendly young soldier lying frozen in his coffin. She managed at last to bring her breathing under control. To divert her mind from these terrible things, she started questioning her companion, and found he had been a prisoner of war and was returning to his family. Her compassionate expression (he was thin and pale) changed to one of astonished pleasure when she caught the words "Professor Freud of Vienna". "Of *course* I've heard of him!" she said, smiling, all her sadness forgotten. She was a great admirer of his work. She had even thought, at one stage, of consulting him; but the need had passed. What was it like to be the son of such a famous father? Not unexpectedly, he screwed up his face and gave a wry shrug.

But he was not at all jealous of his father's fame. He just wanted to find a young wife, and put down roots. She must find her life as a singer, constantly in demand here, there and everywhere, a terrible strain? Not really, she said; not usually. This was the first time she had strained her voice. Foolishly she had taken on a role which was too high for her register, and demanded too much power. She was not by nature a Wagnerian singer.

The train, which had been travelling non-stop for about two hours, flashing through great cities without even slowing, surprised them by coming to a halt at a small, quiet station in the middle of the great plain. It was scarcely a village — just three or four houses and a church spire. No one was waiting to get on, but the corridors of the train filled with struggling movement, confusion, shouts, and they saw a mass of travellers disgorge on to the platform. As the train pulled out again they watched the disgorged host put down their cases uncertainly on the platform. The hamlet was soon out of sight. The plain grew dustier, more desolate.

"Yes, we can certainly do with rain," said the young man. The woman sighed, saying, "But you have your whole life before you. You shouldn't have such gloomy thoughts at your age. Now, for me, it's certainly true. I'm almost thirty, I'm beginning to lose my looks, I'm widowed, in a few years my voice will start to go altogether, there seems little to look forward to." She bit her lip. He felt mildly irritated that she ignored or misunderstood all his remarks. But the renewed rise and fall of her bosom produced a tightness at his groin which was luckily hidden by his newspaper.

When — still clutching his newspaper — he went up the corridor to wash his hands, he saw how empty the train was. They seemed to be the only two travellers left on it. Returning, he found that his absence, short though it had been, had broken the intimacy. She was reading her score again, and nibbling a cucumber sandwich (he glimpsed her small, pearly, even teeth as she bit). She smiled at him briefly before burying herself in the score. "What a lot of crows there are on the wires," he found himself saying. It sounded — to him — boyish, uncertain, stupid; his maladroitness disturbed him.

But the young woman smiled a joyful agreement, saying, "It's a very difficult passage. *Vivace*." And she broke into a husky, pleasant hum, running up and down the bristling semi-quavers. She stopped as suddenly as she had started, turning red. "Lovely!" he said. "Don't stop!" But she shook her head and fanned her face with the open book. He lit another of his cigarettes, and she shut the book and her eyes at the same time, leaning back. "It's Turkish, isn't it?" She thought there was opium in the smell, and began to feel drowsy again in the warm, stuffy compartment.

He had changed, during his brief absence, into a smart light-blue civilian suit. The train entered a tunnel, turning their small travelling room into a sleeping compartment. She felt him stretch across and touch her hand. "You're perspiring," he said sympathetically. "You should let the air get to your skin." It did not surprise her when she felt his hand part her legs. "You're running in sweat," he said. It was very peaceful and free, letting the young officer stroke her thighs in the dark. She had already, in a sense, slept with him, allowing him the much greater intimacy of watching her while she was asleep. "It's stuffy," she said drowsily. "Shall I open a window?" he suggested. "If you like," she murmured. "Only I can't afford to become pregnant."

Finding it almost impossible to breathe, she spread her thighs and made it easier. He was looking into the dark blur of her face where now and then the whites of her eyes glowed. Those plump delicious thighs under the stretched silk were all too tempting, for someone who had been caged up for several years. Over her eyes appeared a small patch of red. It increased in intensity and grew larger. It separated into little spurts of crimson, and he realized her hair was on fire. He whipped off his coat and smothered her head with it. She came up choking for breath, but the flames were out. The train moved into the sunlight.

The fire and the harsh sunlight had broken the mood, and the young man stubbed his cigarette angrily. The woman jumped up and stood before the mirror, rearranging her hair, covering the burnt patch with a glossy black lock. She took down her white bonnet from the rack and put it on. "You can see how easily roused I am." She chuckled nervously. "That's why it's best for me not to start. It doesn't take much." He apologized for being so careless, and she perched on the edge of her seat, taking his hands tenderly and anxiously, and asked if she could be pregnant. He shook his head. "Then," she said with relief, "there's no harm done."

He stroked her hands. "Do you want me?" she asked. "Yes. I do. Very much," he said. She blushed again. "But how would your father feel about your marrying a poor widow, so much older than you? With a four-year-old son? And that's another thing — my son. How would *he* take it? You'd have to meet him and we'd have to see how you got on." The young man did not know what to say to this. He decided to say nothing, but to begin stroking her thighs again. To his relief her thighs parted at once, and she leaned back, her eyes closed. Her bosom heaved and he laid his free hand on it. "We could spend a few days together," he suggested.

"Yes," she said, her eyes still closed. She gasped and bit her lip. "Yes, that would be lovely. But let me see him first and prepare him for meeting you." "I meant you and I," he said, "on our own. I know a hotel in the mountains, by a lake. It's beautiful. They're not expecting you?" She shook her head, with another gasp as his finger slid into the opening. The young man lost interest in the woman, through the mystery of his finger having disappeared inside her. He could feel it gliding through her flesh, yet it had vanished. She grew so wet he was able to cram more into her. She cried out — so many fingers gliding in her, as though she was a fruit he was paring. She imagined both his hands crammed into her, to get at the fruit. Her dress was up around her waist, and the telegraph poles flashed by.

Gradually through her distracted senses she heard torrential rain falling on the corridor window; while on the other side the plain was still barren and dusty and the sky a yellow glare. The rain stopped, and when they glanced aside they saw the ticket collector cleaning the window with a soft brush. His startled face looked in at them but they carried on with what they were doing as though he was not there. The thump of her buttocks against his fingers caused her book to fall to the floor, creasing the second act of *The Masked Ball*. "Oughtn't we to stop?" she gasped, but he said he needed his fingers there.

He needed them there, as they ran past streets of neat houses and then high tenement slums with lines of washing stretched from window to window. And besides, they were so jammed he doubted if he could remove them even if he had wanted to. She nodded, convinced it was not possible to stop.

But without difficulty he extricated his fingers when their train pulled into the junction; and in the small train which took them up to the mountains, there was no chance to resume. She sat pressed against him, contenting herself with kissing his

fingers, or squeezing his hand against her lap. Their fellow
travellers were in high spirits, gasping their wonder as the train
pulled them slowly higher and higher into the mountains.
"There's plenty of snow still!" chattered the lady who sat
opposite — a baker's wife, judging by the moist floury smell that
came from her body. "I think so." The young woman smiled
back. "I don't feel sullied in the least." The baker's wife smiled
vaguely, turning her attention to her young daughter, who was
squirming impatiently. The little girl was excited, since this was
the first real holiday she had ever been taken on.

The lake, even in the late afternoon, was a brilliant emerald.
They were happy to be alone again, walking the short distance
to the white hotel. The vestibule was empty, except for the
porter behind the desk; and he was snoring, put to sleep by the
stifling afternoon. The young woman, weak after the passion of
the train journey, rested against the desk while the young man
— who had phoned through from the junction to book a room —
looked at the reservations list, unhooked a key from the board of
rings, and scribbled a name in the register. On the desk was
a bowl of amazingly big yellow peaches, and the young man took
one, bit juicily into it, and offered it to his friend to bite. Then
he caught hold of her hand and pushed her in front of him up
the stairs. The sweet bite of the peach refreshed her, and she
almost ran up the stairs; and as they ran he was already sliding
her dress up to her waist. The silk whispered. Her hand, sliding
round, felt his erection. He entered her and they entered the
room, she was not sure in which order; but without pausing to
take the room in, she was lying back on the bed, her thighs
spread wide, and taking his thrusts. They did not stop their love-
making while he took off her bonnet, and sent it, skimming, into
a corner.

The young woman felt broken in half, and saw the end of the
relationship, before it had properly begun; and her return
home, split open. A trail of splashes ran between door and
bed, and when they had finished she made him ring for a maid
to come and wipe it up. While the maid, an Oriental girl,

crouched, wiping the peach stains from the faded carpet, they stood at the window overlooking the veranda, enjoying the blue sky of the early evening, in the last minutes before the sun would start to set, changing the sky's colour.

The next day brought a renewal of blue, outside their room, but on the second night (she *thought* it was the second night, but had lost all sense of time) a flint stone, as big as a man's fist, came hurtling through the open window. It was the wind which had risen during the evening, and now whistled through the larches, breaking the vase of flowers which the maid had placed on their chest of drawers. The young man leapt to the window and closed it. Now the wind threatened to break the window, and they heard a muffled crash, which was the collapsing roof of the summer-house. It was shaped like a pagoda, picturesque but vulnerable, and the fierce wind blew it away. For a long time there was no answer to the bell they rang, but at last the maid came to clear up the broken vase, and the spilt water and flowers. Her eyes were red, and the young man asked her what was the matter. "Some people have drowned," she said. "The waves are very big tonight. Their boat was overturned." The maid looked wonderingly at the lump of flint stone, lying where it had fallen. "Leave it," said the young man. "It will be a souvenir." She picked it up though and gave it to him, and he weighed it in his hand, wonderingly. He could not imagine the force that had torn it from the mountain and impelled it into their room.

She asked later: "Is my breast softer than the stone?" He nodded, resting his head on it to prove its softness. They heard distinctly, yet distantly, the noises of troubled people scurrying through the corridors; and when they rang for dinner they were told they would have to make do with sandwiches, as all the waiters were helping with the victims of the flood. They were famished, and he asked if they could have some chocolate sent up with the sandwiches. He fondled her breast that was so much softer than the flint, and bent to suck the nipple. The young woman yearned towards the lips that sucked her; the orange nipple was being drawn further and further out. She ran her fingers through his short curly hair as he went on sucking. They heard the sound of something breaking — perhaps a window or crockery — and shouts. The noises of panic. Also they heard guests crying. It reminded her of her baby crying, and she stroked the man's hair. Her breast seemed swollen like a drum, to three times its normal size. The wind flailed against the window. He took his lips from her breast to say anxiously, "I hope it won't break." She directed her nipple again into his mouth and said, "I don't think so. It swelled like this when I was feeding my son."

The hotel was swaying in the gale, and she thought she was on an ocean liner; she heard the creaking of a ship's timbers, smelt the salt tang through the open porthole, and, from the galley, the faint smell of the evening meal, tinged with seasick. They would have to dine with the captain, and he would ask her to sing in the ship's concert. Perhaps they would never reach port. She felt close to tears because her nipple was being drawn so far out it began to be painful; pain was concentrating there, and yet in a way the nipple did not belong to her, it was floating away, a raw appendix removed by the ship's doctor. She wanted him to rest but he would not. To her relief his lips moved to her other breast, and began drawing that nipple out, though it was already quite swollen from its sympathy for the twin. "Are they tender?" he said at last; and she said, "Yes, of course, they love each other." She heard the porthole in the next cabin along, behind their bunk, shatter.

With his hand he opened her vagina, and forced his penis in so hard she jolted back. He lifted himself to look down at where he had so mysteriously disappeared into her body. He made himself appear and disappear at will. There was the lightest of light touches on her hair, and when she put her hand there she touched something dry and papery. It was a maple leaf, which must have blown in unnoticed when the storm began, before the stone had been thrown in. She showed it to him, and he smiled, but his smile was caught back in a grimace, from the pleasure of thrusting in and out and of holding himself on the verge of coming. She put her hand behind his buttocks and stroked him with the dry and papery maple leaf. He tensed, and shuddered.

The light rain had ceased, the wind had dropped; they opened the window and walked out on to the balcony. He held his friend by the waist, and they watched the storm clouds part, revealing stars larger than they had ever seen. And every few moments a star would slide diagonally through the black sky, like a maple leaf drifting from the branch or the way lovers rearrange themselves with gentle movements while they sleep. "It's a shower of Leonids," he said softly. She rested her head on his shoulder. Dimly they could see activity down by the lake shore: bodies being brought to land. Some people were wailing; another voice shouted for more stretchers and blankets. The couple went back to bed and lost themselves in each other again. This time she could feel one of his fingers moving inside her, besides his penis; it fluttered her crosswise to the movement in and out of his penis; and quicker. It reminded her of the shooting stars across the sky, and it created whirls and vortices like the stormy lake. Clearly the storm was not over, because a streak of white lightning flashed vertically to the lake; they saw it from the corners of their eyes, bisecting the black window space, and the curtains billowed. "That was fierce," he whispered; and so she took care to stroke him more gently, with the very tip of her fingernail. At the same time one of his fingers was in her anus, hurting her, but she wanted to be hurt more.

On the lake, there were a few lights where rescue boats were still searching for bodies. The rescuers were themselves recovering from the rumble of thunder that had crashed round their heads just before, rather than after, the lightning stroke that had turned night into day. The wind rose again, and they made haste to row ashore, because there was no hope of finding any more bodies that night. The hotel was alive with excited or demented people; the glass doors kept banging, as more and more bodies were brought in. The flood water in the billiard room, which was in the basement, had risen almost to the level of the pockets, but the army major waded unperturbed round the table, intent on finishing his break. He had taken the last red, and all the colours to pink. It was a difficult straight pot, the whole length of the table, but he struck it cleanly and it slammed into the pocket. As the water rose to his hips he sipped his beer and chalked his cue. The black nestled against a cushion but he gave the white ball spin to try to make the black cleave to the cushion. It was a beautiful stroke and the black thudded into a watery grave. The major had been playing against himself for the duration of the break, because his opponent, a priest, had rushed out to give the last rites to the dying. With a grim smile of self-congratulation the major hung up his cue and swam out of the billiard room. In a high room the lovers were asleep, despite the blustery wind shaking the windowpane; and as they slept they kept their hands resting on each other, as if scared that somehow they would vanish in the night. A black cat crouched, frightened out of its wits, on the pitching and tossing branch of a fir tree, opposite their balcony. It tensed to jump, but sensed it was too far.

Not for two days did anyone find out that the cat was stranded in the tree. The young lovers heard a scraping noise outside their window and got out of bed to see what was happening. They saw an army major climbing a long ladder, which was bending and creaking under his weight. From behind gently blowing curtains they watched the difficult rescue operation. The cat arched her back and spat at the man, and clawed him when he stretched out his hand. The soldier let out an obscene word, which made the young woman blush because she was not used to such language. Eventually the major backed down the ladder, the cat clinging round his neck.

As soon as the young woman had seen the scarlet stigmata spring to the major's hand she felt the noisome fall of a blood clot through her own body, and told her lover the bad news. It surprised and pleased her that he was not upset. There was a problem, though. She had no luggage whatever. She had left her heavy suitcase in the corridor of the main-line train, and when all the travellers tumbled out at the tiny hamlet in the middle of the burnt plain one of them must have taken her suitcase by mistake. She could not believe it had been stolen. Anyway, it had vanished by the time they came to change trains at the junction, taking with it dresses, underwear, toilet articles, and gifts for her son and her mother.

They had to ring for the maid. The polite girl, a Japanese student earning her tuition money, had difficulty understanding the young woman's problem. She had to draw, on a sheet of hotel notepaper, a crescent moon beside a stick-woman. The maid blushed and departed. Fortunately she was herself menstruating, and came back with a towel. Shyly she scuttled away, refusing a tip.

They lay looking at photographs of his family. She was tickled by the shot of Freud at the seaside, wearing a black-and-white striped bathing suit, which could have been cut out of the same material as her dress. The young man chuckled too; he seemed particularly fond of his younger sister. His smile faded into sadness, looking at her.

They went down to dinner and he asked her if she felt well enough to dance to the gypsy band. She nodded. As they shuffled around between the tables she leaned on him. "Can you feel the blood falling?" he asked. "Always," she said. "I fall ill every autumn." The scent of her cherry lipstick stirred him and he kissed her; the warm sticky flavour of it made him want more. She had to draw away to take breath, but she loved the cherry flavour of her lipstick on his lips and they kissed again, endless brief lip-brushes. She broke away again, saying the music made her want to sing. But already too many dancers and diners were staring at them. He pulled up her dress at the front; weakly she tried to push it down, but her throat ached with pleasure and he insisted: "Please, you must let me. Please." It was a purr at her ear, mingled with the dart of his tongue. "But you'll be covered in blood," she whispered. "I don't mind," he said. "I want your blood." So she put her arm again around his neck and let him do what he liked. The dancing and dining men winked at them, smiling, and they smiled back.

"Is it rare enough?" he asked, as he cut the fat from his meat. She caught his fingers in hers, and kissed them. "It's better than I've ever known," she said. "Can't you tell?" The steak put back the blood she was losing, and afterwards they ran down to the trees, and made love again, on the grass by the lake. Sometimes, when a door was opened, they heard the gypsy music, and always there were the exceptionally large stars. It was not so comfortable making love while she was losing blood, but on the other hand she could let herself go even more because there was no fear of any consequences. When they climbed the stairs after midnight more maple leaves had blown into their room. She said, jokingly, that she could make use of them. She borrowed his toothbrush and as she cleaned her teeth he put his arms round her and gave her nape gentle kisses. There were more lightning flashes; sheet lightning and without thunder, bringing the snowy mountain peaks very close and lighting the trail of debris left by the storm and the flood.

POSTCARDS FROM THE white hotel:

An elderly nurse:

> I've been doing what I can for a sweet young couple who are both paralysed. It's very brave of them to come on holiday together. They sit hunched up in their deck chairs sharing a blanket (we're on a yacht in the middle of the lake). The food is excellent, and Elise is picking up, she sends love.

A secretary:

> Your last day hope it is warm & dry where you are, where we are it is very hot, there isn't a cloud, it's all hazy, we are on a boat on the lake, gnawing chicken bones and drinking wine. Hotel marvellous, better than the brochure and a good class of people.

A priest:
I see its three masts as an emblem of Christ's passion and the white sail as his beloved shroud. It makes me feel less guilty for deserting my flock. Mama, I hope you are keeping fine. The weather is nice. A sweet young Catholic girl drowned in my arms a few days ago. Don't worry about me. I am reading the little book you sent.

A Japanese maid:
Wonder to relate, my lovers (the moon couple) up at dawn's crack and out on a boat. It means I and my friend must make their bed all day, their bed is undescribable. I no time to write even haiku.

A corsetière:
The water seems fearfully cold, but tomorrow I must take the plunge. I am trailing my hand over the side of our boat. I would not like to say where the young man next to me with his girl has got his hand. Well, life must go on. Of course, it's not the same when your partner is gone, but I must try to enjoy the rest of the holiday for my dear husband's sake.

An army major:
It's more like a troop ship than a yacht. It's changed since before the war. We're jammed against one another. I'd like a good Gatling to clear a space. The flood didn't get rid of enough. Bodies! Everywhere! Dick arrives tomorrow by the first train.

A watchmaker:
It went up like an oily rag. One moment we were enjoying the pleasant boat trip, the next, we could see our hotel burning away like plywood. We lost sight of the sun, it was so bright. Well, there goes all our possessions except the clothes we stand up in.

A botanist:
It's heartbreaking. Yesterday I found a very rare specimen of edelweiss. I left it back in the hotel, of course, and now it's gone up in flames.

A banker's wife:
I couldn't believe my eyes. There was our hotel burning to the

ground in front of us across the water, and this young fellow pulled his girl on to his lap and settled her on it! You know what I mean? Like deck quoits! And here were these people screaming all round, some with relations back at the hotel!

An insurance broker:
It was just awful to see them jumping out of upstairs windows. They had jets playing on the fire but it didn't seem to do any good. Elinor, thank God, was with me. I'd tried to get her to rest up in the hotel today. Anyway, we're safe & sound and hope to see you.

His wife:
Thank the dear Lord Hubert was with me. He wasn't so keen on a boat trip since we had the flood, but I made him come along. The weather is lovely, tho' it gets very cool at nights. I feel a lot better for the break, and we've met some lovely people.

A boy:
They were hanging from the trees like magic lanterns.

A pastor:
But the dead shall be raised, I have no fear of that. And this corrupt flesh shall put on incorruptible. The old lady we took the trip with, into the mountains, died in the fire. Yet my soul shall magnify the Lord.

A honeymoon couple:
It's clouded our holiday, but just the same we are very happy. This is the lake and the mountains, it is a beautiful place and the scenery is breathtaking.

A baker's wife:
Our hearts are breaking. Dear mother has died in a terrible fire at the hotel. Thank God we were out in a boat, but we saw it all. It went up like paper. And we could see the room where she was. But she was an old lady, so we mustn't grieve over it too much. We are trying to keep cheerful for the children's sake, and you must do the same.

A salesman:
One of the bedrooms had had the curtains drawn for a long time but yesterday they were open, and they think this may

have had something to do with it, though I can't see how.

His mistress:

They think it was probably one of the maids having a quiet smoke when she made the beds. I've seen the Japanese maid smoking in the corridor, which looks funny as they're so lady-like usually. Luckily it was a wing away from where we are, so our things are all right.

A retired couple:

They're saying something about the mountain (where there's still lots of snow) reflecting the sun's rays. Like the glass we use for reading, I suppose. Anyway it's a terrible tragedy so take care of fires, dear. The hotel staff are marvellous. It's still been worth coming, a holiday of a lifetime. Thank you for making it possible.

An opera singer:

I've gone to the mountains for a few days to rest before coming home. I think it's doing me good. The last few weeks have been a strain, and it's lovely not to have to do anything but enjoy the good food and the wonderful scenery. I'm not sleeping well, which is the only drawback, but beginning to relax a little. I'll be seeing you soon.

A seamstress:

My little girl is dead. My heart is broken. I promised to send you a card, my dear, but such a message! She is being buried here. I am leaving straight after.

A lawyer:

The only drawback is, the noise at night. Of course one must have sympathy with them, but we too have had a loss, and it's no excuse for ruining people's sleep. We have complained but the manager seems unwilling or unable to control them.

A retired prostitute:

A gentleman complimented me on my good figure, so it obviously doesn't show. I'm picking up a bit more strength every day and getting more used to it. Just feel a bit weighed down on the left, but I suppose that will pass. I am fortunate, there are many worse off here. The weather is good and the food first-class.

No one felt in the mood to dance. The guests ate their dinner quietly and listened, much moved, to the gypsy band, who played sweet and melancholy tunes. One of their own number, a violinist, had been trapped by the fire in a lift, and burnt beyond recognition. The young lovers, possibly, might have danced, but they did not appear for dinner.

During one of the pauses between melodies, when only the low tone of sombre conversation prevailed, and the politely hushed clink of serving dishes, the army major rose from his table (he always dined alone, at a small table in the corner), walked to the rostrum, murmured something to the plump, sweating band leader, who gave a nod, and spoke to the guests through the microphone. He said he would like to speak to as many of them as possible, on a matter of some urgency, and would they care to take a drink from the bar, after they had eaten, and assemble in the billiard room. There was silence after he had spoken, then a rise in the level of conversation. Perhaps a third of the guests decided to see what the "mad major" (as he was known to many of them) wanted to speak to them about. When the coffee cups had been drained, and the brandies and liqueurs gathered from the bar, a sizeable crowd made its way down to the billiard room and sat on the rows of seats around the table. The green mat was still drying out from the flood, and shimmered under the spot-light like a rectangular scum-covered swimming pool.

The major, who was English and named Lionheart, stood at the baulk end of the table and waited for latecomers to crowd in at the back. "Thank you for coming," he began in a firm but resonant voice. "Let me break the ice by saying that I haven't brought you here to talk about death. Death and I are old acquaintances and he holds no terrors for me. We mourn those who died in the flood and the fire, but this is not what I want to speak to you about. Such things happen. They are acts of God. We should not allow these events to cast too great a cloud over us." A quiet ripple of assent passed through the guests at these words, and one or two of them looked at the tall and distin-guished-looking soldier with a new respect.

The major looked down, stubbing his cigarette, very slowly, as though needing time to marshal his thoughts. There was a deep silence in the billiard room, broken only by the purring of a black cat, the hotel pet (and a great favourite with the guests) who had stolen down with the throng and was curled up, now, in the lap of the watchmaker's wife, who was stroking her. The cat had been badly singed in the fire, but luckily had escaped with no great harm done.

"Odd things have been happening, however," the major went on, crisply. He paused, waiting for his words to sink in. The words had had the ring of military authority. He would have had a good war, thought Henri Poussin, an engineer. A nonentity before, and a nonentity of a different kind after, but when the keynotes of the times were urgency and violence, Lionheart must have been pretty good.

"Would you care to justify that statement, Major?" said Vogel, the German lawyer, sharply.

The major looked at him with scarcely veiled contempt. Vogel was a cynic and a poltroon; he had been caught cheating at cards. "Of course," said the major quietly. "The falling stars." The silence of the assembled throng fell into a deeper stillness, with all of them at once — except Vogel — holding their breaths. "Everyone has seen them," the major went on quietly. "Not just one or two people, but everyone; and not just on one night but almost every night. Large, bright, white stars."

"Large as maple leaves," said the salesman's mistress, in a soft, half-drugged tone. She squeezed her hands together, as if frightened that she had spoken out.

"Exactly," said the major.

"And the elm leaves are red," said the watchmaker, springing up, shaking off his wife's hand. "Has anyone else noticed that?" He looked around him excitedly, and several heads nodded. He was referring to the cluster of elms at the end of the lawn behind the hotel. The people who had nodded dropped their gaze and licked their lips nervously. But other voices agitatedly claimed that this was not true. These voices carried little conviction, and were soon silent. Total silence fell again, and a distinct coldness had spread in the room. Anxious to avoid a spread of alarm and despondency, the major proposed that they should break off for a few minutes while people went upstairs to recharge their glasses. The major sat down, suddenly tired, and in the hubbub of talking and pushing towards the stairs Vogel glided up to him, his rimless glasses glinting maliciously. "I'm surprised at you, Lionheart," he said — lightly enough, but with an iron edge of contempt and resentment.

The major leaned back in his chair. "Are you? In what way?"

"Spreading panic among the ladies. Why couldn't you have kept them out of it? I don't accept your alarmist ideas for one moment. But just supposing they're true, why couldn't you have left them out of it?"

"In the first place, Vogel, you are under-rating the ladies' intelligence. It's a habit with people in sedentary occupations — always unwise, and in some cases dangerous."

Vogel flushed slightly, but he remained controlled.

"In the second place?"

"For their own safety — for the safety of all of us — they've got to realize we may be menaced by things we don't understand. At least, *I* don't pretend to understand them. But then, I haven't had the benefit of a German education."

The lawyer turned away abruptly. The soldier felt annoyed that he had allowed himself to be goaded into a discourteous remark. But he quickly brought his thoughts back to the serious business in hand, as his fellow guests had reassembled with their drinks and were waiting for him to resume the discussion. He got to his feet. Momentarily dizzy, swaying slightly, he gripped the damp cushion of the billiard table.

"The important thing," he said, "is for us to share frankly what we have seen, or think we have seen; and if possible to find rational explanations. For instance I don't know if I'm alone in having seen lightning striking the lake? A livid stroke, absolutely vertical." He looked around questioningly. After a short, tense silence, an elderly nurse flushed and said quietly, "No, I saw it too." "And I," said a gaunt, hook-nosed accountant. His wife, too, nodded her head vigorously. Several others gave subdued, embarrassed gestures of assent, and sipped thoughtful, perturbed drinks. The major asked if anyone else had any odd occurrences to report.

"A school of whales," said a nice-looking blond young woman, an office secretary. "Yesterday morning, when I went down for an early swim. I thought I was seeing things, or rather *not* seeing things, if you know what I mean, because the lake has no outlet. It's just not possible. But now you've made me think again. I'm sure they weren't low-lying clouds."

"Perhaps you were seeing your hangover," said Vogel, sniggering.

"No. *I* saw them too," said his pale sister. "I'm sorry, Friedrich," she added hurriedly, "but I must tell the truth. I had to get up at dawn, for some reason which I needn't go into, and I looked out of my window."

"And you saw whales?" pressed the major, with a kind and gentle smile.

"Yes." She twisted her handkerchief, and Vogel looked at her with contempt and loathing.

It appeared that no one else had seen the school of whales; but no one else had been up at dawn, the previous day, and the painfully honest evidence of Vogel's sister had been impressive.

"Any other testimonies?" inquired the major curtly. "Odd events, odd sightings?"

Eyes shifted round the room, in the blank silence.

"Then let us consider what we have. Falling stars. Red leaves. Lightning. A school of whales. . ."

Bolotnikov-Leskov, who had sat watchfully and remote, stroking his short and elegant beard, in the furthest corner, broke in at this point. The voice of such an eminent statesman earned instant respect, even from those who disagreed with his politics. "I can suggest nothing in the way of — " (he sighed and spread his hands) "explaining the falling stars, the red leaves, or the lightning. But I *believe* I may have an explanation for the whales. Madame Cottin" — he bowed to the plump, blue-dressed lady, who inclined her smiling face in response — "is a corsetière. And part of every corset is — to speak bluntly — dead whale. It seems to me not impossible that her presence among us — which has so cheered us all because of her exceptional warmth and vitality — has 'called' the whales, so to speak. Attracted them, sung to them, lured them home, call it what you will."

Madame Cottin, fanning her flushed cheeks, said that, indeed, she had known occasions before when ladies had seen whales, when she — Madame Cottin — was near at hand.

Bolotnikov-Leskov nodded at her, gratefully, blushing like a boy.

The rational, or almost rational, explanation for the whales' appearance cheered the company, and emboldened a few of them to mention phenomena they had witnessed but been too frightened to declare. A Lutheran pastor said hesitantly that he had seen a breast flying through the yew trees when he had strolled up to the church one evening before dinner. "I thought at first it was a bat," he said, "but the nipple was clearly visible."

A heavily busted woman with greying hair said that she had recently had a breast removed because of a growth. Major Lionheart thanked her for her frankness, and there was a low murmur of sympathy. Vogel, looking distinctly yellow, said he *thought* he had seen a petrified embryo floating in the lake shallows, but it could just as easily have been a piece of fossilized tree. His sister, beginning to weep, confessed to an abortion, ten years ago. There was a painful and shocked silence, and it was clear to everyone that Vogel had known nothing of this. The muscles of his face trembled, and the major felt a shaft of compassion for the dried-up German lawyer.

Vogel's sister was now sobbing uncontrollably. It was a dry, racking sound, almost unbearable to listen to; men who had survived the flood and the fire without flinching were lighting up cigarettes and cigars in an effort to calm their nerves. It was a huge relief when the pastor leaned across Vogel, took the woman's arm in a kind but firm grip, and led her from the room, threading a path for her between guests and billiard table. While she was being escorted out, the baker's wife could be seen, by those near, nudging her husband and whispering to him, and he was shaking his head. But when silence had fallen again the baker got to his feet and in a stumbling working-class voice, barely audible, said he had seen a womb gliding across the lake. He had been out alone, fishing. The womb had barely skimmed the surface, and quickly vanished. "Sometimes you do start seeing things when you're out fishing alone, especially at dawn or dusk. But there was no mistaking this." He sat down, glancing at his wife for support.

Major Lionheart could not suppress a yellowish-toothed grin at the baker's comical, low accent, though he tried to pretend he was flexing his cheek muscles; and even Bolotnikov-Leskov, for all his revolutionary ideals, covertly smiled. The major asked if anyone else had seen a gliding womb. In the silence, someone said that possibly he had seen a loaf of bread, and there were tension-easing chuckles. But then an anonymous male voice, from the corner shadows, cracked out, "Has anyone seen the glaciers? In the mountains." It wiped all the smiles off and renewed the chill in the room.

There were various attempts by sundry guests to explain the falling stars, the lightning, the red leaves and the glaciers. None of them carried conviction, even to those who put forward the explanations. The major, bringing the meeting to a close, counselled vigilance. Bolotnikov-Leskov thanked the major on behalf of all present — there was another murmur of assent — and proposed that, in the event of anyone witnessing any further inexplicable occurrences, they should straightway inform the major; who would be empowered to call another meeting if and when he thought it necessary. The proposal was carried by subdued acclamation.

As the guests trooped two abreast up the stairs, the baker found himself next to the elderly nurse. She took the chance to tell him that her grand-niece, who had not felt well tonight and so had gone to bed early, had only a month ago undergone an operation for the removal of her womb. "I've brought her here to recuperate," she said quietly, not wishing to be overheard. "It's very sad, because she's only in her twenties. I didn't want to say it in public because it would upset her to have it known. She's disturbed enough already. But I wanted you and your wife to know." The baker squeezed her arm, gratefully.

IT WAS SEVERAL evenings before the young lovers again ventured down to dine. When they did, they found their table had been allocated to new guests. There was simply no end to the stream of hopeful visitors who turned up at the white hotel, and an empty table was a luxury it could not afford. The head waiter explained this, apologetically, to the young couple, saying that he had assumed they wished to take every meal in their room. He asked them to wait while he went and had a word with a buxom, brassily attractive, artificially blond woman, Madame Cottin, who sat alone at a table for two. Madame Cottin smiled agreement, nodding a welcome to the young couple across the dining room; and the head waiter quickly produced an extra chair, and escorted the couple to the lady's table. It was a tight squash, and the young man was full of apologies for breaking in on her privacy; but Madame Cottin laughed away all his regrets and shrieked good-humouredly as legs embarrassingly collided under the table.

She was delighted, she said, to have some company. Her husband had perished in the flood, and solitude did not come easy to her. She took out a handkerchief and dabbed a tear from her eye; but was soon, in her turn, apologizing to them for forcing her grief upon them. "I try not to cry very often," she said. "At first I was inconsolable, and I'm sure I made everybody's life a misery. But I told myself I had to pull myself together. It wasn't fair to others, who are here to have a good time."

The young man said he admired her bravery very much. He had noticed her on the previous occasion when they dined; had seen her laughing and dancing, the life and soul of the party. Madame Cottin gave a wry smile. "It wasn't easy," she said. In fact, it had been terribly painful, to be pretending jollity while her heart was there in the coffin with her husband.

It had become a little easier, she added, since the awful tragedy of the fire. Seeing the fresh grief of others had had the effect of putting distance between her and her bereavement. And besides, in comparison with being burnt, drowning was a kind and merciful death. You could always see someone worse off than yourself, she said. She dabbed her eye again; but then, not wanting to make their evening a misery, she grew cheerful, and started telling hilarious stories, especially about her customers. They both fell in love with Madame Cottin. She had the tears streaming down their cheeks, with her droll tales of fitting ladies (and even gentlemen) with corsets. Having eaten heartily, she smacked her well-supported stomach, saying that she was a living advertisement for her goods. "I'm really out here!" She laughed, spreading her hands like a fisherman recounting his catch. In fact the baker, catching her eye across the room, misunderstood her gesture and capped it with a full spread of his arms, grinning delightedly. The evening sped by, as though the watchmaker, at the next table, had trebled the speed of all the clocks and watches.

The lovers escorted Madame Cottin to her room — which was actually the one next to theirs, behind their bed-head. Night after night they had overheard heart-rending sobs from that room. Their admiration and respect for her increased still further — they sensed the cost to her of bottling up her grief all day. And again, tonight, as they fell into each other's arms and began undressing each other impatiently, they heard the sound of Madame Cottin's grief, behind the wall. They quickly lost the sound, however, in their own hunger.

Later, they had their first lovers' quarrel. It was very good-humoured, and never rose above a whisper. He was convinced that stars were falling through the black sky outside their window, and she argued that they were white roses. But then something that was unquestionably a grove of oranges floated down past, and they gave up whispering, in the wonder of watching it. The brilliant oranges glowed in the dark rustling foliage. The lovers went on to the balcony to see the orange grove fall in the lake. Each separate fruit hissed and was extinguished as it touched the calm water.

Hidden from their view, Madame Cottin was at the same time standing on her balcony. She was unable to sleep. She saw that there were hundreds of lanterns on the lake, and one by one they were covered by a black cloth. She had cried herself out for another night. Having undressed and put on her cotton nightgown, she poured away the almost-full glass phial of her tears.

Entirely spent, the couple lay side by side in bed. It was strange and refreshing not to have to listen to any sounds of grief. They had no idea what time it was. Time, that had raced during the evening, now dragged for Madame Cottin, lying open-eyed in the dark; and did not exist, in different ways, for the sleeping guests, for the dead down in the cool store rooms, and for the lovers. Their souls, balancing on the edge of sleep, like someone oppressed by heat who makes his bed perilously on the balcony, attuned themselves to total silence. Her hearing was keener than his, and she heard silences he was unaware of. Not even their fingers touched. Occasionally his hand tiredly brushed the tangled mound of her pubic hair, in affection rather than lust; she liked him doing that.

He broke the stillness by whispering that it reminded him of a hill he had often played and picnicked on as a boy. The hill was covered in ferns, and he had played hunter and hunted with a cousin. He remembered the fearful pleasure of stalking or being stalked through the stiff ferns with their heavy summery smell. It was the only time he had ever felt really close to the earth.

"My father says there are four people present whenever love-making takes place," he said. "They are here now, of course. My parents."

The young woman saw the stern figure of Freud, beside his timid wife, at the bed's foot. Freud's black suit and his wife's white nightgown dissolved and melted into her dress, lying shadowily on the floor where he had flung it.

They loved the sunsets best. The mountains spun pink clouds out of themselves, like flowers. (The old nurse, in fact, one evening saw the whole sky turn into a huge crimson rose, with endlessly inwoven petals; and dutifully she went straight to the major to report it.) The rose, though eternally still, seemed to spin within itself, and the lovers had the eerie impression that the whole earth was turning. So were her breasts turning, in his hands, as night stole over them; and his tongue turned too, as it delicately tilted at her sex, or tried to get deeper and deeper in, as if wanting to force her into the mountainside. She was opening up so much that she felt her vagina hollowing into a cave, so that it expelled air in a way that was like breaking wind and brought a blush to her face, though she knew and he knew it was not.

Time, with his bland surgeon's hands, was quietly healing Madame Cottin. While the lovers spent their day in the stuffy room, she was out walking around the lake with Father Marek, the kindly old Catholic priest. His certainties were a great comfort to her. He urged her to return to the Church, likening its effect to one of her stout corsets. The Church's dogmas, he said, smiling, were the whalebone of the soul. The analogy delighted her, and she chuckled. After a beautiful long morning's walk through woods and wildflowers, the priest and the corsetière stopped at a pleasant lakeside inn, miles from anywhere, for refreshment. Carrying their bread and cheese out to the lakeside tables, they spotted Vogel and Bolotnikov-Leskov. They felt bound to join them, though neither party relished the meeting. Bolotnikov-Leskov was midway in a political peroration, and had built up too much momentum to stop. The problem, he explained (while Madame Cottin smiled sadly and let her gaze stray over the lake), was that his party was best for the masses but unfortunately the masses could not see this. The only answer, he feared, was the bomb.

Vogel's eagle eye noticed the tremor in the priest's hand as he drank his plum juice; noted also the red complexion. His legal training told him that the priest had been sent on a vacation to dry out. The male and female corseters finished their bread and cheese quickly and apologized for their haste in leaving. They wanted, they said, to walk the circuit of the lake.

The young lovers were having their second disagreement, a more serious one. He was interrogating her jealously about her sexual relationship with her husband; which irritated her, because all that was so far in the past, and so irrelevant. The argument brought out, for the first time, his immaturity; the few years' difference in their ages had never before seemed significant. Indeed she had never even noticed it. But it was all too clear now, in this childish outburst of jealousy over the dead. It made her irritated with other things, such as the foul Turkish cigarettes he kept smoking, filling the room with stale scent and no doubt ruining her singing voice forever.

In the end, of course, it was even more enchanting than before. Lying joined in love, gazing into each other's eyes, they could not believe unfriendly words had passed between them. But she had to show that she thought more of him than she had of her husband by doing something strange — taking his penis into her mouth. It was horribly intimate to be eye-to-eye with that rich tulip bulb, that reeking dewy monster. Actually to take it in her mouth was as inconceivable as taking in a bull's pizzle. But she closed her eyes and did it, fearfully, to show she loved him more than her husband. And it was not unpleasant, it was so far from unpleasant that she became curious; squeezing, caressing and sucking the shaft so that it swelled even bigger in her mouth and spurted into her throat. In his jealousy he abused her in foul terms, which stirred her most peculiarly.

It was a new excitement, just when they thought they had reached the end of novelty. By a curious transubstantiation, about the same time her breasts began to give out milk, so endlessly had they been sucked on.

When they went down to dinner, her breasts felt bursting.

They enjoyed the hubbub of activity, the laughter of guests, the dash of waiters, the sparkle of the gypsy band, the aroma of dishes; her breasts, full and bouncing under silk as she walked between the tables, enjoyed all this. The atmosphere of the white hotel had been restored. Time had healed. Animal spirits had revived. The gypsy band had found an Italian guest who played the fiddle with one of the great orchestras and who was incomparably better than the fiddler who had died, and so, though they mourned their comrade, they rejoiced in the splendid sound they were making, because the new player challenged their own modest skills to fresh heights.

Since several guests had moved out, the head waiter had been able to offer the young lovers a better, bigger table. They sat down to dinner with Madame Cottin and the priest. They were in a relaxed, jovial mood after a whole day in the sunshine and fresh air. The red-faced old man waved his hand in a permitting, approving gesture when the young women opened the front of her dress, explaining how sore and full her breasts were. He was sympathetic, because his mother had suffered from that trouble in her younger days. The young man, dabbing red wine from his lips with a napkin, leaned across to take the nipple into his mouth, but before he could do so her milk spurted out and landed on the table cloth. She blushed scarlet and was full of apologies, but Father Marek and Madame Cottin laughed deprecatingly and a waiter hurried up smiling and adroitly cleaned up the splash with his white towel, leaving just a faint stain. He asked if they would like another table cloth, but everyone said it was not necessary; it was only harmless milk.

The young woman saw the priest looking wistfully at her plump breast as her lover sucked. He was toying with his glass of water, and inwardly yearning for something a little stronger. She asked him if he would care to take out the other breast, and drink from it.

"Are you *sure* you don't mind?" the old priest said, touched and flattered. "I admit it's very tempting." He glanced at Madame Cottin who smiled agreement. "It *is*. Yes! We've had a long walk, after all." She drained her wine glass and poured herself another. "It'll do you good. Water is no drink for a man!" He still looked hesitant, embarrassed.

"I really wish you would," said the young woman. "Please." And the young man took his mouth from the fat nipple to say, "Please do. It's too much for me, honestly." The priest needed no further invitation, and was soon sucking away contentedly. The young woman leaned back, no less contented and eased, and stroked her lover's thick glossy hair and the priest's thin dome. The top of his head had caught the sun, she noticed. Over their heads she smiled at the people at the next table, the baker and his wife and their two children. They were sipping glasses of water. The baker had saved up for years for this holiday, but still could not afford to be extravagant. He smiled back, though, at the thirsty quartet.

"I don't blame them, do you?" he remarked to his wife and children. "If you can afford it, why not enjoy it while you can?" His wife, her envy dowsed by the aroma of the roast duck placed before her at that moment, cut off the tart comment she was about to make, and said simply, "Well, it's nice to see everyone looking cheerful."

Indeed, there was not a doleful face in the whole big dining room. As if everyone had decided simultaneously to compensate, this evening, for the gloom of previous dinners. The waiters were in a holiday mood all of their own, doing little skips to the music as they scurried around, and pretending to juggle with their loaded trays. Even the portly cook quit his ovens to come through and see what all the fun was about. He was given a tremendous cheer, and he grinned his delight, wiping the streaming sweat from his round face. Madame Cottin stood up, walked across to him, and presented him with her empty wine glass. She indicated her engrossed friends, and tugged the chef's arm. Shy, reluctant, he allowed his portly frame to be tugged across the room, his wide grin showing a gap where he had lost a tooth. There were cheers and the stamping of feet as Madame Cottin pulled him to their table. The young bare-breasted woman smiled and nodded at the shy, grinning giant, and gently detached her lover from her nipple — the priest went on sucking contentedly, not even noticing the good-humoured events taking place around him. The young man, his lips circled in white, smiled his willing agreement, and the chef, stooping, tenderly took the plump nipple between thumb and finger and milked it into the wine glass. When it was filled, he lifted the glass triumphantly and drank the sweet milk in one satisfying draught. To grateful comments from all sides, on the quality of his cuisine, he rolled grinning back to his kitchen, the swing doors springing shut behind him.

At one of the other tables, a large one for a family of eight, the celebratory hubbub rivalled even the young lovers' table for the other guests' amused attention. Whole magnums of champagne were being got through in record time; glasses were being smashed; roaring toasts drunk; tuneless but joyful voices raised in the gypsy songs. Word spread that the head of the family, an ancient Dutchman, almost blind, had climbed the mountain behind the hotel and returned with mountain spiderwort, so named because it grows only in high places and in rock crannies accessible only to the spider. The old man had turned to botany late in life, and today's find was the realization of his most cherished dream.

When they heard of this, Madame Cottin and the young woman had a whispered exchange and summoned their waiter. He sprang to their side, all attention, then as nimbly skipped to the Dutch table with their invitation. Almost before he could get his words out they were leaping from their chairs and pouring across to take up the kind offer. And after they had drained their glasses, or drunk directly from her breast, other smiling, slightly merry guests got up to join the queue. The band, too, demanded their refreshment. And even Vogel, without ever losing his supercilious expression and air of boredom — as if to say, I'm here, so I'd better join the herd — came over and sucked briefly at the breast. Returning to his sister, he wiped the milk from his lips with a sarcastic grin.

The sun, dropping suddenly, spread butter on the trees beyond the french windows, and the guests sobered. The priest took his mouth from the nipple, contentedly, and thanked her; then feeling a stab of pain in his heart as he remembered his mother, his guilt at her loneliness and poverty, so far away in his native Poland. Also, sadly, he had broken his vow. He had to get himself ready for the funeral service for those who had died in the flood and the fire. He felt more in the mood for a nap; but his duty had to be done. He stood up and looked for the pastor. They were to share the duties. The young woman fastened her dress.

She could feel her lover's hand touching her beneath the table cloth. Her head was spinning from their having drunk too much. Her lover and Madame Cottin had to support her as they made their way slowly out of the dining room. She protested that she could manage perfectly well, and for Madame Cottin to go upstairs ahead and get her coat for the funeral procession. But Madame Cottin said she was not going. She could not face it.

In the bedroom Madame Cottin undressed the young woman and laid her gently on the bed. Her young lover's penis had been inside her even while they were struggling up the stairs; and now Madame Cottin left her corset and stockings on so that he could stay in her all the time. Vaguely she heard the chants of the mourners as they set off for the cemetery, and she lay peacefully enjoying him. Her eyes were shut, but she felt him take her hand and guide it to where he wanted to press her fingers a little way into her vagina beside his penis. He felt, beside the stroke of the young woman's fingernail, the hardness of Madame Cottin's ring. "It's helping me to get through," whispered Madame Cottin, and the young woman mumbled that she understood: her own wedding ring had been a help to her in her sorrow, and she still could not bear to take it from her finger.

The corpses were being taken on carts, which they heard for a while rumbling through the pines, before fading to silence. The young woman felt empty where she was most filled, and asked for more, sleepily. Dragging her eyes open, she watched

Madame Cottin and her lover kissing passionately.

The path around the shore to the mountain cemetery was very long, and the priest had made this journey on foot once today already. Also, he felt weighed down with the food he had eaten and the strong liquor he had drunk. Clearly others felt much the same as he, and they soon grew tired of singing the funereal hymns. They fell silent, listening to the grumbling of the cart wheels on the sandy path.

The priest fell into hesitant conversation with the pastor. It was the first time he had talked at some length to a minister of the opposite faith; but disaster makes strange bedfellows, he thought. It was an interesting talk, on matters of doctrine. They could agree at least that God's love was beyond analysis. It ran without a seam or join through the whole of His creation. They were stumbling now with fatigue — because the pastor was not a young man either — and stopped talking to conserve their strength. The priest's thoughts went back to the breast at which he had sucked. He tried to remember its roundness and its warmth. He thought also of Madame Cottin, who had given him such good advice, in their trek today, about his feelings of guilt.

Madame Cottin's ample flesh, released from the whalebone that dug into her after her heavy meal, was being tickled and poked by her two young friends, and she was threshing, crying and laughing as she fought to escape from their hands. Foolishly she had said she was ticklish, and they were taking full advantage. She was no match for a strong young man, let alone a young woman bearing down on her too. Once or twice she was almost free and off the bed, but each time the young man dug his thumbs into the tenderest part of her thighs, and she had to submit, lying back panting. Then, while she was weak and off balance they caught hold of her legs and pulled them wide and she was shrieking and struggling again, and rumbling with laughter as they tickled her feet. The young man got between her legs and stopped her cries with his mouth, and she had to promise, in order to be able to breathe, to be a good girl and let him do it. She panted and laughed, more quietly, and her laughter faded into quick-taken breaths, through lips that gently smiled, or joined his in brief, swift kisses.

A stiff breeze tugging the hem of his military coat, Major Lionheart recalled other mass graves he had stood over, and all the letters he had had to write. As colour began to leave the sky and the day to darken under the mountain's shadow, he believed he saw an orange grove floating down towards the lake; and roses too. The impression was strong enough for him to decide to mention it at his next meeting, planned for the next night. The roses matched oddly the vision of the rose seen by the elderly nurse. He had not paid much attention to that before, as she was very nearly in her dotage. He felt sorry for the quiet, sad, charming girl who was in her charge. But maybe she *had* seen a rose at sunset. The mountain spiderwort — that too was strange. Father Marek began to address the line of stiff, cold mourners, and the major turned his thoughts to the handsome young lieutenant, his nephew, who would be arriving on the first train tomorrow. They would have some good skiing. Up there was his favourite ski slope.

The universe, thought Bolotnikov-Leskov, is a revolutionary cell comprising one member: the perfect number for security. God, if he existed, would clench his teeth under the bitterest torture, and no word of betrayal would spring from his lips, because he would have nothing to betray, he would know nothing.

Only half listening to the mumbles of the priest, he looked down with curious dispassion at the coffin lid which hid from sight the naïve young woman who had shared his zeal; so dedicated, in fact, that often she had talked to him about the coming millennium even while they made love.

Cats, thought Enrico Mori, a violinist, have no one to read consoling lies over them. Cats know there is no resurrection, except in transplantation to my music. He stroked the head of the black cat who had followed them all the way from the hotel. She lay now, purring, in the arms of the cancer-troubled prostitute. He knew she was a prostitute because he had been entertained by her once when he was a music student in Turin. They had recognized each other on the first night, and the whore had flushed, and looked away.

Father Marek in his address was speaking about the shroud of Jesus, stained with His blood. The miraculous face was saying, Trust in me, I have borne for you the grave's darkness and chill. Mori noticed that the pastor at the priest's side was looking uncomfortable. Of course, he thought, he doesn't like this talk of images.

As the pastor took up the service, reading the Protestant committal, Mori glanced down and to his right, where a tiny coffin lay. The weeping parents were throwing down flowers. Mori had met the little girl only for a few minutes; the girl had asked if she could try his violin. But they had made friends in those few minutes, and it had shocked him when he found that she had burnt to death.

He was amused, though, when the black cat sprang out of the prostitute's arms and bolted down the path as if seven devils were after it. It was soon lost to sight, on the path back to the hotel. Summoned to vespers, thought Mori; for the bells of the church that stood behind and above the white hotel had started to chime; the sound carried dimly across the lake, and a lone fisherman in the middle of the lake started taking off his hat. The mother of the little girl, to his right, crumpled to the ground, and, as if on cue, other women fainted in the line. That was the trouble with having a mixed funeral service, thought Mori: it went on too long, it was too great a strain.

A thunderclap smote in their ears, and Lionheart, looking up, knew that the end had come. He had heard even louder thunderclaps, in his time, and had threaded through safely; but now there was no escape. The mountain peak had dissolved, and giant boulders were rumbling down the mountainside. The mourners had broken into a sustaining hymn, and for a little while it looked as if the music was holding the boulders in mid-air. The ground was opening under their feet.

The young woman saw the mourners fall, one by one, into the

trench, as if intolerable grief afflicted them, one by one. She watched as they twitched a little and the earth and rocks began settling on top of them. Darkness fell very suddenly that evening, and they lay, listening to the silence again after the thunderclap. Cold under the mountain's shadow, the air was still warm around the white hotel, and they kept the window open. The lake drank the sunlight in one draught, and there was no moon to take its place. They all felt very thirsty, and the young man rang the bell for the maid. The little Japanese girl was startled when she saw three heads on the pillow, and they chuckled at her bewilderment. She brought them a litre bottle of wine and three glasses.

The full-bodied wine revived them. The experience had been unique, for all of them, and they talked about it happily. Madame Cottin was pleased to see the young lovers showing unharmed affection for each other by their kisses and playful nibbles.

Far from damaging their love, the experience had strengthened it; or so the young woman believed. Generosity always rewards the giver, and their kindness to the lonely, bereaved woman had drawn them closer to each other. So she felt happy. And her lover was happy because he lay snugly in between them, the tasty meat between two fresh slices of bread. He drank, lit a Turkish cigarette for Madame Cottin and gave it into her hand; lit another for himself, took a draw, exhaled with a sigh of pleasure, turned to give his mistress an affectionate kiss.

Madame Cottin envied them their firm young bodies, for at thirty-nine she knew she was well past her best. And the church bells, sounding as if they came from the room above, made her gloomier. Probably the most she could hope for, at her time of life, were a few brief adventures like this one; but for the most part, solitude. She reached for the wine bottle and poured herself another glass; but the wine stopped pouring when her glass was only half full. "Is this all there is?" she asked, apologetically.

"It's all we know about," said the young woman, in thoughtful tones. "It's all we can be sure of. Fairly sure."

Since they had finished the wine, the young man started fondling Madame Cottin's plump, rather slack, breasts. Parting her thighs he clambered on to her again. The young woman offered her a nipple, because the wine had gone into milk and her breasts felt full and painful again. She took it into her mouth gratefully. At the same time he began to suck at her own breast, and the circle of pleasure was almost complete. The young man was very excited, very erect, and thrust so hard that Madame Cottin screamed; and, as she screamed, brought her teeth together and bit the young woman's breast, drawing blood mingled with milk. It was late before Madame Cottin dressed and went back to her room. The hotel was dark, silent.

The dozing night porter was woken by the night bell. When he opened the door it was Bolotnikov-Leskov and Vogel; they slid in looking tired, unkempt and dirty. They each ordered a pot of coffee, a large brandy, and a round of sandwiches to be sent to their rooms, and ordered their usual newspapers for the morning. Bolotnikov-Leskov gave Vogel a curt good night as they parted on the first floor. He did not even like the fellow, but they shared the same general principles in life. Besides, Vogel was a survivor, like himself, and such men are worth a thousand virtuous losers.

TOWARDS EVENING OF the next day he became restive, and suggested they get out of bed and take a walk up in the mountains. She felt tired, and would rather have taken a short stroll by the lake: perhaps with Madame Cottin. But he had in mind a bigger expedition, just the two of them.

He rang the bell, summoning the maid to bring tea and to open the curtains. Adjusting to the flood of sunlight, the young woman saw that the little Japanese maid had been crying. She inquired if anything was the matter, and the maid told her of the disastrous landslide that had buried the mourners. She was very upset because she had grown fond of the English major who was one of the victims. To her surprise, she had discovered that he had visited her homeland, and even knew a little of her language. Lonely, waiting for the arrival of his nephew, an army lieutenant, he had asked her to go with him on walks, during her hours of freedom in the afternoons. He had been very interested in her studies, and altogether had proved a kind, intelligent friend. She would miss him.

Grateful for the young woman's sympathy, the maid excused herself for a few moments, and returned clutching to her heart a slim book, which she said the major had given her only yesterday, on their last walk together. The young woman took the book and saw, on the plain cover, "*Meadowsweet*, Poems by Harold Lionheart". She flipped quickly through the twenty or so little poems in the volume, and gave it back, with a sympathetic nod. "It's something to remember him by," she said. The maid, her eyes moistening, opened the book at the title-page and handed it back. The young woman saw some lines of verse written out in copperplate, and signed "With love from Major Harold Lionheart". The maid explained that she had spoken to him some little verses which she had been ordered by her teacher to write during her vacation. And yesterday, on taking him his morning tea, he had presented her with this book, his translations of her verses written out on the first page. She had been so touched she had burst into tears. The young woman read the copperplate lines:

> At sunset, even
> the stone of the plum can turn
> the green lake crimson.

> The plum who marries
> an ox can anticipate
> great sorrow, great joy.

Like biting a plum
to reach the stone, is passion
for this hour only.

When the plum ripens
the swan flies. When my love is
nigh me, my heart sings.

Behind the hotel, the path up the mountain was steep and
stony, winding between clumps of larches and pines. At first
they walked with their arms around each other's waists; but as
the path narrowed and grew steeper he let her climb ahead. She
was in quite the wrong clothes for a mountain climb, but it was
the only dress she had. In the lifeless heat her sweat made the
dress cling to her buttocks and thighs; and he could not resist the
temptation to slide his hand, now and again, up the cleft
between her thighs. They came to a cool, grassy terrace where
the church spire nestled among yew trees. Stopping to breathe,
he put his arms around her waist and turned her face so that he
could kiss her throat, her lips. He pulled her down on to the
cropped grass.

"Someone might come," she whispered, as his hand tugged
her dress up round her waist. "It doesn't matter," he said. "I
want you. Please. Please."

A donkey, tethered, was grazing the short grass, twisting the
rope round a fence post and drawing his domain smaller and
smaller. The animal belonged to an order of nuns who lived and
worshipped in the convent house attached to the church.
Unknown to the lovers, an old and stooping nun had hobbled
out with a basket of linen to wash; for near where they lay there
was a spring. They thought they heard the noise of falling rocks
above them, but it was the old nun flailing the dirty clothes with
a stout stick.

Embarrassed, the young woman slid away from her lover and
flustered her dress down. The old nun stopped her flailing for a
moment and flashed a toothless grin in their direction. "It's all

right," she said. "Nothing is sinful here because of the spring, you know. Have a drink before you leave. But don't hurry. I'm sorry I interrupted you. I won't be long." She explained that the nuns needed fresh linen for the memorial service for Father Marek and the other Catholics who had died in the avalanche. She crossed herself piously.

The lovers resumed their lovemaking, pausing again to smile their thanks as the nun wished them good day and good luck, and hobbled off with her heavy basket of wet clothes. The lovers cupped their hands and drank from the spring. The water was ice-cold and refreshing. As they brushed the grass off their clothes they looked down at the lake, amazed how red it was, like the juiciest of plums.

The path upwards lost itself in boulders and deceiving patches of snow, and they had to go carefully. Sometimes they had to scramble on hands and knees; and the rapidly falling darkness only made it more difficult. "I've torn my dress," she observed; and he said that tomorrow they would check at the station, and maybe her suitcase would have turned up. If not, perhaps they could ask the maid if there was a shop where they could buy dresses. "And a toothbrush," she said. "I wouldn't mind if I only had a toothbrush."

The object of their climb was a small observatory which had been built on this mountain but later abandoned. They found it just as the sun dropped behind a peak, bringing instant night. It was fearfully cold, and the young woman wished she had brought her coat. They entered the black shell. There was nothing inside except a slit in the roof for the telescope that had never been installed.

He had badly misjudged the time it would take to climb the mountain. There was no chance of making the descent that night. "I'll keep you warm," he said; and they lay on the icy floor and he held her tightly in his arms. Wisps of snow fell on them, through the slit in the dome.

"Please, you mustn't make me pregnant," she whispered. He could see the whites of her eyes, whiter than the snowflakes. She

thought, This is the way it could so easily happen. Not, iron-
ically, in a warm bed in a fall of roses and orange trees, but on a
freezing night when the stars fall as snowflakes through a tiny
slit. A cold wisp fell on her cheek and she thought, These are the
seeds of God. The fierceness of his lovemaking warmed her. She
heard mountain cascades, faintly, not on this mountain only,
but from all the mountains surrounding the lake and the white
hotel. And the cascades sang, because the night and the snow
allowed the mountains to meet; they sang as the whales had
sung, at dawn, unheard, when the office secretary and Vogel's
sister had glimpsed them.

The young woman was warmed, also, by the depths of snow
that fell, half burying the igloo. The whole sky fell in the night,
all the stars and constellations. She listened to the very beginning of the universe, a very soft, sighing sound.

By morning they were rimed with frost, and famished; but
had to content themselves with gathering up snow, a whole
cluster of white stars, and drinking it as it melted. They broke
through the wall of stars that had piled up in the doorway, and
gasped to see how everything was white below them. Even the
lake was ice-covered. Only the dark green of some of the pines
and firs showed through the snow and ice. The white hotel itself
was lost in white. There was simply deep snow where they
thought the white hotel must be.

"We must try to find the path back," he said hopelessly.

"You know that's not possible," the woman said. "We can't
retrace our steps; and anyway why should we ? Remember what
the nun said, that here there is no sin."

The young man made no reply; just touched his neat moustache as if to reassure himself that he still existed, and set off
floundering. As the sun broke through and the clouds swiftly
parted they felt more cheerful. The labour of wading through
the snow sent the blood coursing again; they tingled with
warmth and energy. They could see the ice of the lake breaking
up into floes, and the floes vanishing into the blue water. A few
birds were whistling. Snow slid, hissing, off the church spire,

and — aiming for that — they found it not difficult to keep to the path. Midway between the observatory and the church, there was a flat resting place with a wooden seat and a telescope, through which you could watch climbers attempting the sheer mountain face across the lake.

They sat on the seat, and happily pecked a kiss. The day was turning fine; the melting snow was tumbling from a thousand cascades into the lake, and there was, by now, not a cloud in the sky. Still they could not see the white hotel.

The young man stood up and went to the telescope. He trained it down in the general direction of the hotel, and, as a patch of snow broke off and fell on to a veranda, he saw their bedroom window. For there were the words she had traced with her breath and her finger, just before leaving, a phrase of Heine. He called her to come and look. She smiled in relief as she saw, vaguely inside, his hair brushes and the uncollected tea tray, and the unmade bed. She began to worry, though, at not having explained to the maid about the bloodstains on the sheet. Yet she must be used to chaotic beds, the diaries of people's loves.

She let her lover take the telescope from her, and he started turning it at random. He could see edelweiss rippling in the breeze, probably ten miles away. Turning the telescope away from the distant mountain to the blue over the lake, he caught reflected sunlight and had to pull his eyes away. He looked again, more cautiously, and saw it was the reflection of a metal clasp on a white corset suspender. The metal had slightly frayed the elastic, and, thinking he recognized it, he drew breath sharply.

"Isn't that Madame Cottin?" he said.

She put her eye again to the glass, and saw a pale, stout thigh against the dazzling blue, and a fading bruise. And there — tilting the glass up slightly — was a strained pink face.

"Yes, it's Denise," she said. He looked again, and smiled. There were other people falling near her; yet with the naked eye nothing could be seen but a cable car crawling minutely along between two mountains. The bruise he had made on her fleshy thigh made him roll with his startled friend on the short, wet mountain grass. She tried to cry out that the air was too thin; his sudden passion made her gulp for breath.

When the cable car had broken from one of its strands, and sent them screaming out through the open top and down through the air, the baker's son had had the presence of mind to keep tight hold of the black cat that had crept aboard after him. Just because he had given it a stroke on the hotel steps, the cat had followed him all the way up the path to the cable car. The cat, now, was miaowing and scratching, but the boy kept hold.

He was not sucking at her nipple but vibrating it rapidly with his tongue; like a child setting up ripples by skimming the sea with a flat stone. Their skirts blown up around their waists by the motion of the air, the women fell more slowly than the men. Madame Cottin, her heart in her mouth, saw a handsome Dutch lad falling only a few feet away from her, quite vertical, as was she, and she had the strange impression that she was not falling to her death but being lifted high by his strong arms. She had once, unforgettably, seen Pavlova dance; now, young and thin, she had become Pavlova. The men and boys struck the ground or the lake first. Madame Cottin saw the baker's boy land in a pine tree, feet-first, and contriving somehow to turn on to his back (which instantly snapped) in a way that made sure the cat was safe. The black cat tore itself out of his arms and clawed its way down the trunk.

The women and young girls fell next; and last of all, after what seemed an eternity, a hail of skis, glinting in the sunlight, tumbled into the pines and the lake.

They rested again by the spring — where the donkey still browsed — and cupped their hands to drink the pure water. They visited the church, which had been filled with flowers for the memorial service, and then wandered into the walled graveyard which the local inhabitants preserved for their own. The graveyard, and the tall yews, trapped the heat. Each grave carried a smiling photograph of the dead person, on the stone; and there were many glass jars holding immortelles. At one of the graves, an old woman in black was bending to look at a photograph, and the young woman felt ashamed to be seen in her torn dress. "I don't like the immortelles," she said, drawing her arm through his and leading him out of the cemetery.

As the lake rose nearer, she could see the fish swimming around in it: millions of gold or silver fins twisting and turning aimlessly forever and ever. Or so it seemed to her. Actually they were not aimless; she could see they were hunting for food; their round, mindless eyes were staring curiously at the huge grey shapes drifting down through the water, to feast them. The wriggling fish reminded her of tadpoles in a pond, and then of sperm, a picture her governess had shown her, sperm magnified a thousand times. They wriggled with apparent aimlessness, yet were seeking.

At dinner that evening the young man was puzzled because she was quiet and depressed. It was not on account of a depression in the general atmosphere, because on the whole cheerfulness prevailed. A whole new crowd of tourists had moved in, and naturally they could not be expected to eat their hearts out over misfortunes that had preceded them. On the contrary, they were in excellent spirits at the start of their holiday. There were only a few familiar faces left: Vogel, the older members of the Dutch family (eating in silence), Bolotnikov-Leskov, and the pale, sad, pathetically thin young woman with her elderly nurse.

Both the gypsy band and the waiting staff tried to keep up an air of jollity, for the sake of the newcomers; though they themselves had suffered losses. The accordion player had persuaded the popular little Japanese maid to give skiing a try, on her free half-day. The young woman was upset when she heard about this from their waiter. She recalled one of the maid's little verses, translated by the English major, and she repeated it to her friend:

> The plum who marries
> an ox can anticipate
> great sorrow, great joy.

She did not think it amusing, as her friend did; she found it disturbing, moving, even erotic. She put herself in the position of the plum, exuding its dewy moisture and trembling in the marriage bed as the hour for the coming of the ox drew near. She anticipated the fearsome breaking of her hymen, the horrific penetration. It made her shiver and break into a sweat.

But she knew she ought not to feel that way. This was what was making her depressed; and finally, while they were eating a lemon sherbet, she explained. She wondered if she had grown obsessed with sex. She admitted to thinking about it almost all the time. She even enjoyed, in her heart, the dirty word for it which had brought a blush to her cheeks when she overheard the English major say it, in the branches of the fir. And other words she was ashamed even to know. She rejoiced in them because they were so dirty. She had never told anyone else about this wickedness of hers.

He smiled indulgently, and took her hands. She removed them from his grasp and ran them, absently and in agitation, round her coffee cup.

"It's not as if," she said, "the world around me is sexual. It would excuse me, to some extent, if it were. If there were fish spawning in millions, grapes loading the vines, dates weighing the palm trees, peaches lusting for the bull to come in the night."

She looked up from the coffee cup, looking for his green eyes to help her; but he avoided her gaze by resting his cheek on his finger and looking round at the band. His refusal to help angered her, because he was much to blame for her obsessions. Before meeting him, she had held them under control.

"And if I'm not thinking about sex, I'm thinking about death," she added bitterly. "Sometimes both at the same time." She took a knife from the cheese board, and twisted it in tense hands.

She did not add that she had foreseen the deaths of Madame Cottin, and of the Japanese student, and of the lady with one breast, and all the others; or that she foresaw his death, and her own.

The young woman cheered up after he had bought her a liqueur at the bar and taken it through to the pleasant terrace to catch the last warm rays of the sun. Some of the newcomers were eager to talk to them, knowing they had actually witnessed the tragedy of the ski lift. The new arrivals wore looks of horror and pity, but beneath that played a much more powerful feeling of excitement at the stunning drama they had just missed; as well as an infinite relief that the break had occurred today rather than tomorrow.

Vogel, standing or swaying beside Bolotnikov-Leskov, in a near-by group of newcomers, was drunk. He was saying in a very loud voice that it might have been worse — there were a large number of Yids among the victims. He was thinking of Madame Cottin and the young members of the Dutch family.

It was an unspeakably offensive remark, in the presence of the old Dutch couple and of the invalid young woman. A hush fell. His Russian friend, embarrassed, led Vogel away. When he returned, he apologized to the Jews who had heard Vogel's words. It was inexcusable, he said; but they must in charity recall that Vogel had suffered more than most from the disasters of the white hotel, having lost a cousin in the flood, a dear friend in the fire, and his sister in the landslide. Also, he — Bolotnikov-Leskov — and Vogel had both had extremely narrow escapes, since they had gone to the ski lift ahead of the main party, intending to take a ride, but had changed their minds at the last minute owing to the uncertainties of the weather. They themselves could have been falling down through the air.

So one could perhaps excuse Vogel for getting drunk and giving vent to deranged remarks. Though — he had to say it — he was not the nicest of men at the best of times.

One of the newcomers, a Belgian doctor, asked if they thought the broken strand might have been an act of political terrorism. Bolotnikov-Leskov said it might conceivably be the case. If so, he deplored it; though he thought such desperate acts were bound to continue so long as there was injustice in the world, and violence against the people.

The new guests were beginning to get uneasy with this talk of violence and terrorism, and the conversation on the terrace turned gradually to more pleasant themes, such as the likelihood tomorrow of firm snow and calm water.

The young lovers took themselves off to bed, where they were disturbed by nothing more ominous than the faint but frequent ringing of the telephone in the depths of the hotel. The calls were almost always requests for rooms, because the white hotel was extremely popular and there were, summer and winter, more requests than they could possibly accommodate. From this point of view alone, the catastrophic deaths of the past few days were a godsend; but even this unusually rapid turnover could not keep pace with the demand, and many had to be turned away. The hotel staff worked wonders in fitting as many people in as possible. On the very day of Madame Cottin's death, the young lovers heard a camp bed being dragged in next door, so that room could be found for a young married couple and their child.

A place was found, too, for another young couple who had a baby well on the way. There was really no room for them, but the girl was crying and distraught, so finally a trunk room was cleared. The lovers were woken by the girl's cries in the night; after which they heard the tireless staff scurrying about with towels and hot water and the other necessaries of childbirth. It was another night of bitter cold and snowfall, and it was a mercy that room had been found for the poor young woman. Though it was foolish of them to have come, without being sure of a room, so far on in her pregnancy.

It was to the credit of the overworked staff that they never grumbled. They were simply marvellous — a description that occurred, in various guises, over and over again in the guest book. . . "Wonderful food, and nothing too much trouble. See you next year". . . "The best of everything. We were treated like royalty". . . "Thanks for having us. Tip-top service and accommodation. We'll be back". . . "Good value". . . "Nowhere else like it. Enjoyed every minute." The whole staff, from shoe-cleaner to manager, piled in to help restore the damaged wing, in their time off, so that all the rooms should be available. Even the chef, the portly beaming chef, took a hand in the refurbishing — embarrassingly, for one day the lovers were disturbed by a scraping at their window, and when they looked across they saw the jolly chef beaming in, paint brush in hand. The young woman was being mounted from behind; pink with shame, she tried to pretend she was kneeling in prayer. But they were so far gone, and he gave them such a jolly wink, that there seemed no harm in calling him in and asking him to join them. And he must been good for more things than steaks, because, with her eyes closed and her face buried in the pillow, she could not tell which of them was making love to her, it was all equally rare, tender, and full of good juice. She felt happy that part of her body was occupied by someone else. The spirit of the white hotel was against selfishness.

Sometimes she felt uneasy and closed in, but if she suggested going out, he took her in his arms again and said they had so little time. Outside, it was sad not to see the familiar baker, casting his nets in the middle of the lake. The baker's lad flying his kite. The old priest reading in his deck chair. Madame Cottin sharing a laugh with the cheeky young waiter. But swans were soaring between the mountain peaks; whether gliding down to the lake or rising to leave it. Their feathers were so white, the dazzling peaks seemed grey in comparison.

III

Frau Anna G.

IN THE AUTUMN of 1919 I was asked by a doctor of my acquaintance to examine a young lady who had been suffering for the past four years from severe pains in her left breast and pelvic region, as well as a chronic respiratory condition. When making this request he added that he thought the case was one of hysteria, though there were certain counter-indications which had caused him to examine her very thoroughly indeed in order to rule out the possibility of some organic affection. The young woman was married, but living apart from her husband, in the home of an aunt. Our patient had had a promising musical career interrupted by her illness.

My first interview of this young woman of twenty-nine years of age did not help me to make much progress in understanding her case, nor could I glimpse any sign of the inner vitality I was assured she possessed. Her face, in which the eyes were the best feature, showed the marks of severe physical suffering; yet there were moments when it registered nothing, and at these times I was reminded of the faces of victims of battle traumas, whom it had been my melancholy duty to examine. When she talked, it was often difficult for me to hear, on account of her hoarse and rapid breathing. As a consequence of her pains, she walked with an awkward gait, bending forward from the waist. She was extremely thin, even by the standards of that unhappy year, when few in Vienna had enough to eat. I suspected an anorexia nervosa, on top of her other troubles. She told me the mere thought of food made her ill, and she was living on oranges and water.

On examining her I understood my colleague's reluctance to abandon the search for an organic basis for her symptoms. I was struck by the definiteness of all the descriptions of the character of her pains given me by the patient, the kind of response we have come to expect from a patient suffering from an organic illness — unless he is neurotic in addition. The hysteric will tend to describe his pain indefinitely, and will tend to respond to stimulation of the painful part rather with an expression of pleasure than pain. Frau Anna, on the contrary, indicated where she hurt precisely and calmly: her left breast and left ovary; and flinched and drew back from my examination.

She herself was convinced that her symptoms were organic, and was very disappointed that I could not find the cause and put it right. My own increasing conviction that I was, despite appearances to the contrary, dealing with an hysteria was confirmed when she confessed that she also suffered from visual hallucinations of a disordered and frightening nature. She had feared to confess to these "storms in her head", because it seemed to her an admission that she was mad and should be locked away. I was able to assure her that her hallucinations, like her pains and her breathing difficulties, were no sign of dementia; that indeed, given the intractable nature of reality, the healthiest mind may become a prey to hysterical symptoms. Her manner thereafter became a little more relaxed, and she was able to tell me something of the history of her illness and of her life in general.

She was the second child and only daughter of moderately wealthy parents. Her father came from a Russian Jewish family of the merchant class, and her mother from a cultivated Polish Catholic family which had settled in the Ukraine. In marrying across racial and religious barriers, Frau Anna's parents proved their own liberated ideals but suffered the consequence of being cut off from their families. The only close relative who did not turn against the couple was the patient's aunt (with whom she was now living), her mother's twin sister. This woman had married a Viennese teacher of languages, of her own faith, whom she had met when he was attending a conference in Kiev, the sisters' native city. Hence the two sisters were forced to live far apart, but their close bond remained undiminished.

As a result of her loyalty to her twin, Frau Anna's aunt also became increasingly estranged from her family, with the exception of her father who came to live with her in his old age. The patient felt that her own life had been impoverished by these family estrangements. Nor were there many relatives of her own generation to compensate. Her mother had given birth to a son early in her marriage, followed five years later by Anna. The aunt, to her sorrow, had remained childless.

The patient had the fondest memories of her mother. She possessed a warmly maternal nature, handsome looks, a creative spirit (she was a water-colourist of some talent), and an impulsive gaiety. If she had grey moods, usually in response to miserable autumn or winter weather, she indulged her children all the more when they were over. She and Anna's father made a handsome couple. The father also had great energy and charm, and the child adored him though she wished he were not so busy. He had worked immensely hard, without parental support, to establish himself in business. Shortly after Anna's birth, he had moved his family to Odessa, where he became the owner of a grain-exporting firm. Almost his only relaxation was sailing: he was the proud owner of a splendid yacht.

In the pleasant seaport, each summer, they were joined by the patient's uncle and aunt. The little girl looked forward to these visits, which, thanks to the Viennese custom of long summer vacations, lasted for several weeks. With the family guests, and with pleasant yachting weather, her father took more days from his business, becoming more genial and approachable; and her mother positively spread her leaves with the arrival of her beloved sister and the sun, together. Naturally her sister, childless herself, was devoted to her little niece. The aunt was of a quiet and devout disposition. A gifted pianist, she preferred the tranquillity of the music room to the possible turbulence of the yacht. Anna's uncle was more outgoing: a hearty, jovial man, as uncles are supposed to be. The patient recalled his fondness for jokes, such as donning a white officer's cap for sailing. Her uncle and aunt were important to Anna, as her only 'family' apart from her parents and her brother — and to her brother she was not strongly attached.

If I had not been familiar with the idealizing tendencies of our adult years, I should have believed that the patient's early childhood held no tedious or unpleasant interludes, but consisted entirely of building castles of sand on the beach, and gliding along in her father's yacht, under the blue sky, past the cliffs of the Black Sea coast; and that this happy state lasted interminably. In fact, these happy and vivid memories extended only to her fifth summer; for the shadow of the event which would bring a cruelly sudden expulsion from her paradise was already hanging over her — her mother's death.

Her mother was in the habit of varying the tedium of the winter by making occasional visits to Moscow, for the shops, galleries and theatres. For Anna, there were two consolations: she had her father to herself, and her mother always came back laden with presents. This year, just before Christmas, she did not return with the expected gifts. Instead, a telegram arrived with the news of a fire that had destroyed the hotel in which she was staying. To Anna's immature mind the news meant only that her mother would be away a few days longer. Yet, as she was being undressed for bed, she was disturbed by her nurse's crying. She recalled lying awake, wondering where her mother could be, and listening to the storm which happened to be raging. Two of her recurrent hallucinations in adult life — a storm at sea, and a fire at a hotel — clearly related to this tragic event.

Her grief-stricken father withdrew more or less completely into his business affairs; and in any case preferred the company of his son, now old enough to hold a sensible conversation. Anna was left in the hands of her nurse and her governess. There were no more visits from her aunt and uncle, for by a melancholy coincidence her uncle also died, a few months later, of a heart attack. As a teacher, his income had not been large, and his still youthful widow was forced to sell her home, move into a cheap apartment, and make a meagre living by teaching the piano. Except for letters and occasional small gifts, the burdened and unhappy woman lost touch with her sister's children. Neither she nor the patient's father had ever remarried.

One may easily conceive the young girl's loneliness and misery, deprived so cruelly of her mother, abandoned by her aunt and uncle (as it must have seemed), and treated indifferently by her father. Fortunately she was in the care of sensible and devoted attendants, particularly her governess. By the age of twelve or thirteen, Anna could speak three languages besides her native Ukrainian; was familiar with good literature, and demonstrated a considerable degree of talent in music. She enjoyed dancing, and was able to attend ballet classes at the *lycée*. This had the advantage of giving her an opportunity to form friendships, and she became, by her own account, quite sociable and popular. Altogether, then, she survived the loss of her mother better than many, or perhaps most, children would have done.

When she was fifteen, an unpleasant incident occurred which left its mark on her. There were political disturbances; an uprising of the fleet; violence and street demonstrations. The patient, with two friends, ventured imprudently into the docks area of the city, to observe events. Because of their genteel dress and appearance they were threatened and insulted by a group of insurgents. No physical harm was done to the girls, but they were badly frightened. What affected the patient more was the attitude of her father, when she returned home. Instead of comforting her, he coldly rebuked her for having exposed herself to danger. Perhaps he was merely hiding his concern, and was genuinely upset at the grave risk his daughter had run; but for the young girl his hostile air was the final proof that he cared nothing for her. Henceforward she returned reserve for reserve, coldness for coldness. It was not long after this episode that she had her first experience of the breathless condition, which was treated as asthma but to no avail. After several months it subsided of its own accord.

Shortly after her seventeenth birthday, she left Odessa, and her father's house, for St Petersburg, on no other basis than the prospect of an audition with a ballet school. She was without friends in the capital, and had no means of support except for a small inheritance from her mother which she was now old enough to claim. She was successful in her audition, and lived frugally in a rented room in a poor quarter of the city. She formed an attachment with a young man living in the house: a student, A., who was strongly involved in the movement for political reform. He introduced her to a circle of friends of like commitment.

Her interest in the political struggle was wholly subordinate to her involvement with A. She brought to her first love all the pure and generous ardour of that state; their relationship was an *affaire de cœur*, not of the flesh. But after a while he abandoned her for more important concerns — the coming conflagration. Almost at the same time she was abandoned by her chosen profession: not because she failed in skill or application, but simply that she was becoming a woman, and gaining flesh which she could not lose, even though she was eating next to nothing. She was forced to conclude that nature did not intend her for a prima ballerina. Fortunately, at this distressing time, one of her ballet teachers, a youthful widow who lived alone, befriended her, and invited her to share her home until she had planned what to do with her life. Madame R. became her mentor as well as her friend. They went to concerts and theatres together, and during the day, while Madame R. was at the ballet school, Anna read from her well-stocked library or went for pleasant walks. It was a quiet and happy period in her life, restoring her to good spirits.

The comfortable and mutually convenient arrangement ended when Madame R. unexpectedly decided to remarry. The man in question, a retired naval officer, had become a congenial friend to them both, and Anna had not suspected any attachment threatening her own tranquil existence. Yet she could not but rejoice at her friend's well-deserved good fortune. Madame

R. and her new husband begged Anna to stay on, but she did not wish to interfere in their happiness. She was uncertain where to go and what to do; but, at just the right moment, an unusually kind fate pushed the young woman towards a new country and a new profession. Her aunt wrote to her from Vienna to say that her father — Anna's grandfather — who had been living with her for some years had died, and she was alone again. She asked Anna if she would consider coming to live with her, at least for a few months. The young woman did not hesitate to accept the invitation, and left for Vienna, after a sad leavetaking with her kind friend Madame R. and her husband.

Coming face to face with her aunt, for the first time since her mother had been alive, she was overcome by both sadness and happiness. Her first impression was that she was being welcomed by her mother, grown graciously middle-aged.[1] For her part, her aunt doubtless found many poignant reminders of her sister in this sensitive and intelligent young woman of twenty. Aunt and niece slipped at once into a warm relationship, and Frau Anna never found any cause to regret her decision to leave her native country.

As so often happens, the change of environment brought about changes in Frau Anna herself. She had been brought up by her nurse to a somewhat half-hearted belief in the Catholic religion, the faith of her mother's side of the family. During her adolescent years she had drifted away from it, but now, under her aunt's influence, she became devout. More practically, again as a consequence of being in her aunt's musical environment, she found an enthusiasm, and a skill, which promised to fill the gap left by the failure of her attempt to become a dancer. Under the tuition of a close friend of her aunt's, the young woman learned to play the cello; and rather to her astonishment discovered that she was highly talented musically. She made such rapid progress that her teacher was predicting, within a few months, that she might become a virtuoso performer.

---

[1] Almost literally so, for the two were identical twins.

Within three years of her arrival in Vienna, she was playing in a professional orchestra and was also engaged to be married. The man in question was a young barrister of good family, deeply attached to music, who had made her acquaintance during a social occasion at the Conservatorium. The young man was well-mannered, modest and rather shy (a combination that appealed to her), and an attachment very soon grew up. He was thoroughly approved by her aunt, and Anna got on well with his parents. He proposed to her, and — after a very brief struggle between her wish for domestic happiness and a professional musical career — she accepted.

They spent a honeymoon in Switzerland, and then settled into a pleasant house. Her aunt, a frequent and welcome guest, was happy in knowing that a grand-nephew or -niece would soon console her for any pang she felt at being alone again; for she knew how much Anna wanted a child.

The only cloud on the young couple's horizon was the rumour of war. When hostilities broke out, the husband was called to serve in the army's legal department. Their farewells were sad, but there was the comfort that he would be out of the combat zone and was stationed close enough to be able to return home often. They wrote to each other every day, and the patient was fruitfully occupied with her musical career, in a city hungry for the last remnants of civilized culture. Indeed, as her playing improved with experience, her career began to flourish. She had her aunt and plenty of friends for companionship. Altogether, except for the major drawback of being apart from her husband, she was busy and contented.

Just at this time, as her husband was expecting his first home leave, she suffered a recurrence of the breathlessness that had afflicted her in Odessa, and also developed incapacitating pains in her breast and abdomen. She lost all desire to eat, and had to abandon her music. Informing her husband that she had fallen ill, and that she now realized she could never make him happy, she went back to live with her aunt. Her husband, obtaining compassionate leave, came to plead with her, but she remained adamant. Though he would never forgive her for the hurt she was causing him, she begged him to forget her. He had continued to try to win her back; and only in the past few months had he consented to a legal separation. For the past four years Frau Anna had lived in almost total seclusion. Her aunt had taken her to see many doctors, but none had been able to find the cause of her illness or to effect any improvement.

This, then, was the story which the unfortunate young woman told me. It threw no light on the causes of her hysteria. There was, it is true, a rich soil for the growth of a neurosis, notably the early loss of her mother, and her father's neglect. But if the early death of one parent, and the inadequacy of the other, were sufficient grounds for the formation of an hysteria, there would be many thousands of such. What, in Frau Anna's case, was the hidden factor which had determined the creation of her neurosis?

What she had in her consciousness was only a secret and not a foreign body. She both knew and did not know. In a sense, too, her mind was attempting to tell us what was wrong; for the repressed idea creates its own apt symbol. The psyche of an hysteric is like a child who has a secret, which no one must know, but everyone must guess. And so he must make it easier by scattering clues. Clearly the child in Frau Anna's mind was telling us to look at her breast and her ovary: and precisely the left breast and ovary, for the unconscious is a precise and even pedantic symbolist.

For many weeks I was able to make very little progress in my attempt to help her. Partly the circumstances in which we worked were to blame; it was difficult to create an atmosphere of confidence, in an unheated room in winter, with patient and physician dressed in coats, mufflers and gloves.[1] Also the analysis had often to be interrupted, many days together, when

[1] [Fuel for heating and lighting was in desperately short supply after the war. — Ed.]

her pains became so distressing that she was forced to take to her bed. There was, however, some remission of her anorexia; I was able to persuade her to take solid food — in so far as nourishing food was obtainable at all in the city at that time.

A much more decisive factor in the slowness of our progress was her strong resistance. Though not as prudish as many of my patients, the young woman was reticent to the point of silence when any question of her sexual feelings and behaviour rose in the course of the discussion. An innocent inquiry, as for example on the subject of childhood masturbation (an almost universal phenomenon), was met by blank denial. I might, her attitude implied, have been asking the question of the Virgin. I found I had good cause to doubt some of the superficial memories she had related; which did not bode well for any deeper investigation. She was unreliable, evasive; and I became angry at the waste of my time. To be just to her, I should add that I soon learnt to distinguish her truth from her insincerity: if she was hiding something, she fumbled with a crucifix at her throat, as though asking God's forgiveness. Thus, there was in her a *propensity* for truth, even if only on the grounds of superstition, which made me persevere in helping her.[1] I was forced to lure the truth out of her, often by throwing out a provocative suggestion. As often as not, she would take the bait, offering a retraction or modification of her story.

One of her retractions related to her affair with A., the student whom she had loved in St Petersburg. So far, she had told me only trivial facts about him: such as that he was a student of philosophy, of wealthy and conservative background, a few years older than she, etc. She stuck to her story that it had been a 'white' relationship. I was struck by the adjective she used, and asked her what she associated with the word "white". She said it conjured up the sails of a yacht; and it seemed reasonable to suppose that she was recalling her father's yacht. But one should never jump to conclusions in psychoanalysis: she said she was

[1] She told me one day that the crucifix was an heirloom from her mother. Thus, filial piety reinforced religious awe.

thinking instead of one weekend in Petersburg when she and other members of the political group, including of course A., went out sailing in the Gulf. It was perfect summer weather, and a relief to her to be sailing again and to have a break from the 'serious' discussions which were beginning to bore her and even frighten her. She had never felt so much in love with A., and he was tender towards her, and respectful as always. They had to share a cabin, but he never once tried to touch her; their consciences remained as white as the sails, or as the white nights.[1]

She was nevertheless fumbling with her crucifix, and her face wore an expression of sorrow. I told her, sharply, that she was not telling me the truth, and that I knew there had been a sexual affair. Frau Anna confessed that she had slept with him a few times, towards the end; he had begged and begged her, and at last, almost in weariness, she had "fallen". She used the English verb; our discussions were in German, but it was not unusual for her to interject foreign terms now and again. I had learned to be alert to their possible significance.

I decided to "chance my arm", as the saying goes. "I'm glad you're being honest," I said. "There's nothing to feel ashamed of. And why, while you're about it, don't you confess that he got you with child, but you lost it in a fall downstairs?"

The poor girl struggled with her feelings, and then admitted that I was right; not downstairs, but from a bad fall in the dance studio. No one had ever known of this, except Madame R., or even suspected it, and she was astonished that I had found out her secret. She asked me how I had been able to tell.

I replied: "Because your story of putting on weight, and so having to stop dancing, didn't ring true. I should guess *you* would find it difficult to gain weight, at any time, much though it would improve you. It was an obvious way of telling me what happened, indirectly — for you really wanted me to know. You probably went on dancing too long, in your condition, and were worried sick about *beginning* to put on weight; and generally

[1] An allusion to the long summer nights, in the far north, where the days are only divided by a brief dusk.

wondering what to do in an impossible situation."

The young woman's silence told me I had struck home all too truly, and I was glad I had not taken my interpretation to its logical end — that by continuing to practise energetically, she had been secretly hoping for just such a consequence; indeed, may even have precipitated it. She was sufficiently disturbed by the bringing to light of her youthful sin.

From this point, however, she became a little livelier and more frank, as though relieved that her burden of unreal perfection had been lifted. She even revealed, shortly afterwards, a flash of sly humour. She was describing to me one of her recurrent hallucinations, of falling through the air to her death. Her eyes twinkled for a moment and she said, "But I'm not having a baby!"[1]

She came one day with a dream. Normally she slept poorly and dreamt little: itself an aspect of her resistance. So a complete dream was a welcome rarity, and I expended a good deal of effort in trying to make sense of it. Here is the dream as related by Frau Anna:

I was travelling in a train, sitting across from a man who was reading. He involved me in conversation, and I felt he was being overfamiliar. The train stopped at a station in the middle of nowhere, and I decided to get out, to be rid of him. I was surprised that a lot of other people got out too, as it was only a small place, and completely dead. But the platform signs said Budapest, *which explained it. I pushed past the ticket collector, not wanting to show my ticket, because I was supposed to go on further. I crossed a bridge and found myself outside a house which had the number 29. I tried to open it with my key, but to my surprise it wouldn't open; so I went on past, and came to number 34. Though my key wouldn't turn, the door opened. It*

[1] [In the text there is a play on the word *niederkommen*, which means both "to fall" and "to be delivered of a child".]

was a small private hotel. There was a silver umbrella drying off in the hall, and I thought, My mother is staying here. I went into a white room. Eventually an elderly gentleman came in and said, "The house is empty." I took a telegram out of my coat pocket and gave it to him. I was sorry for him because I knew what it contained. He said, in a dreadful voice, "My daughter is dead." He was so shocked and sorrowful I felt I didn't exist for him any more.

At my first hearing of the dream, I became alarmed, for it told me that the dreamer was quite capable of ending her troubles by taking her life. Train journeys are themselves dreams of death; and in this case all the more so, since she had got off "before her stop" and "in the middle of nowhere". Avoiding the guard was an obvious allusion to the proscriptions against suicide; and the bridge was yet another symbol of dying. In a sense, Frau Anna's dream could not have been clearer; yet I was also sure it contained many other elements of a more personal nature. I therefore asked her to take the dream bit by bit and tell me what occurred to her in connection with it. She had already had some training in dream interpretation from having previously analysed a few minor specimens; furthermore, since she was intelligent, I had encouraged her wish to read up some of my previous cases.

"Something occurs to me," she said, "but it cannot belong to the dream, for it happened a long time ago, and really was of no importance in my life."

"That makes no difference," I said. "Start away!"

"Very well, then. I suppose the man in the train reminded me of someone who pestered me when I was travelling from Odessa to Petersburg to try and make a life for myself. It's — what? — twelve years ago and I had forgotten it completely. It wasn't particularly scaring, because there were plenty of other people about. But he leaned across and kept talking to me, in a rather obvious way; asking me what I was going to do when I reached Petersburg, and offering me his help in finding somewhere to live. It just got annoying, and in the end I had to move to a different compartment."

I asked her if anything had happened to her recently to make her dream of the experience; and prompted her by recalling a few details, such as the book her companion had been reading in her dream.

"Well, yes, as a matter of fact I remember the young man in the Petersburg train was a nuisance because he was talking when *I* wanted to get on with my book. It was a copy of Dante, which I had to concentrate on to understand because my Italian was not very good. And now you mention it, I suppose my brother comes into the dream."

I should interrupt at this point to say that Frau Anna had recently experienced a rather disturbing event. Her brother, with his wife and two children, had decided to leave Russia, because of the revolutionary turmoil, and emigrate to the United States; and they had stopped off in Vienna to say, as it were, hello and goodbye to Anna and her aunt. The patient had not seen her brother for several years, and now might never see him again. Although — or even because — they had never been very close, the reunion and parting had depressed Frau Anna still further.

"When we were saying goodbye at the station, my brother covered the awkwardness by taking his time in choosing books for the journey. I recall thinking that Dante's *A New Life* would be appropriate; except that my brother is not interested in the classics, he's a very practical person. He bought himself some thrillers. It was absurd to think you could buy Dante at a station bookstall anyway."

I was beginning to see the way the dream was going. I recalled to her the numbers of the houses, and asked her if they were of any significance.

She thought hard, but admitted bafflement.

"Could it be that you yourself are twenty-nine years of age?" I suggested. "And your brother is — how many years older? Five?"

Frau Anna agreed, surprised by her dream's mathematical logic.

"You stopped first at the door of your own house. It should have been the right key but it wasn't. Instead, you were able to walk into number 34 — your brother's residence, so to speak. You're only a guest there, so you see it as a private hotel." I asked her if she recognized the man who came into the room. I called to mind his words, "The house is empty."

After a time, she was able to summon up the association. Her brother had rather tactlessly remarked how upset his father was at their going; for he had gone into his father's business and continued to live near by, after his marriage. Frau Anna remembered thinking rather bitterly that *now* her father would feel lonely, in his empty house; whereas he had never expressed more than conventional regret at her leaving home, nor any keen desire to see her again.

At this point my impressions of her dream became a certainty. Her brother's departure, complete with wife and family, *en route* for *a new life*, contrasted with her own sense of having reached a dead end, or rather, of being on a pointless journey. Her brother had always had the assurance of being his father's favourite, and he knew where he was going: unlike Anna's girlhood journey to a distant city, which had clearly been a last desperate attempt to make her father take notice of her existence. He had been quite willing to let his innocent daughter battle with physical or moral dangers — foreshadowed by the pressing young man on the train.

Two phantasies, I suggested, mingled in her dream. If her father should receive a telegram saying she was dead, then at last he might be sorry. But side by side with that wish, not contradicting it so much as reinforcing its tragic thought, was the wish that she might never have been born — as a girl, as Anna. If only she could have taken her brother's place! She quits the train journey which is her own destiny, to enter an impossible existence as her brother. In the private hotel, the white room stood for the womb of her mother, which awaited only the coming of Anna's father to conceive the male child. The drying-out umbrella in the hall was symbolic of the discharged penis. Her father brings the new life, because without a *son* his "house is empty". Anna was dead — by suicide or prophylaxis; it did not matter which, and he did not care. His shocked and sorrowful reaction was the product of her wish-fulfilment. Her dream knew that too: she "did not exist" for him.

The young woman was overcome by the sadness of her dream, and disinclined to dispute my interpretation to any serious extent — except on one point, of a melancholy nature, which she did not have the heart to tell me about, and which I myself will reserve till the proper time. In any case it did not affect the overall meaning, which was altogether apparent.

During our discussions, while I was questioning her about the nature of the young man's overfamiliar attentions on the train, she recalled a forgotten fragment. She did not think the new material of any importance, but I have learnt from experience that dream elements which are forgotten at first but remembered subsequently are usually among the most vital. So it was to prove in this case, though its full meaning was not to become clear until much later on in the analysis.

I said to the young man I was going to Moscow to visit the T——s, and he replied that they wouldn't be able to put me up, and I'd have to sleep in the summer-house. It would be hot in there, he added, and I'd have to take all my clothes off.

The T——s, she explained, were distant relatives on her mother's side, who had settled in Moscow. Her mother and aunt had spent holidays with them in their youth, and they had maintained affectionate contact with Anna's mother after her marriage. Frau Anna had never met them, but according to her aunt they were a warmhearted and hospitable couple. Her aunt, in fact, had mentioned them only the day before: recalling wistfully the holidays she had spent there, and wishing she could take Anna to meet them, since she was sure a break would do her niece a world of good. But they were old now, and might not even have survived the troubles.

The fragment appeared to me to express the young woman's yearning to free herself from the sad constraints of her present life and to reclaim the lost paradise of the years with her mother: that is, in effect, to be naked in the 'summer-house' or house of blissfully hot summers. She did not disagree with this interpretation; and also brought to mind a memory of those far-off years which she found amusing, as well as affecting, to recall.

Their house in Odessa lay in many acres of semi-tropical trees and shrubs, which ran down to the very edge of the sea. There was a tiny private beach. The summer-house was in the midst of a grove of trees in a remote part of the garden. The previous owners had let it go to ruin, and as a result it was little used. One scorchingly hot afternoon, everyone had scattered in the grounds and the house, driven into isolation by the heat. Anna's father was probably at work, and she believed her brother had gone off for the day with some friends. Anna was hot and bored, playing listlessly on the beach, where her mother was standing at her painting easel and so not willing to be disturbed. Having been scolded for chattering, Anna thought she would try to find her aunt and uncle. She wandered through the grounds, and eventually came upon the summer-house. She was pleased to see her uncle and aunt inside, but they were behaving in a way she could not understand; her aunt's shoulders were naked, though normally she kept them covered from the sun, and her uncle was embracing her. The embrace continued, they were too absorbed to notice Anna's approach through the trees, and she slipped away again. She returned to the beach to tell her mother the strange story; but her mother had abandoned her easel and had gone to lie on a flat rock, and appeared to be sleeping. The child knew there were two circumstances when on no account must she disturb her mother: when she was painting and, even more so, when she was asleep. So, disappointed, she wandered away again, back to the house to have some lemonade.

What was I to make of this memory? It was very much an

adult's view; but this was not proof that we were dealing with a phantasy. I have my doubts if we ever deal with a memory *from* childhood; memories *relating to* childhood may be all that we possess. Our childhood memories show us our earlier years not as they were but as they appeared at the later periods when the memories were aroused. The young woman was amused by her recollection of her first glimpse of adult sexuality; while at the same time her heart was touched by the knowledge of her aunt's tender intimacy with her uncle, in the recreative atmosphere of a summer holiday in Odessa; more especially as her aunt now found it too painful to talk about those times.

However, it was necessary for me to ask whether she had perhaps witnessed more than she recalled? If she had, her memory could take her no further; and indeed it seemed highly improbable that a young married couple, who might withdraw to the privacy of their room, should take such a risk of embarrassment. Nevertheless, the memory's appearance in Frau Anna's dream seemed to suggest that it was significant. It was not impossible that it was connected with her hysteria; for those whom Medusa petrifies have glimpsed her face before, at a time when they could not name her.

The days and weeks following brought little advance. For this, probably both patient and physician were to blame. Frau Anna, for her part, withdrew altogether behind her defences, and sometimes made a worsening of her symptoms an excuse for not coming to me. To be fair to her, I am sure that she felt her pains to be unbearable. She pleaded with me to arrange for an operation, for the removal of her breast and her ovary. For my part, I confess that I grew irritated by her unhelpfulness, and infected by her apathy. She remarked once that she had thrown a scrap of food to a dog in the street and it was too feeble and emaciated to crawl to it; and that she herself felt much the same. I found myself abandoning analysis altogether, on occasions, and simply urging her not to think of taking her life. I pointed out that suicide is only a disguised form of murder; but it would be a pointless exercise, unlikely to have any effect on its intended

victim, her father. Frau Anna said it was only the unspeakable
pains which would ever make her think of ending it all. She was
quite rational during these discussions. Apart from her debili-
tating symptoms, no one would have taken her for an hysteric.
There was something impenetrable, which increased my irrita-
bility. I considered using her evasiveness as an excuse for bringing the treatment to a close; yet in fairness I could not bring
myself to do this, since, in spite of everything, she was a young
woman of character, intelligence and inner truthfulness.

Then occurred a melancholy event which might have provided
me with a perfect excuse for breaking off treatment: the sudden
and unexpected death of one of my daughters.[1] Perhaps my
oppressed mood of the preceding weeks had been a preparation
for it. Such an event is not to be lingered over; although, were
one given to mysticism, one might well ask what secret trauma in
the mind of the Creator had been converted to the symptoms of
pain everywhere around us. As I was not so given, there was
nothing for it but "*Fatum & Ananke*". When I returned to my
duties I found a letter from Frau Anna. Besides condoling with
me on my loss, and informing me that she had gone with her
aunt to spend a short holiday at Bad Gastein[2], her letter
contained an allusion to the dream of some weeks previously.

> I have been sorely troubled by the element of prediction in my
> dream. I would not mention it except that I am sure it will not
> have escaped your memory either.
>
> At the time, I was half convinced that the man who received
> the telegram was you (at least in part) but I feared to upset
> you needlessly, knowing of your tender feelings for all your
> daughters. I have long suspected that, together with my other
> infirmities, I am cursed with what is called second sight. I
> foresaw the deaths of two of my friends in the war. It is some-
> thing I have inherited from my mother's side, apparently —

[1] [Freud's second daughter, Sophie, aged twenty-six, who died in
Hamburg on 25 January 1920. She left behind two children, one of
whom was only thirteen months old.]
[2] [A popular health resort in the Austrian Alps.]

a strain of the Romany; but not a gift that gives me pleasure — quite the reverse. I hope that this will not have upset you more than you already are.

I have no comment to make on Frau Anna's 'prediction', except to say that the sorrowful news did arrive (not unusually) by telegram. It seems plausible that the patient's sensitive mind discerned in me anxieties, much below the level of consciousness, over a daughter with small children, living far away, at a time when there were many epidemics.

What happened on Anna's return from Gastein was totally unexpected and illogical. So much so that, were I a writer of novellas instead of a man of science, I should hesitate to offend against my readers' artistic sensibilities by describing the next stage in our therapy.

Arriving five minutes late for her appointment, she breezed in with the carefree air of someone merely wishing to say hello, before going off to meet a friend for the theatre or the shops. She spoke loquaciously, in a firm, vibrant voice without a trace of breathlessness. She had put on perhaps twenty pounds in weight, so gaining, or regaining, all the attributes of personable womanhood. There was a lively glow in her cheeks and a sparkle in her eyes. She wore a new dress of an appealing style, and a new coiffure which suited her face. Here, in short, was not the painfully thin, depressed invalid I expected, but an attractive, slightly coquettish young lady, bouncing with health and vigour. She hardly needed to inform me that her symptoms had disappeared.

I had often spent vacations at Gastein, but never in my experience had its thermal springs been so miraculous. I said as much, adding drily that perhaps I ought to abandon my practice and become a hotel-keeper there. She positively roared with laughter; then, recalling my bereavement, fell into a penitential expression at her thoughtless gaiety. I assured her that her good spirits were a cordial to me. However, it soon became apparent that, far from her having thrown off her hysteria, it had simply changed direction.[1] Whereas before, it had sapped her bodily strength with fierce pangs, yet left her mind rational, now it had released her body at the cost of her mind. Her unbridled talkativeness soon gave evidence of a wild irrationality. Her cheerfulness was the desperate humour of soldiers joking in the trenches; and her efforts at a sustained discussion drifted into a dreamlike monologue, almost a hypnotic trance. Before, she had been miserable but sensible; now she was happy and demented. Her speech was full of imaginative products and hallucinations; at times it was not so much speech as *Sprechgesang*, practically an operatic recitative, elevated and lyrical-dramatic. I should add that, since joining the orchestra of one of our leading opera companies, she had become devoted to the art.[2]

She seemed unconscious of the effect she was producing, and remained joyfully convinced of a full recovery. Failing to make any sense of her account of her stay at Gastein, I suggested to her that she try to write down her impressions. She had, on a previous occasion, responded well to such a proposal, since she had a taste for literature and enjoyed writing — she was, for example, an inveterate letter-writer. However, I was not at all prepared for the new Anna's literary productions, with which she came armed on the day following. Hesitantly she put into my hands a soft-covered book. I saw it was the score of Mozart's *Don Giovanni*. She had, I discovered, written her 'impressions' of Gastein between the staves, like an alternative libretto; and had even attempted rhythm and rhyme, of a sort, so that her script could be read almost as doggerel verse. Had Frau Anna's version of Mozart been sung in any of our opera houses, however, the

[1] In actual fact, ground *had* been won back from the enemy. What we were seeing was the hysteria fighting back in some desperation.
[2] ['Frau Anna G.' was, in fact, an opera singer, not an instrumentalist. Freud's desire to protect her identity gave rise to the change; though he always regretted having to depart from the facts, even in apparently trivial details.]

house manager would have been prosecuted for the abuse of public morals; for it was pornographic and nonsensical. She had used expressions heard only in slums, barracks and male club rooms. I was astonished where she had learned such terms, for she had not, to my knowledge, frequented the places where they were spoken.

At first glance, little was evident to me except some references to her hallucinations, and a bold acknowledgement of the transference. In her phantasy Don Juan's place was taken by one of my sons — with whom, I need scarcely add, she was unacquainted. It was fairly clear that she was expressing a wish that somehow she might take the place of my missing daughter, through marriage. When I confronted her with this inference, Anna rather shamefacedly said it was only a joke, "to cheer me up".

Finding the flood of irrational images too much to deal with, I invited her to go away and write down her own analysis of the material she had produced, in a restrained and sober manner. She took my request not unreasonably as a rebuke, and I had to assure her that I had found her 'libretto' of great interest. After a gap of several days, she handed me a child's exercise book, filled with her untidy writing. She waited breathlessly (literally so, for she had suffered a slight return of the asthmatic symptom) while I glanced through a few pages. I saw that, instead of writing an interpretation, as I had asked, she had chosen to expand her original phantasy, embroidering every other word, so that I seemed to have gained nothing except the herculean task of reading a document of great length and untidiness. Though she had, to some extent, tempered the crudity of the sexual descriptions, here was still an erogenous flood, an *inundation* of the irrational and libidinous; the billows were less mountainous, but they covered a greatly enlarged terrain. I was now dealing with an inflated imagination that knew no bounds, like the currency of those months — a suitcase of notes that would not buy a single loaf. We spent a fruitless hour, after which I promised I would read her document carefully when I should be at leisure.

Upon doing so, I began to glimpse a meaning behind the garish mask. Much was the purest wish-fulfilment, mawkish where it was not disgusting; but here and there, also, were passages not without a touch of skill and feeling: natural descriptions of an 'oceanic' kind, mixed with the erotic phantasy. One could not avoid thinking of the poet's words:

> The lunatic, the lover, and the poet,
> Are of imagination all compact. . .[1]

By the time I had put down the notebook I was convinced that it might teach us everything, if we were only in a position to make everything out.

There is a joking saying that "Love is a homesickness"; and whenever a man dreams of a place or a country and says to himself, while he is still dreaming: "This place is familiar to me, I've been here before", we may interpret the place as being his mother's genitals or her body. All who have hitherto, in a learning capacity, had the opportunity to read Frau Anna's journal have had that feeling: the "white hotel" is known to them, it is the body of their mother. It is a place without sin, without our load of remorse; for the patient tells us she has mislaid her suitcase on the way, and comes without even a tooth-brush. The hotel speaks in the language of flowers, scents and tastes. There is no need to attempt to apply a rigid classification of its symbols, as some students have done: to claim, for instance, that the vestibule is the oral cavity, the staircase the oesophagus (or, according to others, the act of coitus), the balcony the bosom, the surrounding fir trees the pubic hair, and so on; what is more to the point is the overall feeling of the white hotel, its wholehearted commitment to orality — sucking, biting, eating, gorging, taking in, with all the blissful narcissism of a baby at the breast. Here is the oceanic oneness of the child's first years, the auto-erotic paradise, the map of our first country of love — thrown off with all the *belle indifférence* of an hysteric.

[1] [Shakespeare, *A Midsummer Night's Dream*.]

Here, it seemed to me, was evidence of Anna's profound identification with her mother, preceding the Oedipus complex. Nor, except in its degree of intensity in Anna's case, should this particularly surprise us. The breast is the first love object; the child sucking at the maternal breast has become the prototype of every relation of love. The finding of a love object, in puberty, is in fact a refinding of it. Anna's mother, warmhearted and pleasure-loving, bequeathed to her child a lifelong auto-erotism,[1] and therefore her journal represented an attempt to return to the time when oral erotism reigned supreme, and the bond between mother and child was unbroken. Thus, in the "white hotel" there is no division between Anna and the world outside; everything is swallowed whole. The newly born libido overrides all potential hazards, like the black cat she describes as making hair-raising escapes from death. This is the 'good' side of the white hotel, its abundant hospitality. But the shadow of destructiveness cannot be ignored for a single moment, least of all in the times of greatest pleasure. The all-giving mother was planning her visit to the doomed hotel.

I now had the ludicrous sensation that I knew absolutely all there was to know about Frau Anna, except the cause of her hysteria. And a second paradox arose: the more convinced I grew that the "Gastein journal" was a remarkably courageous document, the more ashamed Anna became of having written so disgusting a work. She could not imagine where she had heard the indelicate expressions, or why she had seen fit to use them. She begged me to destroy her writings, for they were only devilish fragments thrown off by the "storm in her head" — itself a result of her joy

[1] There is also evidence that she helped her daughter through the later stages with a minimum of repression. Passages in the journal hint that Anna possessed a healthy and moderate awareness that the genital apparatus remains the neighbour of the cloaca, and actually (to quote Lou Andreas-Salomé) "in the case of a woman is only taken from it on lease."

at being once more free from pain. I told her I was interested only in penetrating to the truths which I was sure her remarkable document contained; adding that I was very glad she had evaded the censor, the train guard, on her way to the white hotel!

It was only with the greatest reluctance that the young woman would consent to go through her narrative with me, pausing where any associations occurred to her. Her slight recurrence of breathlessness having passed, she was convinced she was fully cured, and could not understand my insistence that we press on. Fortunately the effect of the transference made her also reluctant to bring the analysis to an end.

"The white hotel is where we stayed," she began. "I loved being in the mountains, it was such a relief after the miseries of Vienna; but I wanted a lake too, a huge one, because I feel freer beside water. The hotel had a green swimming pool, so I allowed it to grow into a lake! Most of the people were guests at the hotel. There was an extraordinary mixture — people trying to take up their habits again after the war, I suppose. For instance, there *was* an English officer, very straight-backed and courteous, who had been shell-shocked in France. He wrote poetry, and showed me one of his books. It took me by surprise; even though it didn't seem very good, so far as I can judge English. He kept mentioning a nephew who was going to join him later, to go skiing. But I heard someone say his nephew had been killed in the trenches. The major summoned us to a meeting once, to say we were under threat of attack. I thought I would weave an amusing scene around it — because after all there are so many things we don't understand, such as leaves in autumn and falling stars."

I interrupted to inquire if there was not something of her childhood in the comparison she often made of falling stars to flowers.

"How do you mean?"

"I remember you said the jelly-fish looked like blue stars under the water."

"Oh yes! I used to run down to the beach in the morning, first thing, to see if any more jelly-fish[1] had swum in during the night. Yes, of course, there's a lot of my past mixed up in it. We had a little Japanese girl as a chambermaid, in Odessa, and she used to quote haiku — little verses — to me while she was dusting and polishing. I somehow thought it would be nice if she made friends with the English major staying at Gastein, as they were both lonely and fond of poetry. The major looked so sad, trying to persuade people to play him at snooker. It's a mixture of the past and the present, like I am. The Russian, for instance — he's my friend in Petersburg as I imagine him now. He's risen quite high, I've seen his name in the newspapers."

I remarked that her portrayal of him was very satirical.

"He abandoned me, you see. More to the point, he abandoned himself, because there was a lot of good in him when we first met; he could be affectionate and tender, even shy. That was why I loved him."

Frau Anna paused to gather her breath, then continued:

"There were an awful lot of selfish people in the hotel. They really would have carried on writing their cheerful postcards if the hotel had burnt down, so long as *they* weren't in the fire." (A reference to that part of her journal written in the form of post-cards, of the banal type so often written to friends when one is on holiday.) "There was a gypsy band, and a whey-faced Lutheran pastor, and a nice little man everybody laughed at, because he was only a master baker and spoke roughly; and a large Dutch family. But the old Dutchman wasn't a botanist. The mountain spiderwort was a little gift for you." She blushed, smiling. "I know how you love finding rare specimens. I looked it up in a book of mountain flowers, and it seemed the rarest."

"And how about the retired prostitute?" I asked. "Was she at the hotel?"

"No. Or rather, yes. Myself."

"How is that?"

---

[1] Frau Anna used the Russian term, *medusa*: another example of her occasional introduction of foreign words of which careful note had to be taken.

She paused before saying, "I have unruly thoughts."

I remarked that if the possession of unruly thoughts constituted immorality, all of my patients, indeed all the respectable ladies of Vienna, were prostitutes likewise. I respected her, I added, for the openness of her confession, which had taken much courage.

Two or three weeks after our resumption of analysis, Frau Anna's symptoms returned in full force. The blow was a hard one for her to bear. I told her I was not surprised, and she must not despair. As I had warned her, remissions were common, but the symptoms would always come back unless we got to the root of her hysteria; and I assured her, with more confidence than I felt, that we were moving closer to the light at the end of the tunnel.

Rereading Anna's journal, I was struck afresh by the rank and shameless energy of the sexual products. I asked her if she had had any other relationships besides the student A. in St Petersburg and her husband, and she replied with an emphatic negative. Her sexual life, then, had been limited to a brief liaison in her eighteenth year and a few months at the beginning of her marriage. I could not help suspecting that this woman who was clearly so passionate and so capable of strong feelings had not won her victory over her sexual needs without severe struggles, and that her attempts at suppressing this most powerful of all instincts had exposed her to severe mental exhaustion.

It was time to grasp the nettle of the central, narcissistic love affair described in her journal. For, to use the analogy of her favourite art form: within the theatre of her mother's body, there were really only two important characters on stage singing their love duet, however many supporting figures there were behind them. That, at least, was how it struck me.

Always she spoke of the husband from whom she was estranged in a manner that made it certain she still loved him. She blamed him not in the slightest degree for the estrangement; he had been good to her in every way: faithful, considerate, generous and gentle. The responsibility for the break was entirely hers, but the reason she consistently offered was clearly an evasion: that she desired to give him children, more than anything in the world, but had become convinced that for her ever to have a child would bring nothing but misfortune. Though she felt remorse at having caused her husband unhappiness, it would be far worse to deny him his right to a family. It was fortunate, she said, that at her insistence they had practised coitus interruptus; for this meant he could have the marriage annulled, and marry someone who could make him happy. She would not, or could not, explain further, and needless to say I was not at all satisfied with her explanation.

In the belief that the narcissistic phantasy of her journal must relate very strongly to Anna's nuptials, I asked her one day who she thought the lovers represented. "Apart from the young man's being my son!" I added.

However, her barriers were still erected. She insisted that the lovers were modelled on a honeymoon couple staying in the hotel at Gastein. Their lack of modesty in public had made them notorious. The chambermaids complained because they slept late in the morning; and they had behaved scandalously on an excursion, right under the noses of Anna and her aunt: though admittedly not as scandalously as the lovers of her journal. Their behaviour had both shocked and amused her; but also the young couple had touched hèr heart, for her Cassandra-like gift told her the young bridegroom would not live for many years.

"*You* are not present in the young lady?" I asked, with irony.

"Naturally, yes! I've told you as much."

"With your husband."

"Not specifically. I was mainly thinking of the honeymoon couple." She was fumbling with her crucifix.

"Come now! You will be telling me next that your honeymooners made friends with a corsetière and invited her into their bed!"

"No, of course not! I think she must have been Madame R."

This was not unexpected, for she had always spoken of her Petersburg friend and mentor with exceptional warmth. I inquired why she had made Madame R. into a corsetière. "Because she always stressed discipline, if we wanted to succeed in the ballet. Self-discipline to the point of pain."

"So the white hotel — "

"It's just my life, you see!" she interrupted in some irritation; as if to say, with Charcot: "*Ça n'empêche pas d'exister.*"[1]

"And was your friend given to light adventures?" I asked.

"Most certainly not! She's a Jewish convert to Orthodoxy, and you know there's no one more devout!" Frau Anna went on to say that she had been thinking of her friend's marriage (hoping they were well and happy in these dark times), and of the mystical imagery in the Song of Songs. "They made an ideal couple. She was fortunate to find such a handsome, distinguished man to marry her. He was no longer young, of course, but some men seem to grow handsomer when they're older." She stopped, flustered; and I asked her whether there might not have been some rivalry between her and Madame R. As she denied the suggestion, her breathlessness and hoarseness increased; her hand flew involuntarily to her bosom. I reminded her that their attachment had taken her by surprise. "You never thought his interest was directed at you, Frau Anna?" She did not answer, but shook her head as she struggled to find breath. "Yet are you not pushed to one side by this lady, in your journal?" I persisted. "Your bed is invaded by a rival, is it not?"

"It's nothing to do with that!" she replied, in tones of great distress. Then, in her troubled state, she let slip a surprising admission. "If you must know, it's about my honeymoon with my husband — you are right. That part of it is, at least. The two women are really one. You see, I thought if I had only been blessed with my friend's liveliness and optimism, in spite of all

[1] [One of Freud's favourite quotations. Charcot's dictum in full was "*La théorie c'est bon, mais ça n'empêche pas d'exister*" (Theory is good, but it doesn't prevent things from existing).]

she'd gone through, I wouldn't be so dreadfully tense."

"Why was that, Frau Anna?"

"I was afraid I couldn't live up to his expectations."

"I see. He believed you to be a virgin, naturally, and you feared discovery?"

"Yes." She touched her crucifix again.

I told her she was wasting my time; that I could no longer tolerate her lies; that unless she would be completely frank with me there was no point whatever in continuing the analysis. Eventually, by such threats as these, I managed to drag from her the truth about her marriage. Its intimate side had been, not a disappointment, but a complete disaster — a nightmare, at least from her point of view. What made it so were the hallucinations, from which her life had never been completely free, but which during this period pressed upon her constantly. They rose before her eyes whenever sexual intercourse took place. They were of the obsessional kind described in her journal, and varied only in details. The flood, and the hotel fire, could be related to her mother's death; the other two hallucinations, of falling from a great height and of mourners being buried by a landslide, were inexplicable to her; the last was the most frequent, and also the most horrifying, because she suffered from claustrophobia.

She did not think her husband had suspected anything. Could I not imagine what torment it had been, she said, to see those pictures before her eyes while pretending to transports of happiness? And would I not agree that the marriage could not have been sustained, without doing her husband a great wrong?

She excused herself from having confessed all this earlier in the analysis, by saying that she had no wish to seem to be blaming her husband. And she was adamant that no blame existed. He had been tender, patient and skilful; she had loved all the intimate caresses leading up to coitus; or had done, until the knowledge of the inevitability of hallucination caused her to dread even these preliminaries. Besides, she said, it was not important, for she was sure the hallucinations only arose as a warning to her of what she had already told me: that on no account should she bear a child. Even coitus interruptus carried an element of risk.

At Gastein, she had come to terms with childlessness, and that was why she had regained her health. She had felt able to sublimate her desires and needs; but in the fetor of Vienna they had come back to plague her, and so her symptoms had returned.

I must now agree, she concluded wryly, that the happiness she had described in her journal could not possibly refer to her own marriage; only the catastrophes were 'autobiographical'. She remarked also that if *anyone* had been intended for her husband, it was the German lawyer she had called Vogel. I expressed astonishment, and Frau Anna said she did not know why she had depicted him in such black colours, and she would give anything to call it back. True, her husband and his family sometimes expressed moderately anti-Semitic views; but less often and more moderately than most people. It had not occasioned any unpleasantness between them, for the simple reason that she had not felt it necessary to tell her husband of that unimportant aspect of her background.[1] She was very troubled by her malignant caricature of a fine young man. I had to reassure her that it was perfectly understandable: she had been compelled to hurt him; which was extremely painful to her, and therefore she was angry with him for causing her to feel that pain.

Shortly after her disclosure of the sexual problems she had encountered in her marriage, I was able to evoke another unpleasant memory from her past. I had given her to study a recently published case history,[2] and she had been pressing me to discuss with her that particular patient's obsession with coitus

[1] Anna's father had completely rejected his Jewish heritage, and in consequence she herself felt not in the slightest degree Jewish. She once described herself to me as "mid-European Christian".

[2] *From the History of an Infantile Neurosis* ("The Wolf-Man") (1918). Unknown to Frau Anna, there were a surprising number of similarities in their backgrounds. On one occasion, also, she must have passed that particular patient on the stairs, after spending much time in discussion with me of aspects of his case.

more ferarum (usually with servant girls and common women). It seemed to interest her excessively; and of course it reminded me of an incident towards the end of her journal. À propos of that, I suggested it was surprising that a form of intercourse not commonly practised in polite circles should lie within her experience. The patient thereupon appeared distressed, and found it difficult to speak; but when she had reasonably recovered she revealed an incident relating to A., the father of her miscarried infant in St Petersburg.

The incident occurred on what she had previously spoken of as a singularly happy memory of her relationship with him: a weekend of cruising in the Gulf. They had been seeing each other for about three months, and had formed a deeply romantic attachment — but still a 'white' one, to use Frau Anna's descriptive term. There were perhaps a dozen young people on the yacht. The weekend started harmoniously enough. They enjoyed themselves, mixing serious discussion with an over-indulgence in spirits, provided by A.'s wealthy father. Then, on the second day, Anna and her friend had a serious quarrel. It concerned Madame R., in fact, who had taken to inviting Anna and a few other pupils to her home, for more informal discussions and cultural activities. A. accused Anna of selling her soul to aestheticism. Their quarrel was exacerbated by the fact that he and his friends were beginning to accept the need for political violence; and Madame R.'s late husband had been killed by a bomb intended for a statesman. Anna, having seen at first hand, in her teacher's sorrow and loneliness, the consequence of violent acts, told A. she was withdrawing from the group.

Intoxicated, and in a rage against her, A. became unrecognizable as the young man she loved. The delightful yachting party turned sinister in her eyes, took on the nightmarish tone of Dostoevsky's *Possessed*. Her friend singed her hair with his cigar, and made other aggressive gestures. She told him their relationship was over, and went to her cabin to cry and, eventually, to fall asleep. Some time later she was disturbed, and awoke to the horrifying and degrading sight of A., and another young woman, lying on the bunk opposite, engaging in sexual intercourse.[1] Far from being ashamed of his behaviour, he abused Anna with coarse, jeering remarks, and had obviously intended her to be awakened. Anna did not wait for the end of the yachting trip but, being a strong swimmer from childhood, jumped into the sea and swam ashore.

᛫ To her sorrow she let him persuade her, a few weeks after, that he was repentant and still loved her. He blamed the spirits he had drunk, the overwrought atmosphere of the times, and their sexual abstinence. She took him back and became, for a short while, his mistress. As with her husband later, painful hallucinations occurred. She moved into his apartment. She became pregnant. She discovered that he had taken a train for the south, accompanied by the young lady of the yachting party. At this dreadful time her life was saved by Madame R.'s friendship, for Anna had begun to haunt the Neva bridges, debating whether to put an end to her miseries; and she was convinced that following her miscarriage she would have done so, if she had not confided in her teacher and been welcomed into her home.

So painful for the patient was the experience of reinvoking the images of that period in her life, that I scarcely had the heart to demand why she had talked of the yachting trip, some months before, in glowing terms. When I eventually put it to her, she pretended that I was confusing two different weekends.

Her symptoms continued to be severe; she was sleeping badly, and had lost all the weight she had regained, being once more on a self-imposed diet of oranges and water. She said on one occasion: "You tell me that my illness is probably connected with early events in my life that I have forgotten. But even if that is so, you can't alter those events in any way. How do you propose to help me, then?" And I replied: "No doubt fate would find it easier than I do to relieve you of your illness. But much will be

[1] Evidently in the position to which I had alluded.

gained if we succeed in turning your hysterical misery into common unhappiness."

It was at this moment in the painfully slow unravelling of my young patient's mysterious illness that I began to link her troubles with my theory of the death instinct. The shadowy ideas of my half-completed essay, *Beyond the Pleasure Principle*,[1] began, almost imperceptibly, to take concrete shape, as I pondered the tragic paradox controlling Frau Anna's destiny. She possessed a craving to satisfy the demand of her libido; yet at the same time an imperious demand, on the part of some force I did not comprehend, to poison the well of her pleasure at its source. She had, by her own admission, an unusually strong maternal instinct; yet an absolute edict, imposed by some autocrat whom I could not name, against having children. She loved food; yet she would not eat.

Strange also (though too many years of psychoanalysis had partly blinded me to its strangeness) was her psyche's compulsion to relive the night of the storm when she learned of her mother's death in a hotel fire. I have said that at certain moments Frau Anna's expression reminded me of the faces of the victims of war neuroses. It is still not clear to us why those poor victims of the battlefield force themselves again and again to relive in dreams the original traumatic events. Yet it is also the case that everyone, not only neurotics, shows signs of an irrational compulsion to repeat. I observed, for example, a game played by my eldest grandson, who kept carrying out over and over again actions which could only have had an unpleasant meaning for him — actions relating to his mother's absence. There is also the pattern of self-injuring behaviour that can be traced through the lives of certain people. I began to see Frau Anna, not as a woman separated from the rest of us by her illness, but as someone in whom an hysteria exaggerated and

[1] 1920.

highlighted a *universal* struggle between the life instinct and the death instinct.

Was there not a 'demon' of repetition in our lives, and must it not stem from our human instincts being profoundly conservative? Might it not therefore be that all living things are in mourning for the inorganic state, the original condition from which they have by accident emerged? Why else, I thought, should there be death? For death cannot be regarded as an absolute necessity with its basis in the very nature of life. Death is rather a matter of expediency. So ran the argument in my mind.

Frau Anna was simply in the front line, as it were; and her journal was the latest dispatch. But the civilian populace, if I may so term the healthy, were also only too familiar with the constant struggle between the life instinct (or libido) and the death instinct. Children, and armies, build towers of bricks only to knock them down. Perfectly normal lovers know that the hour of victory is also the hour of defeat; and therefore mingle funeral wreaths with the garlands of conquest, naming the land they have won *la petite mort*. Not least are the poets familiar with the wearisome strife:

> Ach, ich bin des Treibens müde !
> Was soll all der Schmerz und Lust ?[1]

[1] [Goethe, "Wanderer's Song at Night" ("I am weary of it all, where is the sense in all this pain and joy?"). The quotation was an apt one in view of the circumstances in which *Frau Anna G.* was written. In 1930 Freud was awarded the Goethe Prize for Literature. His masterly address of thanks (read in Frankfurt by Anna Freud) so impressed the City Council that he was invited to write a psychoanalytical paper, to be published in an elegant limited edition in honour both of the centenary of Goethe's death in 1832 and the fortieth anniversary of Freud and Breuer's *Studies in Hysteria*. Freud, accepting the commission, proposed to write up the case of Frau Anna. The centenary committee at first willingly acceded to his wish that the patient's writings should appear as an appendix to his study, but reacted with predictable dismay when they discovered the nature of the material. Beyond the substitution of conventional asterisks for indecent words, Freud would not permit any censoring to be carried out. Publication of the

While I was thus dwelling on the universal aspect of Frau Anna's condition, Eros in combat with Thanatos, I stumbled over the root of her personal anguish. I had, up to this point, never been able to establish any particular event which might have been instrumental in unleashing her hysteria. The pains in her breast and ovary had attacked her at a time when she was busy and happy, successful in her resumed career, and eagerly anticipating her husband's first leave, confident that all would now be well. She could not think of any unpleasant episode which might have had a bearing on her illness. She had gone to bed quite happily one night, after writing her husband a very affectionate letter hinting that she would like to become pregnant during his forthcoming leave. The pains had woken her that same night.

One day she arrived for her appointment with me in an unusually cheerful frame of mind. She explained that she had received a letter from her old friend in Petersburg, with the splendid news that she and her husband had survived unharmed, though in much reduced circumstances, and had been blessed with a son. Though he was already three years old, she reminded Frau Anna of her promise to be a godmother, should the happy occasion ever arise. This was Anna's first news of her friend for nearly four years, and the first news *from* her since before the war. Her happiness was therefore easy to understand.

However, while she was expressing her pleasure at the thought of having a little godson, her pains, which had previously been only moderate, greatly increased. They were so severe that she begged to be allowed to go home. I was not prepared to let her go without attempting to find the cause of this sudden deterioration, and I inquired whether she was not perhaps jealous of Madame R.'s happy event. The poor young woman was crying with the pain, while vigorously denying any such unworthy thought. "It would not be at all surprising or discreditable, Frau Anna," I said. "After all, if you had not left your husband you

---

paper was delayed. With the rise to power of the National Socialists, it was abandoned altogether; and in 1933 all of Freud's works were burnt on a bonfire in Berlin.]

yourself would doubtless be equally blessed." She continued, weeping, to deny any jealousy, yet confessed the truth through her gesture of fumbling with the crucifix. I felt it was the right time to tell her, at last, what a 'godsend' I had found her crucifix, on occasions; but even before I could explain why, she was saying, with some excitement, that she now recalled the onset of her pains in more detail.

Before going home to write her nightly letter to her husband, she had dined quietly with her aunt, following an afternoon concert. She now remembered it was on that very day that she had last had news of Madame R. The news had reached her by a lucky chance. Her husband wrote that he had been questioning an officer from the Russian capital; and in a lighter moment they had found a slender thread of coincidence linking their lives. The officer was acquainted with Anna's friend, and reported her as being in good health and (he believed) expecting a child. Frau Anna had discussed the exciting news with her aunt. Could it be true ? Was it not dangerous, to be with child in middle life ? What christening present should she send, when circumstances permitted ? Her aunt had suggested a crucifix, and Anna had concurred. That was all she could remember of the conversation. She had gone home, written a happy, amorous letter, and awoke feeling ill in the night.

The young woman, whose pains had eased somewhat in the excitement of recollection, was stroking her own crucifix during her recital; and I now proceeded to relate the importance to me of these involuntary gestures. My explanation had the effect of bringing back her fierce pains, but also of recalling to her mind a host of forgotten memories of that evening, and thence to untying the knot of her hysteria. Needless to say, it did not happen without much distress on her part and much probing of her defences on mine. The gist of her story was as follows:

She had felt disturbed by the news from Petersburg as well as glad. She confessed it had to do with her knowledge that if she had allowed her husband full intercourse she herself might well have been pregnant by now. But she had shaken off this slight disturbance by discussing the question of a christening gift. Her aunt happened to mention that her own crucifix had come to her at birth, and she had worn it day and night ever since her first communion. On saying this she touched the silver cross proudly. How well worn it was, she remarked — unlike Anna's; for the simple reason, she added, that Anna's mother had ripped hers off on her wedding day and never worn it again. It was an angry gesture against her parents' hostility. Indeed, from that day she had ceased her religious observances. Her crucifix had lain untouched in her jewellery box, until eventually it had come to Anna.

Her aunt had then made a somewhat tactless remark about her sister's character being selfish and worldly; then, quickly repenting, began to praise her and to speak cheerfully about those distant times. It was rare for her to talk about the past, for she found it painful; Frau Anna enjoyed the treat of conversing about the mother she had scarcely known. Her aunt recalled her sister's good looks; and her own too, in those days before she had become old and crippled, for of course they were so alike. She brought out the photograph album to confirm it: and smilingly she recalled that people used to say you could only tell them apart by glancing at their bosoms to see which one wore the cross! Anna, looking at the two lovely young ladies, smiled too, and thought she dimly remembered people saying such a thing. Then an entirely forgotten memory flashed into her mind: the incident of the summer-house. As she recalled it then — and related it now — it differed in one respect from the version I had previously heard.

The child was bored and hot, impatient with her mother for being so engrossed in her painting. Everyone else had vanished after the noon meal. Anna decided to return to the coolness of the house, and torment her nurse for a while. She had forgotten it was the nurse's half-day off, so instead she drank some lemonade and played alone with her dolls in the nursery. It was less hot when she went outdoors again. She went exploring through the trees, and came upon the scene in the summer-house. She was startled to see her aunt's shockingly naked chest and shoulders, and backed away into the shrubbery. She went down to the beach, to ask her mother to explain why her aunt and uncle were behaving so strangely; but by now her mother was dozing on a rock. She knew it was a strict rule not to disturb adults when they were resting, so Anna returned to the house and played with her dolls again. In her heart of hearts she was glad her mother was asleep on the rock — because, of course, she really knew it was not her mother lying there. Besides the hundred secret signs by which a child knows its own mother, there was no mistaking her aunt's high-necked dress, the glint of silver on her chest, in contrast to the shocking nakedness of the woman in the summer-house.

But what, then, were her mother and her jolly uncle doing together in the summer-house? It was too disturbing and puzzling, and the child forgot it in play. The adult Anna, when it flashed back to her with all the accretions of mature knowledge, immediately assumed the worst; and likewise found it impossible to bear. Her fragile sense of her own worth had been sustained by the ikon of her mother's goodness. One flaw and it would shatter, shattering the young woman too. Now, the embrace of a single afternoon became the incest of many summer-houses and many summers. She did not wear a crucifix because she did not deserve to wear one: so her thoughts ran, even as she continued to attend to her aunt's reminiscences. Then instantly another thought — she, Anna, did not deserve to wear it either; she too should rip it from her neck.[1]

But for what reason? She knew of none. She performed her religious duties and led a blameless life. Almost too blameless! In a sense, was she not jealous of her mother? Wicked she may have been; but how much pleasure she must have had, to want to fly into his arms, at the slightest opportunity, whatever the risk. Of course she must have gone to him, all those times

---

[1] Her aunt's account of her sister's impulsive action had a painful effect on the patient, and she was often to revert to it.

she had left Anna with the nurse and returned many days later. There must be something very sadly lacking in me, she thought; for *I* could not imagine travelling hundreds of miles — to endure the rack! What is wrong with me? Clearly her poison still runs in me but in a quite, quite different direction. And I cannot even share my burden with one other person, as my mother could. I am completely alone. Suddenly the truth about herself which the young woman had not acknowledged burned itself upon her like a lightning flash in the dark: I would travel hundreds of miles — at this very moment, if it were possible — to see my friend! But now she is bearing his child, I am more alone than ever!

Everything was now clear. I had listened to her agitated account with a growing assurance of its conclusion; it was by no means entirely at odds with certain suspicions I already had. Yet the clarification had a shattering effect on the poor girl. She threshed about, she cried aloud when I put the situation drily before her with the words: "So you didn't want *a* child, you wanted Madame R.'s child — if only Nature had made such a thing possible." She complained of the most frightful pains, and made a desperate effort to reject the explanation: it was not true, I had talked her into it, she was incapable of such feelings, she could never forgive herself, she had meant only that her friend would now be even less likely to sympathize with her unnatural horror of becoming pregnant. I confronted her with inescapable facts. Was it not significant that she suffered her destructive hallucinations during the only sexual activity permitted by her conscience? That her only long-lasting and fruitful relationships had been with women? That she was strongly maternal in her instincts yet, when it came to the point, was filled with revulsion by the permanent domestic tie which motherhood would entail? That her journal gave a far livelier sense of Madame R.'s personality (in the guise of "Madame Cottin") than of the young man's? In comparison with Madame Cottin, was he not a cipher?

Still the poor young woman struggled against acceptance. For a while, her symptoms remained severe. The degree of suffering, and the intensity of her struggle, did not slacken until I offered her my two pieces of consolation — that we are not responsible for our feelings; and that her behaviour, the fact that she had fallen ill in these circumstances, was sufficient evidence of her moral character. For every gift has its cost, and the price of freedom from intolerable knowledge had been an hysteria. By the time she had returned home that night, she had so completely buried the knowledge of her homosexuality that she could write an unusually ardent letter to her husband. A few hours later, her pains came on. The rejected Medusa had exacted her price. But the price was worth paying; for the alternative would have been still worse.

When I explained all this, her resistance weakened, without ever disappearing entirely. Rather, she accepted it and dismissed it at the same time, in her eagerness to turn our discussions to the less threatening discovery of her mother's behaviour. Her relief at having exposed this childhood memory was palpable; and as we proceeded to explore it there was a progressive improvement in her condition.

I could not help but admire the economical way in which her mind had rendered this memory harmless, by a simple cut as with a pair of scissors, leaving her with nothing more flagrant than a tender marital embrace. Yet I was still not sure *what* she had seen. If it did not mask some much more devastating discovery, if it was no more than her spirited mother and uncle embracing, more or less for anyone to see who happened to stroll that way, it could have been comparatively innocent. She agreed that this was true — in theory; but was nevertheless convinced that her mother and uncle were adulterers, and that she had somehow sensed this, even at four or five years old. She pointed out, as evidence of their guilt, how excited and overindulgent her mother became as her brother-in-law's visits drew near. She recalled her depressions in the autumn and winter, her trips to Moscow, and the lavish gifts she brought home — as though to salve her conscience. She did not believe her mother had gone to

Moscow at all: but rather to some convenient place between Odessa and Vienna — probably Budapest — to rendezvous with her lover. (As a teacher of languages, he doubtless had plenty of conferences to attend. . . .) She recalled an embarrassed silence, both before and after her mother had been brought home for burial; a reluctance to speak of the dead woman, then or later; the fact that her aunt did not come to the funeral, never visited the house again, and now almost never mentioned that time in her life. When I argued that there were perfectly good, and likelier, explanations for all of this, she became angry, almost as if she *needed* to establish her mother's guilt. She recollected, with suspicious suddenness, that the sailors who had insulted her when she was fifteen had made obscene remarks about her mother, saying everyone knew she had perished with a lover in Budapest. They had employed a coarse term to suggest that the charred bodies could not be separated.

She was now arguing, of course, that her uncle did not die of a heart attack in Vienna a few months after her mother's death, but died in the same hotel blaze. Her father and her aunt, between them, had concocted the false story to allay gossip; but, in the way of these matters, probably everyone in Odessa knew what had happened, except Anna and her brother. When I asked whether she ought not to approach her aunt with these suspicions, she said she did not wish to reopen wounds. Still I urged her to do so, or even to consult newspaper files; for I was sure her phantasies were running wild. She was now so much better that she was starting to go for walks on her own around the city. And one day she stormed in with an air of triumph. She flourished before me two photographs. One, somewhat brown and tattered, was of her mother's grave; and the other, a fresh photograph, was of her uncle's. She had found his resting place only after much searching, she said, because her aunt did not visit it. It was overgrown, as the photograph showed. To my surprise, the dates of death on the two graves, faint but discernible, were the same. I had to admit that I was impressed, and that the balance of evidence, such as it was, had swung towards her version of events. She smiled, and enjoyed her triumph.[1]

It is time to summarize what we know of this unfortunate young woman's case. Circumstances from her earliest years had contrived to load her with a heavy burden of guilt. Every young girl, when she reaches the Oedipal stage, begins to nurse destructive impulses towards her mother. Anna was no exception. She wished her mother 'dead', and — as if she rubbed a magic lamp — her mother *was* dead. Thanks to the serpent (her uncle's penis) in her paradise, the field was free to Anna, and she could do what every little girl wants, bear a child to her father. But instead of bringing her happiness, her mother's death brought misery. She learned that death meant being in the cold earth forever, not just staying away for a few more days. Nor was her matricide rewarded with her father's love; on the contrary, he was colder and more remote; obviously he was punishing her for her terrible crime. Anna had brought about her own expulsion from paradise.

Preserved by the affection of mother-surrogates, nurses and governesses, she was punished — again by men — when a mob of sailors frightened and abused her. She learned from them that perhaps her mother had deserved to die, for being a bad woman. But by this time her father's harshness towards her had driven her to an intense idealization of her mother; the sailors' remarks were insupportable, and needed to be buried in her unconscious along with her memory of the summer-house. It was at this time

[1] Her dream (p. 98) appears to have been preparing the way for the uncovering of the trauma. She gets off at a place that is signposted *Budapest*, though it is "completely dead". The man in the train warns her that the T —— s in Moscow would not be able to put her up, and she would have to sleep naked in the summer-house. Frau Anna's reflection on this, during the period of abreaction, was that it was extremely unlikely her mother would have stayed at a hotel, had she been visiting Moscow; she would almost certainly have stayed with the T —— s, her hospitable relations.

that she developed symptoms of breathlessness and asthma — perhaps a mnemic symbol of choking in a fire. Simultaneously her father proved to her once and for all that he was indifferent to her well-being, and she cast him out of her heart, resolving to make for herself a new and separate life.

In the capital, she had the misfortune to become attached to an unworthy lover, of a sadistic and somewhat sinister temperament. Nevertheless, it was to be expected that she would select a lover of this kind, for at seventeen the compulsive pattern of her relationships had become established. It was to be expected that the sexual act with A. should turn out to be a failure; and also that she should be befriended by a woman and 'saved' by her, though not before further damage had been done. In Madame R.'s home, her self-esteem was restored; the widow's motherly affection was absorbed into the idealizing pattern of maternal love — the genuine *first love*. Feelings of a homosexual nature became established in Frau Anna, though she could not admit them to herself, much less to Madame R. Fortunately she was able to survive the shock of her friend's remarriage through the re-entry into her life of her aunt, a woman whose maternal feelings had been thwarted and who was, in fact, the uncanny image of her mother. One is tempted to see Anna's discovery of a musical talent at this time, especially as expressed in the rich tones of her chosen instrument, as a spontaneous 'flowering' from her restored sense of her own value.

Driven by her desire to prove to herself that she was capable of a normal relationship, she found a husband. Predictably it was another disaster, but she was reluctant to admit failure. She must have been secretly relieved when the outbreak of war separated them. However, it required a serious mental illness for her to take action to end the marriage, giving (to herself and others) the reason that she would be unable to cope with having children.

Some news of Madame R., and a stray remark from her aunt, threatened to overthrow all she had so painfully achieved. Her marriage was an hypocrisy; and her music was, at least in part, a sublimation of her true desires. The incompatible idea had to be suppressed, at whatever price; and the price was an hysteria. The symptoms were, as always with the unconscious, appropriate: the pains in breast and ovary because of her unconscious hatred of her distorted femininity; anorexia nervosa: total self-hatred, a wish to vanish from the earth. Also, the breathless, choking condition which had afflicted her during her puberty reappeared, as a consequence of having glimpsed the true circumstances of her mother's death. It remained uncertain why the pains attacked the left side of her body. An hysteria not seldom attaches itself to a physical weakness in the constitution, provided it fits in with the primary symbolism; and it may be that there was a propensity to illness in the patient's left breast and ovary, which would become manifest later in life. On the other hand, perhaps the left-sidedness arose from a memory that was never brought to the surface. No analysis is ever complete; the hysterias have more roots than a tree. Thus, at quite a late stage of the analysis, the patient developed a mild phobia about looking into mirrors, claiming that the act gave her nervous palpitations. This phobia, fortunately short-lived, was never satisfactorily explained.

Frau Anna's analysis was less complete than most. Since she felt practically restored to health, she was anxious to take up again her musical career. There were disagreements, which in a way I was happy to see, since it meant she was regaining her independence. Most of these concerned my estimate of her attachment to Madame R.; she was still loath, at times, to admit openly that it had a homosexual component. We both had a feeling that our discussions should be broken off, and we parted on friendly terms.

I told her I thought she was cured of everything but life, so to speak. She did not dispute this. She took away with her a reasonable prospect of survival, in an existence that would doubtless never be less than difficult, and might often be solitary. By the end, she was able to say that she could understand how her mother might have craved affection and novelty, after the first transport of her marriage had worn off. This acceptance of the unalterable past owed much to the serenity of Gastein and the subsequent writing of her 'journal': an interesting example of the unconscious preparing the psyche for the eventual release of repressed ideas into consciousness.

I have compared the journal to an operatic stage — but it is a stage with one great difference. That is, that the characters in her drama are interchangeable. Thus, the young man is from time to time (or even at the same time) Anna's father, brother, uncle,[1] her lover A., her husband, and even the unimportant young man on the train from Odessa. Anna herself is (at times) the opera singer; but also the prostitute without a breast, the pale, thin invalid without a womb, the dead mistress in the common grave. Sometimes the 'voices' are distinct, but more often they blend, melt into each other: "the spirit of the white hotel was against selfishness." With moderate help from the physician, Frau Anna's journal moved her towards psychological health, through acceptance of her mother's mysterious individuality. There is a symbolism of the corsetière which the patient did not mention: hypocrisy. Her mother was not as she appeared, not nearly so strict — with herself. She was Medusa — as well as Ceres. When she seemed most loving to her child, her mind was perhaps elsewhere. But far below the conscious level, the patient was learning to forgive her mother her fallible nature, and thereby (most profoundly) her own.[2]

[1] For the most part her uncle is the chef: from the white naval cap which he wore jokingly, calling himself the "Chief" to her father's "Captain"; and from his huge appetite which had stuck in her memory.
[2] [Freud's unusual emphasis on the mother's role may have owed something to the recent death of his own mother, on 12 September 1930. Cf. his letter to Jones: "Her value to me can hardly be heightened. . . . No pain, no grief, which is probably to be explained by the circumstances, the great age, and the end of the pity we had felt at her helplessness. With that a feeling of liberation, of release, which I think I can understand. I was not allowed to die as long as she was alive, and now I may. Somehow the values of life have notably changed in the deeper levels."]

I was thus quite mistaken in assuming the central characters to be "a man, a woman; a woman, a man".[1] Whatever the appearance to the contrary, the role of the male, of the father, in the patient's private theatre was subordinate, and we were faced with two 'heroines' — the patient and her mother. Frau Anna's document expressed her yearning to return to the haven of security, the original white hotel — we have all stayed there — the mother's womb.[2]

About a year later, I met Frau Anna again, quite by chance. By a pleasant coincidence, the meeting occurred at Bad Gastein, where I was on holiday with another member of my family. We were out walking when I saw a familiar face. It emerged that Anna was playing in the orchestra of a small touring company, and I was glad to see that she looked well; indeed, she had rather too much flesh than too little. She appeared pleased to see me, and expressed the hope that we would attend the performance that evening. She was on her way to a rehearsal. The opera she was due to play in was a modern piece of some obscurity, and I protested my lack of appreciation of modern music — adding that I should certainly have come had she been performing in *Don Giovanni*! The sly allusion was not lost on her, and she smiled. I inquired if she was familiar with the language of the

[1] [G. von Strassburg, *Tristan*.]

[2] [The manuscript of 1931 continues from this point with a new paragraph: "It seemed appropriate on this occasion to introduce a case in which reason and imagination can be seen as partners in the search for truth, as they were in the mind and heart of the genius whom we honour. Disordered and sentimental though Frau Anna's journal is, I believe Goethe himself would have seen in it more of purity than coarseness; and that he would not have been surprised to learn that in the realm of the libido the highest and the lowest are closely connected, and in a way dependent upon each other: 'From Heaven, across the world, to Hell.' Long may poetry and psychoanalysis continue to highlight, from their different perspectives, the human face in all its nobility and sorrow."]

opera (the score of which she had in her hands) and she replied that, yes, she had added Czech to her repertoire. My companion expressed admiration that she could learn to read so many languages, and Frau Anna replied with a melancholy smile, delivering her words rather to me, that she sometimes wondered from whom she had acquired that gift. It was perhaps inevitable that she should ask herself whether her father's coldness, after her mother's death, sprang from a suspicion that she was not nis child.

Frau Anna said she continued to suffer some mild recurrences of her symptoms from time to time, but not to a degree that would interfere with her playing. However, she feared that her belated start, and prolonged setback, would prevent her from reaching the heights of her profession. I am happy to say that I have continued to hear of her over the years, as a talented musical performer, pursuing a successful career in Vienna, and still living in the company of her aunt.

IV

The Health Resort

IN THE SPRING of 1929, Frau Elisabeth Erdman was travelling by train between Vienna and Milan. She had allowed herself the luxury of a first-class seat, to make sure of being fresh at the end of the journey; and for much of the way she sat alone, enjoying the scenery, reading a magazine from time to time, or closing her eyes and rehearsing, under her breath, the part she had been called upon to sing. The train was almost empty, and she found herself alone in the large and pleasant restaurant car when she took lunch. The attention of so many waiters made her nervous, and she bolted her food and went back to her compartment.

The train stopped at a tiny Tyrolean village — the station was little more than a platform — and Frau Erdman thought at first there must be a dignitary on the train, for the platform seethed with people. But then, to her annoyance, she realized they were travellers, for they were weighed down by rucksacks and suit-cases; they were swarming on to the train. There were far too many of them for the second-class coaches; they spilled over into the first class. Five rucksacked men and women forced their way into her compartment, and she had hurriedly to put her things on the rack. There were even people in the corridor, leaning against the windows and door. After the confusion of settling, rucksacks and skis overhung the rack above Frau Erdman's head, and she felt pressed into a corner by the fleshy bulk of her travelling companions. They wore so many clothes that they looked — even the three men — pregnant; and they talked loudly and laughed with the boorish camaraderie of people who have shared a holiday together, and who therefore, for the

moment, regard any stranger as an intrusion. Frau Erdman
started to suffer mild symptoms of claustrophobia, amidst so
much blubber: that was the word, and image, that came to her.
She stood up, apologized for stepping over their legs, and made
for the door.

She also, as ill luck would have it, felt just at this moment an
urge to go to the toilet. But when she looked along the corridor,
both ways, it was clear she would have an appalling struggle
getting through the press of people, many of whom sat perched
on their suitcases or rucksacks. One young man, a few yards
down the corridor, noticed her anxious gaze, and politely
gestured that she could come through. But with a wry smile she
shook her head, as if to say — *It's not worth it, I can wait!* —
and he smiled back, interpreting her message and amused by it.
Frau Erdman saw that he stood in a small 'clearing', in front of
an open window, so she elbowed her way through to stand by
him. She put her head out through the window and gulped the
air.

Feeling much relieved, she leaned her back against the glass
window of a compartment. The young man asked her if she
minded his cigarette smoke, and, when she said it did not bother
her, offered her one from his case. She declined, whereupon he
remarked that it was noticeable how many more ladies smoked
cigarettes these days: and had she never been tempted to try?
Yes, she said, she had enjoyed smoking when she was a young
woman, but had given it up for fear of damaging her voice.
Immediately she regretted saying it, for it would mean curious
questions, her answers to which might lead him to think that she
paraded her talents. The expected questions came, and she
admitted to being a professional singer; she was on her way to
Milan; she was to sing in the opera house there. And, yes, it was
quite an important role.

The young man was impressed. He scanned her ordinary,
somewhat lined face — but she had expressive eyes and lips —
to try to recall seeing her photograph in newspapers. He knew
little about music, he said, being a geology student at University,

but everyone had heard of La Scala, Milan. She must be one of
the 'greats'. The woman laughed — becoming almost attractive
as she did so — and shook her head vigorously. "Not at all, I'm
afraid!" she said. "I'm only a replacement. You may have heard
of Serébryakova?" (The young man shook his head.) "Well,
she's a great singer. She's been singing the role, but she fell down
some steps and broke her arm. Her understudy wasn't up to it, so
they were in trouble. The opera is in Russian, you see, and there
are not many sopranos who can sing in Russian, and who are not
booked up for months ahead. I was the only one they could think
of!" She gave a ringing chuckle, and the lines at the corners of
her eyes crinkled. She felt pleased by her modesty, which was
genuine, and happy to be free from delusions of grandeur.

The young man made deprecating noises, and she confirmed:
"It's true! That's the only reason I've got the part. It doesn't
worry me. I feel very lucky. I'm not going to get any better — I'm
nearly forty. I shall have sung at La Scala, in a good role. That
will be something to remember!" She gave an amused shrug.

She turned the conversation around to the young man. He
was taking his finals, this summer, he said, and then he hoped to
find a teaching post in Rome and marry his girlfriend there. He
was on his way to see her now, after taking a week's much-
needed rest, climbing and skiing in the mountains, sleeping
under the stars. He felt refreshed. She questioned him on that
interesting experience, but found him disappointingly tongue-
tied when it came to expressing the spiritual aspects of mountain
climbing. His great ambition, he said, was to scale the Jungfrau.
Frau Erdman found his remark, for some reason, rather amusing, but hid her smile in serious nods of the head as he described
how difficult it would be.

After the bright lakes and fertile valleys of the Tyrol, the train
thundered into a tunnel, discouraging conversation. The under-
ground journey was long enough to convince them both that
they had nothing in common, and there was no point in further
talk; and so, when they emerged into light, they remained silent,
until Frau Erdman said she had better make the perilous journey

to wash her hands. When she struggled back, she slid past the young man, exchanging with him a goodbye and good luck. She settled into her cramped seat, and gazed at, rather than through, the window, because heavy rain had started to lash against it.

Fortunately, at the next station, across the Italian border, extra carriages were put on; and the guard came through, ordering the second-class passengers out of the first-class seats. Frau Erdman breathed a sigh of relief, and spread herself again. She thought she had better go through the whole score — there was plenty of time; but the very first chorus, in which the tired peasants were returning from the harvest fields, brought on a dreamy mood, and she read no more. When the train entered the outskirts of Milan, she felt nervous, and had to fight down her breathlessness. She stood in front of the mirror to comb her hair and refresh her lipstick. She worried that they would suddenly realize she was too old to play the part of a young girl. She pictured their faces falling as they greeted her.

But if the welcoming party had any such feelings, they disguised them well. A tall, stooped, balding man stepped forward with a bow, introducing himself as Signor Fontini, the artistic director. His short, plump, fussily dressed wife dropped a curtsey; and Frau Erdman shook four or five hands, too flustered to take in names. Then she was blinded by flashlights, and was half carried by Signor Fontini and the others through a hubbub of reporters flinging questions at her, their notebooks at ready. In the confusion and excitement of arrival, she had left a piece of luggage on the train, and one of the director's henchmen had to run back to get it. At last they were outside the station and — an umbrella held over her to protect her from the rain — she was ushered to a limousine and driven away. At her hotel, in the heart of the city, another reception committee awaited her, and a bouquet of flowers was thrust into her arms. But Signor Fontini, anxious not to overstrain his replacement star, cleared a way for her to the lift, and escorted her personally to her suite on the third floor. A page boy and a porter came behind them, with her luggage. Signor Fontini kissed her hand, saying she must rest now for a couple of hours, and he would call for her to dine at half-past eight. Left alone in the luxury suite, she collapsed on to the sofa. The airy, ample drawing room was fit for a queen. There were vases of flowers everywhere. She undressed, ran herself a bath; and as she lay in it, feeling extraordinarily pampered and indulged, worried that her performance would never justify such treatment.

Having dressed for dinner, she sat at the writing desk overlooking the busy street, and wrote a postcard to her aunt in Vienna. "Dear Aunt," she wrote, "it is raining rain outside and flowers in my suite. Yes, suite ! I'm overwhelmed by their sense of my importance. I don't mean the flowers ! I shan't be able to face dinner, let alone tomorrow's rehearsal — or the actual performance ! I am going to fall downstairs and break a leg. Love, Lisa."

And there, at the dinner table which groaned with flowers, silver and cut glass, was the great Serebryakova, slim, beautiful and elegant, despite having her arm in a sling. One of the world's great sopranos, and still in her early thirties. She had been booked to return to the Soviet Union yesterday, but had decided to stay to wish her successor well. Lisa was overcome by such kindness from such a star. Madame Serebryakova even claimed to be a fervent admirer of Frau Erdman's voice: she had heard her, once, in Vienna, singing *La Traviata*. That was on her first tour abroad, when she herself was still unknown.

Her kindness and good humour set Lisa at ease. She was very funny about her fall, down the La Scala steps, and her attempts to carry on with the role. "I realized it was no good," she said drily, "when the audience started hooting with laughter." They could not 'take' their romantic young heroine, Tatiana, having her arm in a sling throughout the opera, especially as the action covered several years. While complimenting Serebryakova on her courage, one leading critic had expressed concern at the poor standard of surgery in Tsarist Russia.

"So we tried the understudy," said Signor Fontini with a sigh, spreading his hands. "Terrible. Within three nights we were playing to an empty house. But we won't have that problem tomorrow evening, I can promise you. There's enormous interest in your coming."

He laboured the point so much, one might have gained the impression that Serebryakova had been very much a second best; the selection committee had *really* wanted Frau Erdman all the time. Lisa took all the flattery with a grain of salt, and a smile; and began to feel, oddly enough, that she *could* sing Tatiana quite as well as Serebryakova. She also stopped worrying about her age; for the fourth member of the dinner party, a Russian baritone previously known to her only as a respected name, proved to be older than she had imagined. Victor Berenstein, who was singing Onegin, had pure white hair and was surely well into his fifties. Running to plumpness, and sallow in complexion, he peered at her through horn-rimmed glasses, amiably sizing up his new leading lady. Lisa observed him too: reflecting that it was a blessing she was only a medium for Tchaikovsky's music and Pushkin's words, for in real life she could not conceive of falling in love with this man, friendly and charming though he was. The most attractive thing about him — apart from his voice, naturally — was his hands. They were slenderer than the rest of him, somehow; masculine but tender and expressive. His long slim fingers even cut up his beefsteak tenderly and expressively.

Like Serebryakova, he expressed deep admiration for her voice, and delight that she had been able to undertake the role at a moment's notice. He had heard her singing Schubert on a crackly record. But as Lisa had never made a record, and told him so, he blushed with confusion and embarrassment, and became intensely preoccupied with a tough piece of steak.

Both he and Serebryakova (Victor and Vera, as they insisted) were with the Kiev Opera; and Lisa quickly turned the conversation to that beautiful city, where in fact she had been born. The interest aroused by her mentioning this fact, which was not included in her biographical note, allowed Victor to recover his poise. She had been taken from it when she was only a year old, Lisa explained, so she had no experience of it except for a couple of short holiday visits. She liked what she had seen. Her two Russian companions vied with each other in expressing enthusiasm for their city. Of course, conditions had been nightmarish, earlier; but, slowly, things were beginning to get better. Their presence in Milan was an indication of progress; their only previous trips had been in highly regimented teams.

"Don't you ever feel like coming back?" asked Vera. "Don't you get homesick?"

Lisa shook her head. "I'm not even sure where home is. I was born in the Ukraine but my mother was Polish. There's even a trace of Romany, I'm told! I've lived in Vienna for nearly twenty years. So you tell *me* what my homeland is!" They nodded their understanding, and said it was almost as hard for them to tell. Vera was from Leningrad, and Victor from Georgia, and they were of course Jewish. "By race not religion," added Vera hurriedly. Evidently thinking that Signor Fontini might feel left out of this conversation, she asked him what was home to *him*. "La Scala," he said. Everyone laughed, and Victor offered a toast to their host's native land, the beautiful La Scala.

There was a great deal of laughter, from then on. Vera had a dry humour, and Lisa surprised herself, and them, by being at her wittiest. Sparkling from wine and nervous excitement, she had them in stitches with her absurd — but true — anecdotes. Victor Berenstein had a terrible coughing fit when, in the midst of one of Frau Erdman's stories, his wine went down the wrong way.

Serebryakova warned him not to drink too much, for he would have to sing at rehearsal in the morning and would not want a hangover. "He can get drunk on milk," she explained to Lisa, while he protested it was all nonsense — he had never been drunk in his life. Vera rolled her eyes heavenwards. "You're right!" he sighed, pushing away his still half full wine glass; and Serebryakova patted his hand approvingly. He responded by taking her hand in his, and stroking it. They looked full into each other's eyes, and smiled affectionately. Lisa had already formed the conclusion that there was an intimate relationship between them. At first she thought it might be no more than a friendship, the comradeship of having worked together in the same opera house for several years, and now being in a strange land together. It certainly was not surprising that, when they searched in Russian for the right Italian word or phrase, they used the intimate form of the second person. But as time went on, and Victor became a little tipsy, she could see they were in love. She was slightly aghast that Serebryakova, with her flawless oval face, slanting green eyes, and long blond hair (as silver as her name), should have chosen to fall in love with a man so much older and so unprepossessing. There was no accounting for tastes. The discovery upset her, and she did not know why. It was certainly not prudishness, though she knew Serebryakova was married, and Berenstein showed all the signs of marriage also. Perhaps it was the openness of their behaviour. For instance, after they had said goodnight to Signor Fontini and entered the hotel lift, Vera closed her eyes and rested her head on Victor Berenstein's shoulder; and only her awkward sling prevented even closer contact. He put his arm round her and stroked her hair. When they stepped off at the second floor, bidding Lisa goodnight, he still kept his arm around her.

Lisa felt lonely and depressed when she was in her silent suite, surrounded by the meaningless flowers. She found yet another wrinkle in her face, as she prepared for bed. She slept little, and was down for breakfast before they had started serving. She was finishing her last cup of coffee when Victor and Vera came in — together.

When Signor Fontini called to take Lisa to the opera house, he pointed to the pile of suitcases and hatboxes waiting in the vestibule. "The diva's," he said; "you can see she travels light!" She was to leave by the midday train, directly after the rehearsal, which she had begged Lisa to allow her to attend. Lisa, her breast fluttering with nervous excitement, smiled at his dry remark. Then she was out into the warm spring sunlight and stepping into the limousine which would take her the two blocks to the opera house. She had forgotten how Tatiana's opening phrases went, and had to glance at the score to reassure herself.

There were still more flowers in her dressing room. She was rushed straight through into the fitting room, and spent the next hour being adjusted to fit Vera's dresses — that was how it felt. She was too dazed by the unfamiliar star treatment to utter a word, and just let herself be dragged about and prodded, like a queen bee. The beautiful dresses needed to be shortened, and also let out in various places. Then she was rushed to the make-up room, to have her wrinkles smoothed out into a young girl's fresh skin, while the seamstresses made the necessary final quick adjustments to her costumes. Coffee was poured down her throat; she was poured into her dress. They weren't happy with her long, dull hair, beginning to streak with grey. They were not happy with it at all. By this evening they would find her a wig. The ladies clucked also about her oily skin, because she was beginning to perspire a lot. Embarrassed, she confessed to a greasy complexion and a tendency to sweat, especially when she was nervous.

Then she was out on stage. She was being clapped by the orchestra, members of the chorus, hangers-on, and a scattering of people in the stalls (Serebryakova among them). Lensky, a handsome young Italian, doomed yet again to fall in his duel with Onegin, kissed her hand; as did her doting old husband of the last act, the Prince — a bearded middle-aged Romanian. Signor Fontini introduced her also to the conductor, a wasplike man, of whose reputation for unrelenting energy and unfailing brilliance Lisa stood in awe. Past sixty, his manner seemed to be saying, "Why have they burdened me with cripples and old women?" In broken German (for some reason best known to himself), he delivered a few terse words of advice. She went across to shake hands with the leader of the orchestra. Onegin beamed at her. She nodded that she was ready to start. All but her sister Olga and Madame Larina hurried from the stage. The conductor lifted his baton.

And later, when he tapped his music stand to call attention to a mistake, he had harsh words only for the woodwind. To Lisa, he muttered a brief compliment; and Serebryakova, from the stalls, had already given her a nod of appreciation, and a thumbs-up. The rehearsal continued to go well. There were obviously flaws in her performance, but she usually corrected them as soon as they were pointed out. Clearly, too, she would have to learn how to match her movements and gestures to those of the other performers. "That will come very soon," said Victor to her, at the end of the morning session. "Anyone can see you're a born actress. You move like a ballerina. Well, of course, you almost *were* a ballerina! It shows. And the most important thing is — you can *sing*! Thank God you were able to come!" And Vera rushed up on stage, and hugged her exuberantly with her good arm. "*Chudno*!" she said. "Magnificent!" She confessed tears had sprung to her eyes during the Letter Scene. "I was hearing it for the first time!"

Her generous praise moved Lisa so much that she could not even thank her. She had not yet recovered from the moment, near the end, when tears had sprung to *her* eyes. It was when she had to tell the remorseful Onegin that she still loved him, but his response had come too late: she could not betray her married vows. At the phrase "Happiness was so possible, so close!" she remembered a student in Petersburg whom she had loved with all her ardent soul, as Tatiana loved Onegin. And, like Onegin, the young man had cast away her love, her generous gift, and suppressed his own noble impulses, for the sake of a dream, an illusion of freedom. Lisa, even while she sang, had been overwhelmed with unaccustomed memories. For a moment they had threatened to get the better of her singing. She felt angry with herself. One wanted the audience to weep, but the singer must stay cold and dry-eyed.

However, she felt happy again, to have cleared this great hurdle with reasonable success. The conductor gave her a satisfied nod; Signor Fontini said "Bravo!" though with a lugubrious expression; and M. Moreau, the leader, tapped the wood of his violin with his bow, to show his approval. Several members of the orchestra clapped briefly, then everyone scattered to get a drink. There was to be another rehearsal in the afternoon. Vera and Victor invited her to come with them to their favourite little trattoria down a back street, where they could get instant service and good cheap food. Vera said she had no intention of leaving by the midday train; now that she had heard Lisa sing, wild horses would not drag her away from Milan till after tonight's performance. Victor was obviously overjoyed at her change of plans: in full view of the stage hands he hugged her and kissed her firmly on the lips.

Over a light meal, Lisa asked them for their advice, and they made a few suggestions which struck her as excellent; in fact, she wondered why she had not thought of them herself.

In the midst of their happy and creative discussion, they were upset by the appearance of a gaunt, ragged urchin at their table. He held out his hand for coins. His face was being ravaged by some unsightly disease. Before the waiters could chase him out, Lisa insisted on giving him all the change in her purse. Of all suffering, she could least tolerate the suffering of children. Her new friends agreed with her, sadly; and Victor said, *that* was what was hopeful about the Soviet Union. "It can't be done overnight, and there are still monstrous inequalities. But we're heading in the right direction at last."

Vera agreed; and Lisa listened, impressed by their balanced enthusiasm. They talked on, about music and politics — but mostly music — until it was time to return for the afternoon rehearsal. Vera excused herself, saying she was going back to the hotel to rest. Between Onegin and the former Tatiana there was an amorous scrimmage, which embarrassed Lisa, and she turned away.

When the curtain went up on her first night, she found all her nerves had gone; and no personal feeling intervened when she sang "Happiness was so possible, so close". Instead, she found herself responding more and more instinctively and pleasurably to the dramatic voice and gestures of Berenstein. They took their bows to warm, if not tumultuous, applause. Backstage, everyone rushed to congratulate her; but the praise she most appreciated was a silent gesture from Onegin, who crooked his thumb and middle finger into a circle, as if to say, "It worked. We'll be all right." She said, with sincerity, how wonderfully he had sung. At the rehearsals she had not been sure how much she liked his voice, but during the actual performance it had 'grown' on her. Of course his voice was in its autumn, as surely he knew; but the gravelly edge of physical decline only seemed to add to its spiritual richness. He turned her praise aside, with a shrug of dissatisfaction. "It's gone off," he said. "I can't reach the top notes any more. This is my swan-song." But Serebryakova, clutching his arm, said, "Nonsense!"

Bending, he whispered into Lisa's ear: "We've fixed up a little party in our suite. In honour of your first night and Vera's last. Do come." *Our* suite! The effrontery took her aback. She preferred these affairs to be carried on with a certain discretion. Gratefully she accepted, beginning to feel (three hours too late, so to speak) the immense strain of the occasion. It would be good to unwind with a drink. So, having changed, they bundled into limousines and were whisked back to the hotel. "Their" suite on the second floor turned out to be even more spacious and elegant, and bedecked with flowers, than her own. Rapidly it filled and became overcrowded; the air thickened with cigarette smoke and the rumble of voices; waiters whisked around with trays of wine.

When she had drunk a couple of glasses, Lisa told Victor how much she had worried about being too old for the part. He roared with laughter; and said his last Tatiana, in Kiev, had had to be brought on stage in a bath chair! But *he* was certainly the oldest Onegin ever! "You're just the right age. What are you? Thirty-five, thirty-six? Well, at thirty-nine you're not even in your prime, not by a long chalk, and you could quite easily pass for an eighteen-year-old girl! Yes, yes, I mean it! But a white-haired old man of fifty-seven, playing a young man of twenty-eight — that really is straining belief! It's a good thing the Italians are brought up to believe in miracles!" And he roared with laughter again.

Vera glided up, and Lisa explained the joke. "But you're just a spring chicken, Lisa dear!" said Vera. "Truly, your voice is so much better than when I heard you in Vienna — and I loved it *then*. You *must* come to Kiev, mustn't she, Victor? I shall tell the director about you as soon as I get home. Of course, he knows your reputation already and I'm sure he'd be thrilled to have you sing for him. You must stay with us. I'm sure we can find room for you, even though — " her green eyes danced — "I'm having a baby! Yes, but it's a secret. Only you and Victor know, so please don't tell anyone. That's why I'm going home — to rest — though I hate leaving Victor. Look after him, won't you? We're very happy about it. I'm almost glad I fell and broke my arm; though — " her smile dimmed momentarily — "it might have been serious. You see, I couldn't have lasted the whole season anyway! I thought I'd mind having to give up my career, for a time, but now I find I don't. I've never felt happier in my life! So I shall have a little baby when you come!"

Her joy infected Lisa too; and Victor was grinning sheepishly. The moral issue was none of her business, thought Lisa; she knew only that they had been kind and generous to her, and she liked them both very much. She squeezed Vera's hands, and said she was happy for her, and would love to visit, even if she could not sing at the Opera. But they were sure there would be no problem about that: she would be welcomed back with open arms. Lisa was then whisked away by Signor Fontini to be introduced to two wealthy patronesses of the opera — old ladies whose bones rustled like dry leaves and who gushed over her embarrassingly. She was relieved when the director shouted for silence. Gradually the hubbub died away, and he began a slurred speech of welcome to the excellent Frau Erdman and of regretful farewell to the wondrous Serebryakova. Glasses were lifted, toasts drunk, and the waspish conductor called for a farewell song from the diva. This request was supported with acclamation, which grew ever noisier as Serebryakova resisted efforts to drag her towards the piano where Delorenzi, the conductor, was already impatiently seated. (The piano, a grand, went with the suite: Lisa had one too.)

At last the beautiful opera star — the white of her sling contrasting almost elegantly with the plain black of her silk dress — allowed herself to be propelled across the room, smiling through the mêlée of her friends and admirers; and she exchanged a word with Delorenzi. He began the serene, familiar introduction to Schubert's *An die Musik*; and then the soprano took wing. They would not let her escape with just one short song, and so she gave them — Victor having produced a tattered piece of music for Delorenzi — a poignant Ukrainian ballad. The repetitive yet endlessly varied links in the chain of melody, every phrase struck clean, pure as a crystal glass, and full of yearning for the fertile homeland, cast a spell over the audience. One would have sworn that, when the last of many last phrases died into silence, her voice continued to sing, in the heart alone. Everyone was too deeply affected to applaud. The conductor rose from his stool, stretched up on his toes — he was a very small man — and kissed her on both cheeks.

Lisa was suffering. She had found it hard to stay in the room while Vera sang, because she had been overcome by a really bad attack of breathlessness. She thought she was going to die. It had nothing to do with overhearing a member of the orchestra say to the person next to him, after the Schubert, "Now there's a *real* voice." She was not jealous; she knew she could not match that voice, which was as close to perfection as she ever hoped to hear, this side of paradise and perhaps even beyond. She not only revered Serebryakova, she liked her — had even perhaps fallen a little in love with her, in the space of a day.

Partly, of course, it was the heat, smoke, noise, and press of bodies. But more than that, it had something to do with Vera's announcement about expecting a baby; for she had started to become breathless during Vera's rapturous unburdening of her secret. For some reason it disturbed her greatly. Now, as soon as Vera finished the folksong, Lisa went over to her, and in a breathless voice thanked her for her wonderful singing, and for the party, but now she must go to bed, because the smoke was beginning to affect her voice. "Aren't you going to wait for the newspapers?" asked Vera, disappointed.

Safe in her own suite, a faint rumble of conversation underneath the carpet, Lisa threw open a window and gulped cool night air. She began to recover. Am I perhaps an embittered old maid, without knowing it? she wondered, starting to undress. She slept very badly again, tossing and turning. As dawn glimmered through the curtains she slept, and dreamed she was standing over a deep trench filled with many coffins. Directly beneath her she could see Vera, her straight naked body showing through a glass top. As she mourned for her, in a line of crying mourners, there was a rumble above her, and she knew a landslide was going to crash down and bury her. Before it could do so, she was woken by the telephone. It was Vera — who wanted to know if she was all right, because she sounded out of breath and upset. Lisa explained she had been woken in the midst of a bad dream, and was grateful.

"Well, forget about your bad dream — we've just had the newspapers sent up. The reviews are *excellent*! Truly! No more than you deserve. We're going down to breakfast soon — my train goes in an hour. Hurry up and join us. We'll bring the newspapers down. Victor wants to say hello." And after a pause Lisa heard Victor's deep voice intone "Hello!" and then they hung up. Feeling much more cheerful, she jumped out of bed, ran to the bathroom, and quickly dressed. She was down in the breakfast room almost before her friends. They presented her with the newspapers, opened at the review section. But before she could begin to read, Vera laid her hand on hers and said, "Just remember the critics here are cynics. Believe me, these are *good* reviews — better than *I* had — aren't they, Victor?" Victor nodded, after a brief hesitation.

They did not seem at all good to Lisa. "Sadly we have to report that even a one-armed Serebryakova is better than the two-armed Erdman," wrote one of the critics. The other critic said her voice was "raw and provincial", and that she sang with more emotionalism than feeling. There were admittedly some balancing descriptions: "competent", "brave attempt", "Tatiana's Letter Scene movingly acted and sung", "expressive potential". "Believe me, this is high praise from the Milan critics," Vera pleaded, taking Lisa's hand again and squeezing it hard to prove her point; for they saw she was upset.

It was not the reviews, however, which upset her. They were really not at all bad. She had been warned about the Milanese critics, and she knew there was an element of truth in Vera's reassurances. No, she had simply had a shock, and it made her very angry with herself, at her stupidity. One of the critics had written: "The quite exceptional musical and dramatic understanding of the Berenstein–Serebryakova team assuredly owed much to their long association at the Kiev Opera, and also — it goes without saying — to their being husband and wife." Lisa now recalled where she had seen Victor's name most recently — in an article about Serebryakova. Serebryakova, of course, was only her stage name. It now seemed so obvious. Why had she jumped to the wrong conclusion? It was clearly written, she found later, in the programme given to her by Signor Fontini on arrival; but her eyes had somehow skipped over it.

Vera, gulping her coffee, jumped up, and bent to give Lisa a hug and a kiss. As her husband wrapped a red cape round her, and buttoned it at the neck, she told Lisa she would expect to see her in Kiev next year. "Don't come to see me off. Finish your breakfast. And good luck! We'll keep in touch!"

On her first rest day, she went to mass at the Cathedral, but the great building oppressed her, and she resolved not to go again. It was too institutional. She much preferred being in a minority, on the outskirts: it was much easier to believe. Even in Vienna there were too many Catholics; but even so, the Church was not so relentlessly present as it was here. She could not believe in anything so universally acceptable and so infallibly certain.

Even Leonardo's *Last Supper*, which she went to see in a near-by convent, struck a chill in her. It was too symmetrical. People did not eat meals like that.

Perhaps the closer you came to God, the harder it was to believe in Him. That was why Judas had betrayed Him — and the cock crew for Peter too. Walking back from the *Last Supper*, Lisa had to pass one of those smelly tin boxes, by the side of the street, where men urinated. Though she walked hurriedly by, and with averted face, she caught a glimpse of two weather-beaten, olive-skinned faces, overtopping the urinal, deep in conversation. Before she could stop the blasphemous thought, she saw the two men as Jesus and Judas, their robes hoisted, standing in subdued conversation side by side after the Last Supper. It must have been difficult for Judas, being so close, to see Him as the Son of God. And probably even harder for Mary, next to Him in heaven. Which meant it must be impossible for Him too. Sitting up there like Boris Godunov, He must be tormented by the holy sham of it all.

The blasphemous moment passed, but left her feeling terribly oppressed. Before writing a postcard to her aunt, she looked closely at the picture on it. It was a blurred reproduction of the mysterious Holy Shroud, kept at Turin. It was not the first time she had seen reproductions of it, and wondered if it really was the Shroud of Christ; but it meant more here because the Shroud was close. She thought it might help her to feel more spiritual again if she went to see it. So, on another rest day, she took the train to Turin.

She went with Lucia — her understudy. This was the girl, a member of the chorus, whose catastrophic failure had been responsible for the urgent telegram to Lisa. A raven-haired Lombard, with full red lips and lustrous dark eyes under long lashes, she had been chosen more for her looks than her voice. No one had expected Serebryakova, who was notoriously as strong as a horse, to miss any performances. But Lucia had had her big chance, and failed. Her proud parents and six brothers and sisters had been present on the night she was hooted off the

stage. Lisa knew what a terrible blow the young woman had suffered, and made it her business to become acquainted with her
and try to undo some of the damage to her morale. Fearing to
appear condescending, she had at first taken a brisk, professional line, saying she would like to run through some of the arias
with her. Understandably the girl had been reserved and a little
resentful; but she was passionately fond of music, and found the
afternoons in Lisa's suite, studying the score and practising
together, so interesting and instructive that she had shed her
unfriendliness. Lisa, for her part, found she enjoyed helping the
girl to sort out some of the flaws in her technique; she really had
quite a promising voice, and made progress under Lisa's tuition.
If she had to take over again, she could probably now cope reasonably well.

This was important to Lisa, for her attack of breathlessness
that first night — fortunately short-lived — confronted her with
the possibility that one night she might not be able to go on. So
quite apart from the motive of compassion, there were solid professional grounds for trying to help her understudy.

By now they were firm friends: friendship mixed with a good
deal of adoration on Lucia's side, and perhaps of maternal
affection on Lisa's — for Lucia was hardly twenty. Devoutly
religious herself, and knowing Turin well, she was delighted to
accept when Lisa asked her if she would accompany her on her
'pilgrimage'.

Now here they were, gazing, not at the Shroud itself — which,
trapped in iron, had stayed hidden from their eyes when they
had knelt in Turin Cathedral — but at a full-length replica of it
hanging on the wall in the museum, seeing the nail marks, the
scourge marks, the very features of Christ. Those marks and
features had appeared, not in Secondo Pia's photograph of the
Shroud, but in the negative. A nun was gazing at the image,
tears streaming down her cheeks, making the sign of the cross
over and over again, and murmuring, "Terrible! Terrible!
Terrible! The wicked men! The wicked, wicked men!" Lisa too
felt profoundly moved. That gaunt, tortured, yet dignified face

and body — the hands placed becomingly over the genitals. Gazing up at the photographer's image, she became convinced that this was indeed Jesus.

In the confessional, back at the Cathedral, Lisa told the priest that, having seen a replica of the photograph of the Holy Shroud, she no longer believed in Christ's resurrection. The priest, after a moment's thought, said she ought not to judge anything so momentous by a doubtful relic. "We do not claim that it is the Holy Shroud," he said. "Only that it may be. If you believe it is false, that is no reason for doubting the resurrection." "But that is just it, Father," she said. "I am quite sure the shroud is genuine."

The priest's voice was puzzled. "Then why do you say you have lost your faith?"

"Because the man I've been looking at is dead. It reminds me of pressed flowers."

The priest advised her to go home and pray in the quietness of her own room.

Lisa confessed a second time, to Lucia, when they sat on a seat beside the river, taking in the warmth of the sun behind a light veil of cloud, and eating bread and cheese. This time it was a secular confession. She told the girl about some of the disasters in her life: the lack of contact with her father and (of less importance) her brother; her failure in her first choice of career, the ballet, due partly to bad health but mainly to a lack of talent; her annulled marriage — and yet she still had the feeling one was married for life. She envied Lucia's large and loving family circle; she envied her youth, with all its prospects of family happiness. And, because of the late start and a long illness, Lisa would never be more than a *good* singer — whereas Lucia could at least *hope* to be great, one day.

"How have you managed — ?" The girl dropped her head, blushing at her boldness.

"You mean, without love? Oh, I try not to think of it any more. It's not been easy. I'm not without — passions, I can assure you. But you can stifle a lot by getting involved in your work."

"I could never get *that* involved," said the girl, with a sigh. She glanced slyly at her engagement ring.

"You're very wise, my dear," said Lisa.

They fell silent. Lisa was disturbed by the foolish thought that if Christ's hands had not been placed so tactfully, yet suggestively, the Church would not have been able to display His image.

"It's a good thing Rome is too far," she said to Victor. "If I went there I'd become an atheist like you!" He denied being an atheist. You couldn't be brought up in the Caucasus, and look up at the thousands of pure bright stars at night, without having a glimmer of religious feeling.

His remark made Lisa yearn for the tranquillity of mountains. She could get to Como and back within a day. She asked Victor if he would like to go with her. His eyes lit up, flashed for a moment, through his horn-rimmed glasses, with the snowy peaks of his native Georgia.

On a cloudless June day they drank tea on a hotel terrace, overlooking the sparkling lake and with a backdrop of transparent mountains. She felt light enough to float off the terrace and drift over the lake. The cool refreshing breeze would carry her. Victor felt happy too, because of the mountains and that morning's letter from Vera. She was in marvellous spirits, except for missing him. By the same post, Lisa had received a gift from her. It was a print of the Chersonese by Leonid Pasternak. She had mentioned to Vera the Chersonese, as a part of the Black Sea coast dear to her memory. It was a thoughtful, touching gift.

As they sipped their tea, Victor reread his letter, chuckling over the bits he read out to Lisa. "I've bought a maternity corset, darling. I'll be as fat as a sow when you come home." How overjoyed he was, he said, at having a child, so unexpectedly in the autumn, as it were. How much he missed Vera; and how unbearable it would be without Lisa's company. His first wife and their ten-year-old son had been killed in the Civil War. A stray shell had fallen on their house. He still couldn't talk about it. Until he had found Vera he had not expected any more happiness in life.

They went for a ride, up a funicular railway. Still he rattled on, about his wife and coming child, with occasional pauses to point out a fine view. She had never known him so talkative. In fact, without Vera's presence as mediator, she had not found it easy to communicate with him. He spoke very little except when he was drunk; and his wife had given him strict orders about that. But today, in the mountains, he opened out, even if on a line of thoughts as narrow as the railway. Lisa herself did not feel talkative, and was content to smile and nod, while drinking in the scenery.

It was late afternoon when they came down to the town, and neither of them felt like rushing back to the station. He suggested they try to get rooms at the splendid hotel where they had had tea. "We're not needed till tomorrow night," he urged. "Fontini doesn't own us — though he thinks he does! And Delorenzi too, the arrogant little runt! I see what you mean about Milan. Awful place! Well, the Devil take them, let's stay the night!"

Lisa was 'game', after the initial surprise. "Splendid!" he said; and dashed into the hotel. He came out beaming success.

"But I haven't any things!" she suddenly remembered.

"What do you need?"

She considered. "Well, only a toothbrush and toothpaste, I suppose!"

"You wait here." In three minutes he was back, with two paper bags. "We've got our luggage," he laughed. "I needed rather more — some shaving gear, too!"

Rising in the lift, they shared their amusement at the suspicious looks the receptionist and the porter had given them. After settling into their rooms, they had a pleasant, leisurely dinner. The dining room was crowded, but so large and high that it invited people to eat in silence, or to converse in low tones. Victor had recovered from his talkative spell; but the silence was companionable, not awkward. They gazed out through the french windows at the still lake, beginning to ripple towards dusk. Afterwards they had a stroll along the shore. The night fell quickly between the mountains, until the peaks could only be 'seen' by the absence of stars there, for the open sky was full of stars. Lisa felt the Holy Shroud fall away from her, and faith spring alive again. Trite though it might seem, Victor was right — you could not look up at such stars without believing there was *something*.

Outside her door he surprised her by planting a firm kiss on her lips. "I've been wanting to do that for weeks!" He chuckled. "They're so — full and deliciously curved! Vera will forgive me! I hope you didn't mind? See you in the morning."

He had never expressed curiosity about her past; but a remark she threw out at breakfast, about her being "probably half Jewish", did arouse his interest. She found herself, in the quiet train journey back to Milan, telling him things that she had never told anyone. Not being a good talker, he was a good listener; and it relieved her to be able to talk to someone — someone who was sympathetic and yet not too close. Altogether, the trip to Como was a restorative, refreshing her so that she could cope calmly with the two weeks of the season that remained.

A week before the end, she pretended to have a migraine attack before a matinée. Lucia took her place and successfully surmounted the ordeal. So Lisa let her migraine continue into the evening. Again Lucia sang. Victor — and Signor Fontini, and Delorenzi — were astonished by the understudy's secret improvement.

2

VICTOR STAYED OVERNIGHT in Vienna, with Lisa and her aunt, before resuming the long journey to Kiev. He found the old lady charming and cultivated. Indeed, she was not so very old, but

painful rheumatism had aged her. Fortunately it had not yet
attacked her hands, and she was still able to play the piano, with
skill and feeling. She begged them to give her a taste of what she
had missed, lamenting that she had not been well enough to go
to Milan with her niece. To her vigorous accompaniment, they
sang through the closing scene of the opera, with uninhibited
verve and a naturalness they had never quite attained on stage.
Everything always happened too late!

During the months following her return, and for the first time
for several years, Lisa felt troubled by sexual hungers. One night
she was escorted home from a concert by the son of one of her
aunt's friends, an attractive but vain young man, in his early
twenties. He persuaded her to have the cab driver drop them at
his apartment instead, for a nightcap. She told him she was
'unwell', but he said he had no objections to that, if she did not.
Actually she did have objections — such a thing seemed to her
ugly and tasteless — but she allowed him to make love. The most
that could be said was that it partially relieved her physical
cravings, and there were none of the side-effects she had suffered from in former times: no doubt because conception was an
impossibility.

But she felt degraded, because she meant nothing to him,
except as a conquest and an object of prurient curiosity in letting
herself be seduced when she was in that condition. She refused
his attentions for a month, and then went to his apartment
again. When they had finished, he rudely and unforgivably
started to question her about her previous lovers. She said
nothing, of course, but after reaching home and checking to see
that her aunt was all right, she answered his question, silently, for
her own satisfaction, and was appalled by the answer. There was
of course Willi, her husband, and Alexei, the student in Petersburg, her first and possibly her only love. But what could she say
to justify the others? There was the young officer who had
seduced her when she was seventeen, on the train from Odessa to
Petersburg. Well, it was partly the fault of the mixed sleeping
compartments on Russian trains; her sense of devilment on

striking out for independence; the thrill of being borne swiftly through the night; the champagne to which she was not accustomed. Really, though, it was sheer wickedness. Equally brief, meaningless and carnal, and with the added stain of adultery, was the orchestra player with whom she had spent a night soon after her husband had left for the army. She had bumped into him again several years later, at Bad Gastein, and been too embarrassed to speak to him. And finally this young dandy — meaningless and degrading. Including her husband — five men! How many women in Vienna were so promiscuous, outside the lowest class who sold their favours? She was glad she had stopped feeling the need to go to confession. Well, at any rate there would be no more. For fifteen years she had 'sublimated' her desires — until this present shameful episode — and it was much more peaceful to be pure: not to say, neuter.

Fresh from her successful début at La Scala, Lisa found herself much more in demand for operas and recitals, and she threw herself again into music. She heard often from Vera and Victor; and one of their letters brought news that pleased and excited her. Victor wrote that he had been persuaded to sing Boris Godunov next year in Kiev — he was finished as a baritone — this would be his swan-song — and his suggestion that she, Lisa, be invited to sing the role of Marina, the Polish wife of the Pretender, had been enthusiastically agreed. She could expect an official invitation quite soon. They could not wait to see her again. Vera had drawn an asterisk after the word "swan-song" and scrawled underneath: "A likely story!" followed by a sentence or two saying it was wonderful Lisa would be coming to Kiev, and that she, Vera, was bursting out of all her dresses, but would be slim by the time Lisa came, and nursing a fat baby.

But a month or so later, a letter came which, for all its personal warmth, conveyed somehow a sombre message between the lines. The plans to stage *Boris Godunov* had been shelved, they said, as it was thought too heavy for the public taste. They were very upset by this, and they would still love to see her; but perhaps it would be better if she waited a while, until the baby was old enough not to need all Vera's attention. Maybe, by then, the company would decide to put on *Godunov* after all. Though if they did, Victor would not be playing the central role, for he had decided to retire.

Together with a blue baby coat she had knitted, Lisa sent a letter saying she understood; and in any case it would have been difficult for her to leave her aunt, whose rheumatism was much worse.

Two weeks later came a letter which struck her like a blow in the face. Vera had died in giving birth. It was the result of the fall in Milan. So Victor believed, though no one else did. The baby boy was well. Victor's mother had come immediately from her home in Georgia to take care of him. She was very old, but strong; it was good to have her near. People said the baby was the image of Vera. Victor could not believe his beloved wife was gone. He had thrown out all her records, because he could not bear to listen to her voice and know she was dead. He had turned on the wireless — and there was Vera singing a Brahms lullaby to her baby.

On the day following the letter's arrival, obituaries of Serebryakova appeared in the Viennese newspapers: as it were confirming her death.

Lisa wept for days. It seemed incredible to her that she could mourn so deeply, and miss so much, a friend she had known in the flesh only for a single day. Yet such was the case. To Victor, she could not think what to write. Words of sorrow and sympathy sounded false as she wrote them down, though they came from her soul.

Long after the shock had passed, she continued to mourn. In the winter of the same year, she had news from Leningrad of the death of Ludmila Kedrova, her friend and former ballet teacher at the Mariinsky. They had maintained a warm correspondence over the years, whenever the political situation allowed; and Lisa never forgot her godson's birthday. Ludmila was only fifty — stricken by cancer. The deaths of these two friends, both with children who needed them, affected Lisa badly.

She, too, fell ill for a time; with the pains in her breast and pelvic region, from which she had not suffered for many years. It was sheer grief, she thought; and a bewilderment was added to her grief, in that Vera's death affected her worse than Ludmila's. She wondered if she was partly grieving for herself. She associated Vera with the single day in her life when she had been treated, however absurdly and undeservedly, as important. Since then, she had had more singing engagements than ever before, but none had been particularly significant; and now she was less in demand. She woke up one day and discovered she was forty. Others knew it before she did. She was the opera singer who had not quite made it; and few directors are keen to engage such a person for their productions. Of course, if you were a Patti, a Galli-Curci, a Melba, you had hardly begun; but if you were merely talented — you were dead. At least, that was how she felt, and it seemed to her that she was actually not singing so well. She knew her fears were morbid, and put them down to her not having properly lived till she was past thirty, which made her overconscious of the years flying. Now already, whether it was the effect of her throat troubles or simple loss of confidence, her voice was less pure. It was no help, either, that she had bad trouble with her teeth. The dentist saved some with gold fillings, but had to extract four. The dental plate affected her vanity and her voice. It was ludicrous, she thought, to be singing the *Liebestod* and to be conscious of having false teeth.

An event from a long way away, which had nothing to do with her personally, tormented her worse than grief. A man who had committed many murders was tried and condemned to death in Düsseldorf. The case was a sensational one in many respects, and therefore was seized upon by the press, even in Vienna. The condemned man had killed indiscriminately, men, women and children — though mostly women and little girls. He had terrorized Düsseldorf, and now that he was caught there was such a public outcry that the rusty guillotine was to be used — the first execution in Germany for several years. With varying degrees of seriousness and sensationalism the Austrian newspapers were joining in the heated debate about capital punishment. It was a subject, of course, about which everyone felt passionately and self-righteously.

Lisa, though tortured by thoughts of the murdered children, held a passionate, instinctive conviction that it was abhorrent to take human life. Many of her friends agreed. Many others felt just as fiercely and 'morally' that the mass murderer, Kürten, should be put down like a dog with rabies. There were ferocious arguments. One of her friends, a school teacher called Emmy, normally the kindest and gentlest of people, became red-faced with fury, and stormed out of the coffee house where they had been arguing. Before leaving, she threw into her friend's lap the lurid newspaper which contained the most sordid details of the case. Lisa had to fight down the waves of nausea as she forced herself to read the article.

The criminal, of course, had had an indescribably dreadful childhood: ten children in one room with their parents; living on dogs and rats; raped by an older sister; his father a drunken psychopath. Kürten's schooling had been in the arts of torturing and masturbating animals. All this confirmed to Lisa that his criminality was not his fault. The rest of the article made her doubt whether, even in his own interest, he ought to be suffered to live. He killed because he needed to drink blood. One night he had been in such a torture of frustration, not finding a victim, that he had cut off the head of a sleeping swan on the lake and drunk its blood. He was reported as expressing the hope that when the guillotine struck he would remain alive long enough to hear his own blood gush out.

There were other horrific details; such as, that he had dug up some of his victims long after and had sexual intercourse with them; and — more quietly chilling — that he had continued to live placidly with his wife, who had been ignorant of his secret activity and obsession. But it was the image of the swan, and the man's longing to hear his own blood gush, which haunted Lisa for weeks, as a compulsive daylight nightmare. She would stop dead in the street — her head spinning with the thought of the sleeping swan, the falling blade.

And with the thought that it was only by God's grace, or mere chance, that she was Elisabeth Erdman of Vienna and not Maria Hahn of Düsseldorf! Waking up one morning, full of sweet life, with small bright plans to buy some new make-up or go to a dance. . . falling in with a pleasant, charming man, and strolling with him in the woods; and then. . . Nothing. But even more unimaginably horrible, if she had been born as Peter Kürten. . . To have to spend every moment of your life, the only life you were given, as Kürten. . . But then again, the very thought that *someone* had had to be Maria Hahn and Peter Kürten made it impossible to feel any happiness in being Lisa Erdman. . . .

After the execution had gone ahead, she read, in Emmy's newspaper, that while the murderer had been on the loose nearly a million men had been reported to the police as the Monster, and questioned, all over Germany. But Kürten had not been among them; for even the Prosecutor had said that he was "rather a nice man". In jail, he had received thousands of letters from women, about half threatening him with dire torture, and the rest love letters. Lisa cried when she read this; and cried again, later in the day, when she sat quietly with Aunt Magda. Her aunt thought she was still grieving for her dead friends, and scolded her for living in the past.

But it was not the past — the present. For even though this murderer was dead (and Lisa prayed in her heart that he would not *still* be the same Peter Kürten when he entered whatever condition awaits the dead), yet *somewhere* — at that very moment — someone was inflicting the worst possible horror on another human being.

It was many weeks before she lived fully in her own body again, and before her severe pains began to fade into occasional aches. Long after the case had vanished from the headlines, a nine days' wonder, she was haunted by the face of a small boy, lying on a mattress in a room with eleven other people; by a shy, kind man in glasses, liked by his workmates and loved by children; and by a white swan nesting at a lake's edge, lost in a sleep from which it would not awake.

But Aunt Magda had to be helped to dress and to bathe; the shopping had to be got; the *Liebestod* had to be sung; the dentist had to be seen; a friend had to be visited in hospital; a new role had to be rehearsed; a plumber had to be called in to see to a burst pipe; Christmas cards had to be written, and gifts bought and sent off, to her shadowy brother's family in America; followed later by more cards and presents for friends nearer at hand; a new winter coat had to be bought; thank-you letters had to be written.

She exchanged frequent letters with Victor Berenstein, doing her utmost to try to answer his spiritual questionings: the great questions of life, death, and eternal life which were now pre-occupying him. She was, herself, more confused about those questions than she had ever been; and told him so. Yet he seemed to find her friendship a comfort, in black days. Not only personally black, either, because he dropped hints that conditions in general had grown worse.

At this gloomy time of deaths and illnesses, there was also a resurrection from her dead past: none other than Sigmund Freud. A letter came for her out of the blue, saying that he had read with interest and pleasure reports of her appearance at La Scala, Milan, and hoped that her career was continuing to flourish and that she was well. He himself was "subsiding gently and more or less painfully" towards death, with repeated operations on his mouth. The prosthesis he had to wear was a monster. He continued to work, though with great difficulty, and had recently completed a study of her case, which was to be published in Frankfurt, together with her writings. That was his motive for approaching her. Would she be so good as to read the enclosed paper, and a typescript of her own pieces (which she might well have forgotten), and let him know if there was anything to which she objected? He had, of course, thrown a mask over her true identity, but would be reassured to know that he had her full approval for the publication. There would be some modest royalties, of which he would ensure that she received half, for her essential contribution.

Lisa, suffering at the time with her new dental plate, was full of remorse on reading about the Professor's infinitely greater sufferings; and took it as a lesson that she should not complain. She could conceive his misery at not being able to smoke cigars: he mentioned this prohibition, in his letter, as easily the most painful consequence of his cancer and the mutilating device he was forced to wear.

Straight after she had put the breakfast dishes to dry, Lisa took the thick packet to her bedroom. Until the evening, when she had to give a performance, she left her room only to cook her aunt some lunch. Aunt Magda, who still had sharp eyes, saw that she had been crying and that she ate almost nothing. She assumed it was to do with the letter and parcel she had received from Professor Freud and so, wisely, refrained from comment. Composing a reply cost Lisa so much energy that she had nothing left to give her audience that night, and her performance was, as the critic said, "colourless".

Apt. 3
4 Leopoldstrasse
29 March 1931

Dear Professor Freud,

Your letter came as a great surprise to me, and brought me painful pleasure. Pleasure, to hear from someone to whom I owe so much. Pain, to be forced to rake through the dead ashes. Not that I regret it; it has been salutary.

I am sorry to hear about your ill health. I trust that your physician's efforts will lead to a complete recovery. The world needs you too much to allow you to "subside gently", much less in pain. You are kind enough to ask after my health and my aunt's. Aunt Magda suffers greatly from rheumatism, but remains cheerful and alert, and I myself am in quite good health. The past year has not, unfortunately, been a good one in other respects. My friend from Petersburg, Madame Kedrova (Madame R.), died last winter, leaving a husband and a son of fourteen (my godson whom I have never met). And another close friend of mine died in childbirth. I think of the children who are left motherless: and reading *Frau Anna G.* reminded me of that tragedy in your own family circle. I hope your grandchildren are well. They must be quite grown up. I had the dreadful feeling, at the time, one of them would not long survive his mother. Please ease my mind by telling me it wasn't so. I'm sure it was a product of my morbid imagination at that time. Please give my respects to your wife and Anna, and remember me to your sister-in-law. When I met her with you briefly at Gastein I had the feeling that we should be good friends if we had the chance to know each other better.

Reading your beautifully written and wise case study has moved me more than I can say. But I don't think I need to say it. It has been like reading the life story of a young sister who is dead — in whom I can see a family resemblance yet also great differences: characteristics and actions that could never have applied to *me*. I don't mean that to seem critical; you saw what I allowed you to see; no — far more than that, penetrating far more deeply into me than anyone else has ever done. It was not your fault that I seemed to be incapable of telling the truth, or facing it. I can do so now, mainly thanks to you.

To answer your request straight away: of course I can have no possible objection to your publishing the case study. I should be honoured. As for my shameful — or is it shameless? — writings. . . well, if you think they are *necessary*? My face was scarlet on rereading them. I had believed and hoped they were destroyed long since. Surely they cannot be published? But I suppose they have to be included to make sense of the case study? Such obscene ramblings — how could *I* have written them? I did not tell you that at Gastein I was in a fever of physical desire. Yes, sick though I was — or perhaps because I was sick. A very young impertinent waiter, passing me on the stairs, touched me intimately, and then gave me a look of cool effrontery as if it had not happened. He reminded

me in appearance of your son (the one in the photograph).
Anyway, for the rest of my stay I phantasized most dreadfully
about the young waiter. I don't know how he fits in with my
homosexuality, but you know I never accepted that view.

I have to confess that I actually wrote the verses — "doggerel" as you so rightly say — while I was at Gastein. The
weather was atrocious, and for three days we couldn't set foot
outside because of a snowstorm. There was nothing to do but
eat (which I did compulsively), read, observe our fellow
guests, and phantasize about the young man. The English
major gave me the idea of writing some poetry. He showed me
one day a poem he'd just written, about his school days, lying
during the summer holidays with a sweetheart (of doubtful
gender) in an English garden under a plum tree. It was sentimental and terrible. I thought I could hardly do any worse,
and I've always enjoyed trying my hand at poetry. Never
successfully, of course. I wanted it to be shocking; or rather, I
wanted it to be honest to my complicated feelings about sex,
and I also wanted my aunt to know what I was really like. I left
it lying around and she read it. You can imagine how horri-
fied she was.

Well, when you suggested I write something, I thought I'd
try you with the verses. So I copied them out in my score of
Don Giovanni. I don't know why I did that. It shows I was
crazy. When you asked for an interpretation I thought I'd
turn it into the third person to see if that would help me make
more sense of it. But it didn't. It needed *you* to do that; and I
think it is remarkable the way your understanding of it seems
to have deepened in the intervening years. Your analysis (the
mother's womb, and so on) strikes me as profoundly true,
though much too charitable towards its grossness.

The corset as hypocrisy — yes! But also the restraints of
manners, traditions, morality, art. In my indecent revela-
tions I feel as though I were standing before you uncorseted,
and I blush.

I'm sorry I didn't tell you I'd already written "*Don Giovanni* ". I don't imagine it's important. But there are other
deceptions which were, and I've decided I ought to tell you
about them, for you may feel that your case study needs

changing — or even abandoning. I shan't blame you if you hate me for all the lies and half-truths I told.

You were right about my memory of the summer-house being a screen for something else. (Though the summer-house incident *also* happened.) On one occasion in my childhood I wandered on to Father's yacht when I wasn't supposed to, and I found my mother, and my aunt and uncle, there all together, naked. It was such a shock, I thought I was seeing my mother's (or perhaps my aunt's) face reflected in a mirror; but no, they were both there. I thought my mother (or perhaps my aunt) was kneeling in prayer; my uncle kneeling behind her. Quite clearly it was intercourse *a tergo*. You can be sure I didn't stay to inquire. . . . Apparently I was three when that happened.

This only came back to me about five years ago, after a very emotional discussion with Aunt Magda. I heard from my brother Yury (in Detroit) that my father had died. He'd lost his business and his house, of course, and had been living a lonely life in one room. I didn't exactly grieve for his death, but the news affected me, and I was determined to have it all out with my aunt. Poor thing, she was devastated with remorse. She obviously wanted, deep down, to make a clean breast of the only wicked thing she's ever done. She confessed that two or three times in Odessa she and my mother had gone to bed with my uncle. She could only explain her allowing it to happen by saying that a wife will do many things to please her husband; and I can understand that. It seems that my mother and father had had a white marriage for a long time. My uncle persuaded Aunt Magda it would be harmless and even kind. . . . Well, anyway, it happened; but she was thoroughly miserable about it; and when I toddled blithely in, that time, it was the perfect excuse for saying, No more. They all hoped I was too young to understand.

After that, my aunt thought they had all come to their senses. She made her confession (I suppose), and hoped the whole shameful business was in the past. She had no idea they continued to see each other — going to extraordinary lengths to meet, during the winter months; and that it must have been, not just a physical attraction, but a genuine love affair.

She only found out when a policeman knocked on her door, hoping to find a son or daughter — because, according to the hotel register in Budapest, both she and my uncle were dead. . . . I was right, by the way — Uncle Franz was at a pedagogical conference! . . . The bodies were burnt beyond recognition. It wasn't until they showed my aunt some jewellery belonging to the dead woman that she recognized her sister's things. And had to send a telegram to my father. You can imagine that. . . . If I hadn't forgiven my aunt for the sordid events at my home, I should have had to forgive her when I learnt what a nightmare she had been through. Another thought tormenting her was that maybe their 'trio' was not the beginning; that perhaps they were laughing at her. That's something we'll never know.

My aunt is convinced she'll go to Hell for her part in the tragedy, though I've tried my best to persuade her we all do dreadful things but can be forgiven. Of course, when my father died, and all this came out, she also felt dreadful guilt at the way the three of them had deceived *him*. I too have my own 'amends' to make to my father. I was not at all fair to him in my analysis. If there was a bad relationship between us, a lot of it was my fault. You see, I think I knew even then (don't ask me how) that my mother's death had something to do with the scene on the yacht I'd stumbled into; and I'm sure — in the illogical way of childhood — I blamed him for not having been *there*. I blamed *him* for mother's death. And it's true to the extent that, if he'd been with us more, none of it might have happened. It wasn't only his business affairs, by the way; he was also involved in the Bund, the Jewish democratic party. He had a lot on his mind. I should have been more tolerant.

I plead guilty also to slandering Alexei (A.). That weekend on the yacht in the Gulf of Finland — it *was* a beautiful weekend; except for some talk of violence. It was the first occasion on which we slept together, and for me at least it was wonderful. I hallucinated a little — the 'fire' — but nothing to compare with the joy of being completely at one with the man whom I loved. The incident I described didn't take place. Alexei was very correct, even puritanical, where sex was concerned. He was quite capable of shooting people and blowing them up — and obviously has done so since, many times — but not of making love to another girl in my presence. He was very wary of letting emotions get in the way of the cause; in fact, to be honest, we should have been lovers much earlier if it had depended on me. I'm sure it hurt him to abandon me, but he saw marriage and a child as threatening to destroy his mission in life. The young woman with whom he left Petersburg was more a comrade, I think, than anything else. She probably suited him — I was too emotional, too frivolous, to be the comrade of a revolutionary.

But to return to the yachting weekend. . . After we had made love, I *believe* I woke up, in the middle of the night (but it was still quite light in our cabin), and I caught sight of my face in the wardrobe mirror. I *believe* I must have recollected then that childhood scene of my uncle with the twin sisters. Probably, when you asked me about intercourse *a tergo*, I *remembered remembering*, and confused the two yachts. That's the only way I can explain, or excuse, my gross lies. I'm not even sure if I knew I was lying. I was so angry with Alexei for throwing away all we had, I wanted to accuse him of some grossness. I'm sorry. As I said, I think I was incapable of telling the truth. I could easily let myself get carried away in a phantasy. I'm sure I *enjoyed* the idea of me swimming away from the yacht.

He didn't even singe my hair with his cigar. I saw the flash of your match, over my shoulder, and remembered my hair sizzling, but it wasn't on the yacht with Alexei, it was earlier in Odessa when I was 'captured' by the sailors. That was more vile and frightening than I let you believe. They weren't sailors from the *Potemkin* as I think I said, but from a merchant ship that carried grain for my father. They recognized me in the street as his daughter and forced me to go back to the ship with them. They had been burning and looting and drinking, and were altogether in a frenzy. I believed they were going to kill me. From the deck, I could see the burning waterfront across the water (I think that's the burning hotel). They didn't say anything about my mother being loose — as you wisely surmised, I made that up. No, they reviled me for being Jewish. Until then, I hadn't realized there was something *bad* about being Jewish. There was a lot of anti-Semitism in Russia at that time, as well as revolutionary feeling. There was even a disgusting organization advocating the extermination of the Jews as a race. My father gave me one of their pamphlets to read, as part of my 'education' in being a member of a persecuted clan. But I only learnt of such things later, after my baptism on the ship. The sailors saw my father as a filthy exploiter (perhaps I was), and didn't even know he was politically on their side. They spat on me, threatened to burn my breasts with their cigarettes, used vile language I'd never heard. They forced me to commit acts of oral sex with them, saying all I was good for, as a dirty Jewess, was to — But you'll guess the expression they used.

Eventually they let me go. But from that time I haven't found it easy to admit to my Jewish blood. I've gone out of my way to hide it; and I think that may have something to do with my evasiveness and lies generally — earlier in my life; and particularly with you, Professor. Because I knew you were Jewish, of course, and it seemed shameful to be ashamed. I think that was the most important thing I kept back from you. I tried to give you hints in the 'journal'.

My father was very good to me, after that episode; but again he was to blame, in my eyes, for being Jewish. What upset me, what I found unbearable — and I still don't understand it: perhaps you can help — was that on looking back at those fearful events I found them *arousing*. You say I responded to all questions about masturbation as if I was the Virgin. Well, you were quite right to suspect I wasn't telling the truth. I certainly didn't *act* as the Virgin would have; not, at least, after the affair on the ship — I honestly can't recall anything earlier in my life. I would lie in bed and repeat to myself the words they had used, re-enacting in my imagination what they had forced me to do. To a 'pure' girl such as I was, taught by my Polish Catholic nurse that the flesh was sinful, my reaction was more horrible than the event itself. Perhaps that's why I developed 'asthma' not long after. I think I recall reading in one of your case histories that symptoms of throat infection, etc., stem from guilt about such acts.

I poured my complicated feelings and phantasies — even then! — into terribly bad poems and a private diary. One day I caught our Japanese chambermaid reading my diary. I don't know which of us was the more embarrassed. Actually it led to our lying on the bed together, kissing. Ah! you will think, it's just as I always said! She admits it! But isn't adolescence a time of experimentation? It was all very innocent, and never happened again, with her or anyone. We were both lonely and craving affection. I think also — on the basis of what you've taught me — I was trying to move closer to my father, by means of an intermediary. You see, it was fairly clear (in fact she admitted it) that one of her functions was to see to my father's physical needs occasionally. She wasn't alone in this respect. I think almost everyone, from the housekeeper down, had had their 'call'. He was charming and handsome, and of course wielded absolute power. Sonia, my governess, went away for a while in very suspicious circumstances, and I'm sure he'd arranged for her to have an abortion. But the very pretty Japanese girl was his favourite at that period. (She left for home, shortly before I went off to Petersburg.) By getting her to kiss me, that one time, I must unconsciously have been both 'touching' him and also paying him out for his neglect of me.

I realize I seem to be going back on what I've said before. He *did* try his best to make contact with me; was generous with money, and scrupulously avoided favouring my brother. Yet I always felt it was a struggle for him, a matter of *duty*. Possibly he feared women, and was happier with casual contacts. He must have been capable of passion, otherwise he would never have married my mother, against all the odds. But I presume he came to regret giving way to his emotions. When I knew him he seemed cool and calculating, throwing all his energies into his business and — in a hush-hush way — political intrigue on behalf of the Bund. After the shipboard episode I think he realized he'd 'lost' me, and made a special effort to be nice. He even took me on a skiing holiday in the Caucasus. It was disastrous, because I felt he was begrudging every moment away from his work. By now, anyway, I had started to blame him for my terrible crime of being Jewish.

We were both infinitely relieved to get home.

I come now to my husband. He and all his family were horribly anti-Semitic. Much more than I allowed you to think. True, I don't imagine he was anything out of the ordinary in that respect—but literally everything was the fault of the Jews. In all other ways he was very pleasant and kind-hearted, and I was extremely fond of him. I didn't lie about that. But you see, I was *living* a lie. He said he loved me; but if he had known I had Jewish blood he would have hated me. Whenever he said "I love you" I understood it as "I hate you". It couldn't have continued. It upset me dreadfully, though, for in many ways we were well matched, and I wanted to settle down and start a family.

That brings me to the night when I remembered the summer-house incident, and perhaps other incidents. For a few moments I was filled with happiness! Do you understand? I was convinced that my father *wasn't* my father, I wasn't Jewish, and I could live with my husband, and get pregnant, with a clear conscience! But of course, I couldn't cope with feeling *glad* that my mother was an adulteress and that she might have passed me off to her husband as his child — so unutterably sordid and wicked. To be *glad* of such things! And so as you know, I 'buried' it.

We did get an annulment, by the way. I heard he remarried and moved to Munich after the war.

So you see, our separation had very little to do with sexual problems. I have always found it difficult to enjoy myself properly, knowing there were people suffering 'just the other side of the hill'. And there always are. I can't explain my hallucinations; but I do know they were distinct, in some peculiar way, from the pleasure (which I continued to feel). It was the same with Alexei; and I have to confess that I 'experimented' with one of the orchestra players from the Opera, not long after my husband left to go into the army, and I felt the same with him too (though the pleasure was of course superficial in the extreme, and tainted by guilt). I was not lying when I said the hallucinations were bound up with my fears of having a child. If I am right, I should now be in the clear, so to speak, because I have begun to miss my periods — rather early. . . . But there is in any case no prospect of my putting it to the test.

I cannot explain my pains either. (They have recurred from time to time.) I still think they're organic, in some peculiar way; and I keep expecting, every time I visit a doctor, for him to say I've been suffering from some outlandish disease in my breast and ovary for the past fifteen years! The 'asthma' at fifteen may have been hysterical, I grant you that; but I don't think the rest is. Let's try to look at it afresh. I lost my mother when I was five. That was terrible; but as you say, there are orphans everywhere. She died in dreadfully immoral circumstances — and very painfully. Yes, but I could come to terms with it. Is there any family without a skeleton in the cupboard? Frankly I didn't always wish to talk about the past; I was more interested in what was happening to me then, and what might happen in the future. In a way you *made* me become fascinated by my mother's sin, and I am forever grateful to you for giving me the opportunity to delve into it. But I don't believe for one moment *that* had anything to do with my being crippled with pain. It made me unhappy, but not ill. And lastly, yes it is possible there may be a slight bisexual component in my make-up; but nothing specifically sexual, or at least nothing I haven't been able to cope with very easily. On the whole I feel my life has been more bearable by reason of my closeness to women.

What torments me is whether life is good or evil. I think often of that scene I stumbled into on my father's yacht. The woman I thought was praying had a fierce, frightening expression; but her 'reflection' was peaceful and smiling. The smiling woman (I think it must have been my aunt) was resting her hand on my mother's breast (as if to reassure her it was all right, she didn't mind). But the faces — at least to me now — were so contradictory. And must have been contradictory in themselves too: the grimacing woman, joyful; and the smiling woman, sad. Medusa and Ceres, as you so brilliantly say! It may sound crazy, but I think the idea of the incest troubles me far more profoundly as a symbol than as a real event. Good and evil coupling, to make the world. No, forgive me, I am writing wildly. The ravings of a lonely spinster!

Hence the mirror phobia I had for a short while. That was when I was reading the case of the "Wolf-Man", with his compulsive obsession for intercourse *more ferarum*. (Aren't we indeed close to the animals?) I knew him, by the way. Or rather, I knew his family, by repute, in Odessa. It was quite clear from the details. That's why — if I may make a request? — I'd rather you didn't refer to Odessa as "the town of M ——". It won't fool anyone close, of whom few remain. Anyone not close will be sufficiently deceived by my being a cellist (!), for which disguise — thank you.

The Wolf-Man's story haunted me for years; a kind of Christ figure of our age.

At least *now* I have been frank with you, and I can only express my heartfelt regret that I was not frank with you *then*, when you were spending so much of your time and energy on an unworthy patient. I am touched, beyond words, by knowing that so much wisdom, patience and kindness were devoted to a poor, weak-spirited, deceitful young woman. I assure you it was not without fruit. Whatever understanding of myself I now possess, is due to you alone.

I wish you every success with the publication of your case study, should you still decide to go ahead with it. I should prefer my real name to be kept out of any negotiations. If any money should be owing to me, please donate it to charity.

Yours very sincerely,
LISA ERDMAN

She felt a great relief at having declared everything — everything that was relevant. She had intended to tell him also about having slept with the "unimportant" man in the train from Odessa to Petersburg, her first experience of sexual intercourse and also her first experience of hallucination; but her letter had grown so long, and so full of the correction of lies, that she took fright. One more might 'break the camel's back'; and really, it was *not* important, she could not say it had ever preyed on her mind.

Yes, it was marvellous to have poured it all out. She waited anxiously for a reply. As the days, and then the weeks, passed without a response from the Professor, anxiety became a kind of terror. She had mortally offended him. He was in a state of rage. Indeed, how could it be otherwise ? She merited his wrath. Her breathlessness came back (and certainly not because of committing fellatio); she was forced to cancel three engagements because of ill health. She dropped a tray of breakfast dishes one morning, between the kitchen and her aunt's bedroom, because she thought she heard Freud's thunderous voice, cursing her.

She suffered from nightmares, one of which led to her moaning so loudly that it brought her aunt, hobbling on her stick, into her bedroom, her face as white as her nightdress. She had met a man climbing the stairs to the apartment. He doffed his trilby hat and said he was the Wolf-Man, and had come to take her to Freud. She was frightened, but he was very pleasantly-spoken, and explained that Freud only wanted to go over the place names in his manuscript, replacing initials with the real names. So she went with him, but instead of heading for Freud's house he took her into some woods. He wanted her help, he said — showing her some pornographic photographs of a girl scrubbing a floor, kneeling down, with her dress hoisted to her hips. This was the only way he could obtain relief — by gazing at these photos. She talked to him seriously about it, and he appeared grateful for her help. They were by a lake, and she was admiring the swans. When she turned towards the man, he had turned into a real wolf; a wolf's head between his hat and his long, shabby black coat. He snarled, and she ran away, and he bounded after her, intent on biting through her head. Even as she ran for her life, she knew she deserved it, for her letter to Freud. That was when she was shaken awake by Aunt Magda, in her white nightdress, her face as scared as the old granny in *Little Red Riding Hood*.

When at long last a letter arrived, it was several hours before Lisa could muster the courage to open it. Her hands shook as she unfolded the writing paper. And she winced with pain as she read it (but that was mainly because of the paragraph about his grandson). And she flushed scarlet over his reference to her slip of the pen, and agonized over the context, which she simply could not remember. Yet, generally speaking, it was more merciful than she deserved.

> 19, Berggasse
> 18 May 1931

Dear Frau Erdman,

Thank you for your letter of 29 March. I found it of course most interesting; not least your slip of the pen in writing "perhaps I was" for "perhaps he [my father] was". Yet, after all, that is not so diverting as an error made by one of my English correspondents, who has written to commiserate with me on my "troublesome jew", in place of "jaw". Indirectly, that is the cause of my delay in replying. My jaw, I mean. I had to have another operation on it, and I fear I have fallen behind with my correspondence.

I am glad to know you and your aunt are well. In answer to your query, my little grandson Heinz died when he was four years old. With him, my affectional life came to an end.

To the main business. I prefer to go ahead with the case study as it stands, despite all imperfections. I am willing, if you will permit, to add a postscript in which your later reservations are presented and discussed. I shall feel compelled to make the point that the physician has to trust his patient, quite as much as the patient must trust the physician.

I call to mind a saying of Heraclitus: "The soul of man is a far country, which cannot be approached or explored." It is not altogether true, I think; but success must depend on a fair harbour opening in the cliffs.

> Yours very sincerely,
> SIGMUND FREUD

Lisa replied with a short letter, thanking him for his forbearance, and expressing her anguish at the accuracy of her premonition. She confessed to a feeling of remorse, as though her premonition had somehow been responsible for the child's death. She did not expect a reply to her note; indeed she expressly asked him not to burden himself by replying. Nevertheless, within a few days a letter came, from the apartment in the Berggasse:

Dear Frau Erdman,

You are not to trouble yourself about my grandson's death, which is far in the past. Doubtless, already when his mother died, he carried the seeds of his own fatal illness. My experience of psychoanalysis has convinced me that telepathy exists. If I had my life to go over again, I should devote it to the study of this factor. It is clear that you are especially sensitive. You must not let it distress you unduly.

As a matter of fact, one of your dreams during your analysis made me certain you possessed this power. You have probably forgotten it. According to the note I made of it, you dreamt that a man and woman in middle life were being married at a church in Budapest; and in the middle of the ceremony a man stood up in the congregation, drew a pistol from his pocket, and shot himself. The bride screamed —it was her former husband — and fell in a faint. When you recounted the dream, it was perfectly clear to me that it referred to a tragic event, earlier in that year (1919), which occurred in Budapest. One of my most distinguished colleagues, practising in that city, got married to a woman whom he had courted for eighteen years. She had not wished to divorce her husband while her daughters were unmarried. On the very day of my colleague's wedding to her, her former husband committed suicide. I am sure you sensed that knowledge in my mind, and it merged into your mother's situation: which of course I am still convinced was at the root of your troubles.

In your dream you were present yourself, as a "misty" figure, comforting the fainting woman yet also aware that the bridegroom needed your comfort more than was quite proper. And it is a fact that my colleague had had a very ambivalent relationship with one of the daughters of the lady he married. The young woman was in fact a patient of mine at one time.

I should add that no one in Vienna except myself and one or two of my closest colleagues knew of the tragedy touching our friend's wedding, and it was certain you could not have obtained the information from anywhere. I should have liked to include your dream in my study, but its evident application to my Budapest colleague's experience made that impossible; the more particularly as he is not in good health, and believes in the existence of telepathic powers.

I have only told you this to demonstrate to you that your gift is entirely unconscious. There is nothing you can do about it. You can no more alter it than you can make your beautiful voice turn into a raven's croak. So do not try.

I send you my good wishes.

Yours very sincerely,
SIGMUND FREUD

Observing how much happier and livelier she looked, Lisa's aunt wondered if there was a man friend in the offing. Whatever the reason might be, it was a relief to her, for she had been afraid her niece might be heading for another nervous breakdown.

Actually, Lisa had the feeling of being extraordinarily close to Freud: closer, in fact, than when she had been seeing him nearly every day. It was the tone of his latest letter which made her feel this: so unexpectedly warm; paying her compliments on her voice and psychic gift, and the even greater compliment of sharing a confidence with her, the story about his colleague. There was something strange about that. Not that she thought it wasn't true; Freud was incapable of deceit. She remembered the dream — all except that part of it which Freud had separated from the rest, as though to underline it for her. She didn't at all remember being present herself at the wedding tragedy, a "misty" figure giving comfort.

Wasn't this Freud's way of asking for her help and support, in his old age and infirmity? She recalled almost the only personal remark he had ever let fall to her: a hint — no more — that his own marriage, on the physical level, had come to an end when he was forty. Wasn't that in his dream? Freud was the middle-aged husband, whose younger self had already died. He therefore needed comforting "more than was quite proper" from the young woman tending the fainting bride. . . . Well, that would ostensibly be Anna Freud, with her mother. But Lisa was "Anna" in the case study. . . . "A very ambivalent relationship". . . "The young woman was in fact a patient of mine at one time". . . .

He was appealing to her for friendship; but feared she would find it improper if he expressed it openly. Perhaps for more than friendship. If so, she ought not to shrink from trying to console him. Lisa worked herself up into a state of great tension, wondering how to answer his appeal. She decided that the best way was simply to reply in a relaxed and friendly spirit, referring genuinely to matters of the case history — and just see what happened.

16 June 1931

Dear Professor Freud,

I have been touched to the heart by your kind and generous letter. Your compliment on my voice also touched me — till I remembered you have never yet heard me sing! Otherwise you would not call it beautiful. In fact, it has more of the crow in it each day.

I have done little else recently but go over and over that evening when my 'hysteria' began. I remember a few more details, which may be useful to you in writing your Appendix. First of all, I was (as I have said) happy in the thought that I might not be Jewish. Even "might not" was enough to justify my giving myself to my husband completely, with a clear conscience; and with God's grace to bear him a child. Till then, I had been troubled by the approach of his leave (you were right). It was less than a month away. In his letters he had been putting pressure on me to "go the whole way". I couldn't blame him; it was only natural. But I hated the very thought. Now, though, thanks to my uncertain parentage, I felt I could agree, and I wrote him a passionate letter on returning home from my aunt's.

But when I fell asleep I had dreadful nightmares. You see, there were other things I had started to feel bad about. One of Willi's tasks was to prosecute deserters, and he'd just won a case, which meant that the poor soldier would be shot. He had written to me all about his brilliant speech which had convinced the tribunal — he was obviously delighted with himself. I felt sick. I couldn't 'fit' this person in the letter with my memory of his gentleness. So weren't my pains, which came on that same night, the result of my chaotic emotions, and nothing to do with suppressing knowledge? (I'm very good at suppressing uncomfortable knowledge — I once 'forgot', an hour after I'd read it, that my leading man was married to the leading lady — whom I was replacing because she had fallen sick. Just because I'd built up a day-dream that I'd have a beautiful affair with him!) But my convenient lapses of memory don't make me ill.

And didn't I feel better when you'd helped me 'dig out' my mother's affair simply because I felt excited at the way it cleared up mysteries? Clarification! Anagnorisis! I've just sung in a new oratorio called *Oedipus Rex* — can you tell?! I like the idea of clarification. "More light! More light!" More light — and more love.

What do you think? These are just misty ideas, and I'm not at all sure of them.

The tragic business connected with your colleague I shall treat with complete confidence, of course. In spite of that, your letter sounded livelier, and I hope it means your health is better. I am well. Aunt Magda is excited because my brother is coming on vacation from the United States. She has not much of a life any more. We are not quite on our own — we have a mischievous fluffy kitten. Unfortunately it has brought my aunt up in a rash, and I shall have to find her another home. (The cat, I mean!) Sometimes I crave more stimulating company. I would give much for one of our discussions of the old days. Now my aunt is waiting to play two-handed patience. It will stop me from giving way to my weakness for writing long rambling letters.

With cordial greetings,
LISA

Having posted her letter she had the cruel, but not unfamiliar, experience of remembering, or fearing that she remembered, the questionable part of her dream. The only saving grace was that she had not been more outspoken. But she did not expect a reply, and none came.

Lisa and her aunt found themselves entertaining two grey-haired American tourists, George and Natalie Morris. George held a responsible position with a motor company in Detroit and had done very well for himself. Natalie even had a mink coat.

"I don't know what they're doing here," she wrote to Victor.

I keep expecting them to take out little American flags and wave them about as they walk along the streets. I've a friend from New York who met them, and who was repelled by their thick American accents. They miss the milkshakes at their corner drugstore. They don't know how we manage in such a tiny, dingy apartment (it's shrunk since they were here with their children after the war!). They're terrified of catching dysentery. *Nat*alie can't find anywhere to get her hair permed and tinted. George scans the foreign news, in vain, for baseball results. He and I have nothing in common, not even memories. We seemed to occupy different landscapes. How did we come from the same womb? I couldn't bring myself to kiss his morning-shadowed cheek at the station, so we shook hands. *Meine Bruder*! I'm reading the *Inferno* to cheer me up. Of course it's nice for Aunt Magda. To her he's still her little nephew Yury, and it's someone else to talk to.

After two weeks of the infernal visit, it became clear to Lisa why they had come. His children gone from the nest, George was feeling barren, high-and-dry on his menopause. He wanted Lisa and his aunt to come back to the United States with them. He already had their entry permits. Lisa could teach music: there were plenty of opportunities. George brought up the proposition over dinner one night, and Natalie added her persuasions. She would have loved to bring her parents over from Moscow, but that was not possible.

Lisa turned the idea down flat. But Aunt Magda was touched

by the invitation, and promised to consider it. In the end, after many tearful discussions with her niece, she agreed. It would be a terrible wrench to leave Lisa and Vienna. But then, she hardly saw any of the latter any more; just the view from the window, for the stairs were beyond her. Of her circle of friends, most of them widows or spinsters, "some were no more, and others had gone further. . . " — including her dearest friend, Lisa's singing teacher, who had actually emigrated with her children to America. She wrote warmly of the kindliness of the people.

George and Natalie could offer her a pleasant room on the ground floor, and a car to take her out for drives. They had the money to pay for the best medical care, and home nursing if and when she needed it. If she went, it would be best for Lisa too, she said. She was an increasing burden on her (it was true, though she denied it). Lisa could not expect to go on earning good fees for many more years, so what would happen to them? On her own, Lisa would be able to support herself by teaching at the Conservatorium, perhaps.

There was really no decision to be made, though there were tears to be wept, by both Aunt Magda and her niece. "It was amusing to watch my brother's face," Lisa wrote again to Victor. "I'm sure that's what they were hoping for. They don't like me any more than I like them, but they can see Aunt Magda as a pet in the house, a quaint old European lady they can bring out to show their friends. They've even promised to buy her a grand piano, so they can have cultural Viennese evenings. Also, dear George is looking for his mama."

Lisa watched her aunt being eased aboard the train, like an expensive *objet d'art* the Morrises had acquired on their vacation. Lisa and her aunt dared not look into each other's faces, for they knew they would never see each other again. Another layer of skin peeled away, and the apartment was suddenly very big and hollow. Lisa spent more time in it too, as her bookings continued to fall away. She made inquiries at the Conservatorium about pupils. Ever since her afternoons with Lucia in Milan, she had thought she would enjoy teaching, and might even have a talent for it. But the vain, empty years stretched ahead.

Then, in the spring of 1934, Victor wrote from Kiev to say how much better things were. The bad harvests were over. People had enough to eat. He had been asked to produce *Boris Godunov*, and was making it a condition of his acceptance that she be invited to sing the role of Marina. He was longing to see her again. In fact, now that he could invite her in good conscience, he wished to propose marriage. It was not an impulsive gesture; he had thought deeply about it. He had felt more at home with her, those weeks in Milan, than he had with any other woman, except Vera and his first wife. He felt sure it would be Vera's wish. Hadn't she asked her to look after him for her? Little Kolya was running wild, and badly needed a proper mother. Victor's mother had done her best, but she was old, and wanted to spend her last years at home in the village where she had been born and lived her whole life. She was homesick, as only the very young and the very old can be. But he did not want Lisa to think he was asking her just from practical considerations. He felt they had drawn very close to each other through the years of correspondence; but he, too, was ageing, and life was too short to depend on letters. . . . If she could see her way to marrying a man approaching senility, he would be overjoyed.

Lisa compressed into a single day all the neurotic, hallucinatory experiences she had once suffered from. She walked around in a dream — found herself wandering into the bedroom with a jug she intended for the kitchen; poured milk into a sieve she thought was a pan. She didn't know what to do; and there was no one who could help her make her decision, no one she felt close enough to talk to. There was every reason to say yes. She was fond of Victor, and admired him. Her heart was drawn in love and compassion to the motherless little boy. Her own life, in spite of having many acquaintances and a few, not particularly close, friends, was increasingly lonely.

Also there was violence in the city. For several days she heard the rumble of gunfire, and imagined she was back in Odessa at the turn of the century. The political news everywhere was terrible, and it looked as if worse was to come.

For three nights on end she dreamt of children, and saw this as a sign she should go and be a mother to Vera's little boy. But would she know how to? And did she love Victor enough? Certainly she didn't love him as she had loved Alexei or even her husband. And yet, as she read the letter over and over, she began to love him a little more, her heart started to tremble.

From day to day and from week to week she delayed replying. She made herself ill with indecision, every moment of the day — and most of the night. Then her mind locked, and was incapable even of thought. One whole afternoon she sat in a church, but came out no closer to an answer. Her pains were back in full force; she could hardly breathe. She was not eating. She had the wild idea of going to the Berggasse, knocking on Freud's door, and flinging herself at his feet. She would ask him some irrelevant question, and according to whether he answered "yes" or "no" she would frame her answer to Victor.

One morning she took the score of *Eugene Onegin* out of the battered piano stool, and played over some of the passages. Then, because she had too much time on her hands, she began to compose her reply in the form of Tatiana's letter to Onegin. She told herself she would let the rhymes lead her to the correct decision. After writing, and crossing out, all day, it came out like this, just after midnight. . . .

> As if I were a child, I tremble;
> The pen is shaking in my hand.
> Tanya could not her thoughts dissemble;
> My thoughts — I do not understand.
>
> In one way only I resemble
> Reckless Tatiana — that my breast
> Is all on fire and cannot rest.
> Regretfully you are recalling,
> I know, the mood that made you write
> Words which torment me day and night.

Day and night!
Why have you disturbed my peace?
The heart was cool, the embers ashen,
For long ago I found release
From the indignities of passion.
I was contented, in a fashion,
And would have stayed so till I died.
It is too late to teach my heart,
Which is worn through, Tatiana's part,
To flower, and open, as your bride.

Too late!
Her ancient nurse, not Tanya,
Sits listening to the midnight bird —
The kind, dull, ignorant old *nyanya*
To whom love is a foreign word.
A word from a far country. Yet
That is not true; a word — for me —
That has been easier to forget
Than hold in fruitless memory.
I do not know why I am frightened
To pick the blossom that I crave,
As if my body were a grave;
Though, it is true, those fears have lightened
Since I have crossed the Rubicon,
A little early. . . . You will gather
What I am saying. . . . Would you rather
Not choose for your new wife someone
Still young enough to be a mother
To Kolya, and to bear a child
To be his sister or his brother?
He is alone, and therefore wild.

I would be loving to him, tender;
And were you here I should surrender
To all you asked from me, I know.
For I am not indifferent to you;
That night you kissed me — *then*, I knew you
Might make the frozen torrent flow.

Who are you? Angel of salvation,
Or an insidious temptation?
And who am I? A still naïve
Young girl in wrinkled flesh: you, only,
In marrying, might have cause to grieve.
There are worse fates than to be lonely.

So be it, then! I make my choice.
I shall not come to play the Polish
Tsarina. As all else, my voice
Has crossed the line. . . . It would be foolish,
Though I am flattered, to pretend
To be the bride of the Pretender;
The throat is hoarse that once was tender.
Best smile at what one cannot mend!
And cast it off,
And cast it off! Harsh as the raven,
Who was *almost* a nightingale.
Choose someone young. You cannot fail
To think me spiritless and craven.
Now I must close. Some other thing
You asked of me. . . . If you are certain,
Yes, I will come, though not to sing,
Except perhaps — behind the curtain.

She scribbled down, as an afterthought, some of Pushkin's
own artlessly simple lines. . . "Perhaps this is all idleness, /
Delusions of an inexperienced soul, / And what is fated is something quite different. . . / Imagine: I am here alone! / No one
understands me! . . . ." For a few moments, waiting for the ink to
dry, she was a lovesick girl of the 1820s, foolishly and recklessly
laying bare her heart to a loveless cynic. But unlike Tatiana,
Lisa did not hesitate to seal the envelope, with a lick of her
tongue, once she had signed her name; and not having an old
nanny to send out, she put on her coat and hurried downstairs
into the dark night to post her letter at the street corner.

3

AFTER THE WRETCHED doubt-ridden weeks, tiresome packing and sad farewells — the first week in Kiev was a delirium. Victor's broad grin on the station platform; meeting Kolya and his aged grandmother at the apartment; a party at the Opera House, being made welcome by all Victor's protégés — delightful young people; reviving her brief encounters with the city, in walks and rides; and how pleasant (except for her uneasy awareness of being privileged) that their flat was in the heart of the city, the Kreshchatik, with its elegant shops, theatres and cinemas. Then, after a simple ceremony, the wedding party, even wilder than the welcoming party; promises of singing pupils — if Kolya wasn't too much of a burden; celebratory drinks with this, that, and the other person, between helping Victor's mother to pack. There was no time for thought — except that she had come to the right decision.

It was her idea that they take her mother-in-law the long journey by train to Tiflis, and then return by way of the Black Sea; they could pick up a cargo ship at the little Georgian port of Poti, which would carry them to Odessa: and so to Kiev by train. It would be a short honeymoon, and also a happy experience for little Kolya. Lisa thought the excitement of an ocean trip would console him for saying goodbye to his nana, and also provide the right relaxed, peaceful atmosphere for the child and his new mama to get to know each other.

Victor's mother was a tiny, hunched, gay-eyed, balding, sprightly lady of eighty. She was more excited than anyone, because she was going home to her village to die. Her son's marriage did not at all put her out; in fact, it was clearly a relief to her. She loved her grandson dearly, and cried at having to give him up; but he was too much of a handful for an old woman.

At Tiflis she was handed over to a horde of her relatives and neighbours, who keened over her as if they were receiving her corpse. Lisa could see that her husband was overcome by this meeting up with his past, only to say goodbye again; and especially to be embracing his mother, probably for the last time. It was too painful to wish to prolong it, and mercifully there was a swift connection with the train going over the mountains to the coast. They were soon crawling up the steep gradient — their train pushed by two engines, rather like working elephants — through spectacular scenery which both Lisa and Victor, for different reasons, were too distraught to take in. Then the Black Sea came into view, and they were rushing down towards it. They had no trouble, at Poti, in finding a cargo ship which took passengers; and Lisa was on the sea of her childhood.

When she had first been introduced by Victor to his four-year-old son, with the words "Say hello to the lady who is going to be your mama", he had put his hand up to shake hers and said seriously, "Hello Lisa." It had made them laugh, and broke the ice. She had picked him up in her arms and hugged and kissed him, swearing he was the image of his mother, the same straight blond hair, green eyes and mischievous smile. He had smiled when she kissed him — and really the sea voyage did not seem necessary, since he had taken to her. He still called her Lisa. Well, that was fine with her; let him call her Mama in his own good time, if *ever* — she didn't mind. "He's been so *good*, Victor!" she said in amazement, when he had gone off to sleep without a fuss, in their cabin. "I can't see that he's any trouble at all." He chuckled, and said this was only the lull before the storm.

But she couldn't believe there would be a storm. A few gusts, for sure; but she already knew she could cope. Of course, she was old enough to be his grandmother; but she would seem young to him after the bald old soul who had been mothering him. She would make sure he had lots of playmates.

He was an adventurous little boy, and soon found the bridge and appointed himself First Officer. He 'steered' the ship all morning, and had to be brought down for luncheon by a grinning steward. Yet he was pleased to see his daddy and the new lady — hugging her knees and saying, "Hello, Lisa!" She walked with him on deck and they watched the dolphins. She told him how, in winter, the sea was covered in ice; and later, when she undressed him and put him to bed, she told him a story about a huge whale, with the funny name of Porphyry, who hundreds and hundreds of years ago had wandered into this sea, because he loved adventures too. Bad sailors tried to catch him, but he was always too quick and clever for them. The little boy lay sucking his thumb, gazing up at her with round eyes.

While he lay asleep, they had dinner with the ship's officers and a few other passengers. Even the unmusical had heard vaguely of Victor Berenstein, and they were impressed. They begged him to sing at the tinny old piano. Laughingly he protested that his singing days were over; and told them they should ask Lisa instead, for she too was a famous singer. So the happy honeymoon couple were compelled to sing duets. And in the cabin, he scolded her for having pretended her voice had gone off. He ought to be rehearsing *her* in *Boris*, on their return home, not the Leningrad upstart Bobrinskaya! She laughed away his flattery; Kolya was stirring, so she perched herself on his bunk and very softly hummed a lullaby. He was soon sleeping soundly again.

They undressed with embarrassment, even in the dark, for it was the first time they had shared a room. There were only two bedrooms in the Kiev apartment, and at first Lisa had shared with his mother. On their wedding night it seemed embarrassingly obvious to change rooms; and anyway it was only for a couple of nights. Awkwardly, now, he climbed into the narrow bunk beside her; but as soon as they put their arms around each other, they felt at ease, and happy. It was not the wild passion of youth, but that would hardly have been possible anyway, with little Kolya sleeping near them. They had to be very quiet. Perhaps that helped; they were not under pressure to thrash about wildly as lovers are supposed to do. . . which made them both wish, at times, that they could.

They moved gently, silently, with the creaking timbers of the ship and the plash of the waves. She saw no unpleasant visions;

only, through the porthole, the flash of a familiar lighthouse she had forgotten. As they made love she listened to the child's quiet breathing. Almost like another child's was the head resting on her breast. The flashes of the lighthouse lit up her husband's white hair.

The voyage achieved all she had hoped, and more. By the time they berthed at Odessa, on a cool late-summer morning, she felt they were beginning to knit already into a family group. One of their holiday photos, taken by a fellow passenger, brought out the hopeful beginnings of unity: leaning against a lifeboat, there is the tall, heavy frame of Victor, in an astrakhan coat and fur hat, his plump and amiable face glancing proudly towards his wife, her coat collar turned up and her hair ruffled by the breeze; and she in turn is glancing proudly down at the little boy who is between them, holding their hands. He is smiling at the camera, his eyes closed — for he had blinked at the wrong moment.

Lisa did not recognize the city, and the city did not recognize her. As they walked or were driven around the places of interest she felt — not even dead, but unreal, as though she had never lived. Actually, someone did recognize her. A faded, middle-aged woman paused uncertainly on the pavement and, looking straight into her eyes, said, "Lisa Morozova?" But Lisa shook her head and walked on past, pulling Kolya along to catch up with daddy. The woman had been a close friend; they had been members of the same ballet class.

Victor misinterpreted her sombre expression, and sympathetically drew her arm through his. They were in the region of the docks, and he thought she was upset at the air of desolation. "Don't worry; it's all in the past," he murmured. He began explaining to her why most of the business premises along the dock front were shuttered and half derelict, including one that used to be marked: *Morozov: Grain Exports*. There was a government sign over the doors now, but the paint had faded on this too, and the windows were broken.

Kolya wanted to look in through the broken window, and his father hoisted him up to the sill. But there was nothing to be seen inside, except darkness and some broken glass.

They caught a bus eastwards along the coast towards her old home. The rambling white house had been converted into a health resort. Though its facilities were not usually available for the use of passing holiday-makers, Victor, as a leading Soviet artist, was able to buy luncheon tickets. The pleasant dining room was packed; mostly, it seemed, with factory workers from Rostov. None of the furnishings or pictures were left over from the former owners; only the trees outside the french windows were the same. And one old waitress, who served them their cabbage soup, had been a scullery maid in the old days. She served them in a surly manner, and clearly did not recognize Lisa; nor did Lisa feel like making herself known, though in the past she had often exchanged friendly words with her.

After lunch they strolled in the grounds. There was now a concrete path down to the tiny cove and beach; but the latter were no different. Only, now, there were many strangers splashing about in the water, instead of the small family party of her childhood. She helped Kolya to undress, and took off her own shoes and stockings (tucking her skirt into her knickers). Even her husband tucked up his trouser legs and paddled. Lisa looked for jelly-fish under the water, but there were none. They lay then, drying their legs in the sunshine: which was warm, but not nearly so hot as she recalled, perhaps because of the lateness of the season.

Nor were the plants, trees and flowers in the ample grounds subtropical, as her memory said they were. She was surprised by that failure. Perhaps her memory had confused their own garden with some of the other places they had visited in their yacht, further to the south. Leaving Victor sun-bathing on the beach, she took the child on a trip of exploration. Change had not touched the dense trees in that remote part of the garden; except that the summer-house, gone to seed even in her time, was now nothing but a maze of bushes and brambles, growing out of stones and rotten wood.

She had the feeling that she was no more than a spectre. Herself was unreal, the little boy was unreal. She was cut off from the past and therefore did not live in the present. But suddenly, as she stood close against a pine tree and breathed in its sharp, bitter scent, a clear space opened to her childhood, as though a wind had sprung up from the sea, clearing a mist. It was not a memory from the past but the past itself, as alive, as real; and she knew that she and the child of forty years ago were the same person.

That knowledge flooded her with happiness. But immediately came another insight, bringing almost unbearable joy. For as she looked back through the clear space to her childhood, there was no blank wall, only an endless extent, like an avenue, in which she was still herself, Lisa. She was still there, even at the beginning of all things. And when she looked in the opposite direction, towards the unknown future, death, the endless extent beyond death, she was there still. It all came from the scent of a pine tree.

The rest of the day flashed by. She put flowers on her mother's grave, after her husband had helped her clear away the briers; she visited the crematorium, and found her father's name in the book of remembrance; she wrote, and posted, cards to Aunt Magda, brother George, a Viennese friend, and her godson (whom she would soon meet); they took Kolya to the playground in the park, and also bought him an expensive toy, for being so patient and good. They caught the night train to Kiev. They looked forward to a quiet dinner after Kolya was asleep (he should have been worn out). But in fact he hardly slept all night, and made sure they stayed awake too. He whined, sulked, was sick, demanded his grandmother, bit Lisa's finger, disturbed other travellers with his screams. By morning, when they staggered from the train, Victor and Lisa looked so haggard that the friends who met them — influential people who had the use of a car — made ribald comments. Kolya, by this time, was angelic: drowsing in his father's arms.

Apartment 5
118, Kreshchatik
Kiev, U.S.S.R.
4 November 1936

Dear Aunt Magda,

I can't believe it is almost Christmas already. I hope you enjoy the gifts. Your letter was most welcome, as always. I am sorry you are confined to your bed so much; you were always such an active person. But it was nice of George and Natalie to have your bedroom decorated and to give you a radio set. As you say, you are very fortunate to be in such good hands. Please give them my love. It was good news about George's promotion; but I am sure no more than he deserved. And please pass on my congratulations also to Toni, on being awarded her doctorate. Dr Morris! It sounds good. Her parents should be very proud, and I'm sure they are. Good-looking too! She looks marvellous in her gown and hood, and I bet she has lots of admirers. I can't believe it's the same little girl who stayed with us in Vienna. I wish I could meet her now. I'm sure she still thinks of me (if she remembers me at all) as a skinny woman who was so depressed she had no time for anyone else. It's a shame we can't know each other. And the same goes for Paul too, of course. I'm glad he's doing well at Business School.

Our life has been quite hectic these past few weeks. Kolya started school and enjoys it, after a few miserable days. He's such a little dreamer though! One day he wandered home in the middle of the morning — he'd thought it was dinner time when it was only the morning break! Walked home through the streets all on his own! He's growing like a fern, and it's difficult to keep up with his needs. Clothes of course are expensive, and not always easily obtainable. But we manage all right; we're really very fortunate. Victor grumbles now and then about feeling old, which is nonsense, I tell him, because he's healthy, and young at heart. He's been producing a new opera, about building a dam; it's not as bad as it sounds. It has some nice tunes. They had a panic about getting the costumes ready in time, so for two weeks I went along and did my bit, sewing and stitching. It was very good fun, working against time, and sharing a laugh with the girls. And I have two very good pupils, who come to the apartment three times a week. So the time just flies.

Just two weeks before the new opera was due to start, we got news that Victor's mother had died, and we had to rush off to Tiflis for the funeral. It was of course not unexpected, she had lived to a ripe old age and had been ailing for some time; but it's a blow whenever it comes, and it's a good thing he's been so busy, it's helped to take his mind off it. Some friends of ours looked after Kolya. We were only gone a few days, but we missed him; and I think he was very glad to see us back.

It is a shame you have not been well enough to take that trip to visit with Hannah, nor she with you, but nice of her to telephone you on your birthday. (I'm glad our gift arrived in time.) The telephone is a wonderful thing. I keep meaning to write to her, if only to tell her how much I appreciate her superb teaching, now that I have pupils of my own! Give her my very best wishes, when you write.

Yes, it would be lovely if we could take tea together. You are always in my thoughts. I hope the gold treatment has a good effect. It is a blessing that your eyes are clearer. I hope you like the handkerchiefs I embroidered — a little bit of the Ukraine. Now it has begun to snow — the first of the winter — and I must put on my coat and hat to go out and fetch Kolya from school. Our love, and the season's greetings, to you all.

Affectionately,
Lisa, Victor and Kolya

V

The Sleeping Carriage

HE AWOKE, FOR about the tenth time that night, and groaned to himself when he realized it still wasn't dawn. He listened to the sounds of rustling in the wall. He would never hear those sounds again. His mouth was dry with excitement; he wanted to command the sun to rise, so they could start out on their journey. The first time he had 'moved house', it had only been a matter of crossing the city; and a miserable change it was too. This place was a dump. But today they would be crossing borders, deserts, mountain ranges — and it would go on and on. Tomorrow night he would be sleeping in a train! He couldn't wait for it to start. Surely it must be nearly morning and he would hear his mother stirring soon?

They would play cards on the train, Pavel and he. Yet it was a pity the others weren't coming because you could have a more exciting game with four. Pavel was all right, but not much fun on his own. He would miss the rest of the gang. There were several things he would miss: the scavenging around, seeing what you could pick up without getting caught; and not having to go to school. Yes, that would be awful, having to go to school again, though it would please his mother. Not that she didn't keep him busy enough as it was; but after a couple of hours she got tired, fortunately, and let him go out of doors. Would he miss this room? Yes, a little, because although it was a dump it was home. But there'd be plenty of things to make him forget it very quickly.

He would miss Shura, though. Shura was really his best friend. Though he wondered if Shura perhaps liked Pavel better. He would not admit it but he was a little jealous. His mother said that probably the other children would be allowed to follow on, later. He would miss visiting Shura's home, because there was always some food there. He liked Shura's mother; she was young and lively. He wished his own mother wasn't so old. It was embarrassing to have an old woman for a mother. She also had that very bad cough, which went on and on, and he hoped she wouldn't die. He heard her coughing now, on the other side of the curtain. Good, that might mean it was nearly time to get up.

The strange thing about sleeping was that you had no idea what time it was. You could sometimes get an idea from looking at the window, but with the curtain drawn across his bed he couldn't see the window. It was pitch-dark. He had the horrifying thought that it might be only about midnight! Surely it couldn't be! It felt late in the night, somehow; and he knew they were going to get up very early, before dawn.

He turned over in bed, and tried to make the time pass by imagining the place where he was going. The only help to his imagination was the Bible stories his mother told him sometimes; but they weren't much help. They were also boring. It was better to fix his thoughts on the journey. He liked trains. The first time he'd travelled on one he'd been sick, his mother said, and a great nuisance — that was when he was only a baby. He didn't remember it. The longest journey he'd taken was all the way to Leningrad. That was when he had slept in a room of what used to be a real palace. He had been only five or six, but he remembered quite a lot of that holiday. There was an old man and a younger man; and when he looked over the window sill he was surprised to see water. He remembered also being on a ship once, but it was very vague. Yet memories were strange, because he actually thought he remembered his first birthday party. He recalled being held in his granny's arms to blow out the candle on the cake. Yet that was much earlier than when his mother and father had taken him on the ship. Perhaps he only imagined he remembered his first birthday because there was a photograph of it in the album. His grandmother was holding him up to blow out the candle, and his father was there too, smiling.

He imagined the sound of the train wheels taking them to Leningrad and back, and mixed it up with the rustling of the cockroaches in the wall. It made a strange tune. He liked listening to different sounds; and especially at night trying to hear sounds in the silence, or remembering sounds. He had come almost bottom of the class in music at school, and he'd told his parents he hated music; which had disappointed them. And it was true, in a way; the kind of music he was made to learn. All those boring notes. But (and this was a big secret) he was going to be a composer when he grew up. That would be a shock to his mother. If she lived till then. He stirred uneasily.

His father was old too; but nothing mattered as long as he came back. He recalled his last sight of his father — when he was still half asleep, being kissed and hugged by him and told he must be a good boy and take care of his mother. That was the worst memory of his life, just as the holiday in Leningrad was the best. Not just that night, but the weeks after, when the other children bullied him and called him names, saying his father was a traitor. That was even before some of *their* fathers had been put in prison; afterwards, it was even worse. He'd got beaten up. That was when they'd had to move. But he was sure his father was no traitor. His mother was sure too. He couldn't understand why his father should have been put in prison for having travelled abroad, years and years ago, or for putting on an opera about a cruel Tsar. Surely the prison, wherever it was, would be overrun soon; and when his father came back he would come looking for them — and they wouldn't be here! Suddenly it didn't seem such a good idea to be going away. He had a picture of his father knocking on the door, and then turning away with a sad face.

He heard his mother coughing again, and it was clear that she was wide awake. Soon she would get up, light the fire, and make breakfast. Now he snuggled down and enjoyed the warmth of the bed. She stopped coughing, and there was silence again; as if she was making up her mind to get up. He waited for the familiar sounds: the squeak of the bed, the creaking floorboard, the sigh, the swish and rustle of her clothes being put on, the scrape of her shoes. But they didn't come; only his mother's occasional cough; and he drifted half asleep again, and dreamt his father was back and all three of them were riding in a sleigh, through snowy streets.

The old woman lay thinking of the many things she still had to do. Then she climbed out, shivering, for it was a chilly autumn morning, and still dark. Rising so early, they would be in time to get seats on the train. She listened for sounds of stirring upstairs, but the Shchadenkos were not up yet. She dressed slowly, and felt a little warmer, though still she shivered. It was uncertainty and apprehension, she knew, more than the cold night; for she had saved up some warm clothes for just such an emergency, and had likewise put by some warm underwear for Kolya, which she had laid ready on his bedside chair. They would be travelling for one or even two nights on the train and it might get very cold indeed. She shuffled around in her stockinged feet, because she didn't want to waken Kolya with the clump of her shoes. Let him sleep till the last minute. He would be tired enough after his travels.

She lit the candle which she had been saving for Christmas; then kindled a fire in the stove with the last of the wood shavings. By the glow of the fire and the candle you could see she was not such an old woman, in spite of her grey hair and stiff movements — probably no more than fifty. She only seemed old to Kolya and — most of the time — to herself. When the fire was well alight, she slipped into her shoes, pulled a coat round her shoulders, quietly lifted the door latch, and felt her way out into the yard. She pulled open the door of the privy. As she crouched over the hole, trying not to breathe in the foul smell, she heard a rustle behind her, and a long grey blurred form slid past her feet and flashed out through the door, which she had learned to leave ajar for just such an exit. Shuddering, feeling still the rat's soft brush against her ankle, she tore off a piece of *Ukrainskoye*

Slovo, wiped herself quickly, stood, and pulled down her dress. When she was in the yard again, she took a deep breath. It was still not fresh air, for the Podol breathed a perpetual scent of rancid fat and rotting matter from the rubbish heaps; but she had grown used to it and, compared with the privy, it was pure and sweet. Then she returned indoors.

Keeping as silent as possible, she took off her coat, unbuttoned her dress, and poured some of the water from the bucket into the bowl, making sure there was enough left over. Water was precious: one of them had to go every day to the Dnieper to fetch it. Pulling her dress down over her shoulders, she gave herself a wash. Now she could hear the Shchadenkos moving around upstairs, a bustle of hurrying feet. It would be comforting to have Liuba's company. She put the remains of the potato peelings in the saucepan. The pancakes would warm Kolya's stomach for the journey. She relished the smell as the peelings started to sizzle.

It was time to wake her son. Not so long ago, she would have whispered in his ear, and tickled him awake. But lately he had grown modest and private, and she had put up an old curtain to divide the room and give him a chance to feel a little bit independent. So she merely stood at the curtain opening and called his name. When he groaned, she told him breakfast was almost ready. "We've got pancakes!" she said, tempting him. Though he groaned again and turned over, she knew it would not be long before he would be leaping out of bed. He was very excited about the journey.

While she was seeing to the breakfast he appeared, in his trousers and vest, took a good sniff of the delicious pancakes, and sat at the table. She told him he must wash first — but before that he must go to the toilet, because they were short of water and there wasn't enough for him to wash twice. Living in such filthy conditions, she was sure they had only kept healthy during the last three years by being very careful about cleanliness. Grumbling that he didn't need to go yet, he pulled his jacket on over his vest and banged open the door.

When they were sitting and eating the pancakes, he asked her again what she thought the place would be like, where they were going. She could only feed him scraps of her childhood lessons — the fragrant orange groves, the cedars of Lebanon . . . Jesus walking on the water . . . "I am the rose of Sharon". . . . Geography and Scripture were confused in her mind, and it was difficult to paint a convincing picture. She felt hopelessly ignorant. Geography had never been her strong point. It was beginning to get light, and she glanced out at the dreary yard with its rubbish heaps, and the backs of more slums. "It will be a paradise compared with this, Kolya," she said. "You'll see. We'll be very happy there."

But Kolya looked doubtful. He was very upset because two of his best friends, Shura and Bobik, were not Jewish and could not come. And she knew he was also bothered that his father would not be able to find them.

"Don't worry," she said, "he'll find us. They'll have lists of people who have emigrated. When he comes back to Kiev he'll be able to find out exactly where we are, and will come straight over to join us." She tried to make her voice and expression convincing, and briefly touched the crucifix at her throat. Never had it seemed the right time to tell him his father would not be coming back. She would tell him when they were settled somewhere safe, far away, where they could begin a new life.

When they had finished their meal, she washed the dishes in the last of the water, wiped them, and stowed them away in the battered suitcase. Though most of their possessions had been sold or pawned, in the effort to survive, there was still a lot to be squashed into one case. Kolya had to sit on it before she could snap the locks shut. She tied string around the case to make sure it did not burst open on the journey. Luckily it could withstand a lot of battering. It had been expensive when she had bought it, with some of the money her father had given her on her seventeenth birthday. Her mind went back to her departure from Odessa, more than thirty years ago, and she had the same queasy feeling. Her breast felt both hollow and weighed down with lead.

Besides the case, there was a paper package tied up with string. It contained a bottle of water, and some onions and potatoes. Kolya had stolen the food a few days before, during the outbreak of looting. She felt frightened sick at the risk he had run; but had decided to keep the food. It would not be easy to prove that a few vegetables had been stolen; and it would have been almost as dangerous to take them back. She entrusted the parcel to Kolya, and told him to be sure to hold on to it and not let it fall.

They put on their coats, and stood facing each other uncertainly. She knew she must not show how frightened she was. "Say goodbye to the cockroaches!" she joked. Kolya looked close to tears, and it made her realize he was still only a child, for all his grown-up ways. She hugged him and said everything would be fine, and that she was glad she would have him to take care of her.

Dumping their baggage in the tiny hall, they climbed the stairs to see if the Shchadenkos were ready. But Liuba and the children were dashing about in complete disarray still. With three children and a mother-in-law — an old woman who needed tending hand and foot — Liuba looked tired out even before the long day had begun. There were clothes scattered over the floor, and she was struggling to dress Nadia, her youngest. Pavel and Olga were doing nothing to help, as always; the old woman was complaining in the corner; and now Nadia was howling because she had only just realized they would have to leave the cat, Vaska, behind. Her mother was trying to reassure her that Vaska would be fine, she would feed well off the scraps in the back yards. But Nadia was inconsolable. "Can I do anything?" said Lisa; but Liuba shook her head, and said they had better go on, and try to claim an empty compartment; she and her brood would join them later. How she was going to get her mother-in-law to the station she didn't know, but they'd manage somehow; they always did.

Lisa's gaze fell on the cobbler's tools lying by a wood box. She looked questioningly at Liuba, and her friend blushed and dropped her eyes. Lisa knew there was no point in saying anything; she *would* take her husband's tools with her, though it was a million to one against Vanya finding his family again, even if he were released one day. Lisa felt guilty too, because there was almost nothing of Victor's left. Everything had been sold to get food. But then, she had had her parcels and letters returned, which meant his almost certain death; whereas her friend's husband was still alive somewhere, as far as she knew. He had been arrested and sentenced for grumbling to a customer about the shoddy materials he had to work with.

They could hear stirrings of life in the other tenements backing on to the yard. "You'd better go," said Liuba. "With any luck there won't be many about yet." Kolya was edging towards the door impatiently, but Lisa hovered, doubtful. Yet it seemed the best plan, to go early and claim seats. The two grey-haired women embraced, and Liuba shed a few tears. She was very emotional. As she dabbed her eyes, Kolya produced from his pocket the old pack of cards, to show Pavel he had not forgotten them. Then his mother followed him down the stairs, they picked up the case and the package, and went out into the alleyway that led to the street. Dawn had broken, but the light was still weak.

When they came out on to the street they were stunned. The whole of the Podol was on the move. Instead of being able to walk along quite quickly, they had to push their way into a great slow-moving queue as wide as the street. It was like the huge crowd Lisa had once got caught up in, edging its way towards the Kiev football stadium. But that mass had consisted of men, for the most part, and their arms had been free. This mass, surging slowly up the Glubochitsa, carried their houses on their backs, so to speak: old plywood cases, wicker baskets, carpenters' boxes. . . . And in the absence of able-bodied men, who had retreated with the army, here were invalids, cripples, women and their crying children. The old and bed-ridden had taken up their beds and walked. Some of the old women carried strings of onions round their necks, like huge necklaces. In front of Lisa and her son, a sturdy lad was carrying a very old lady on his back. Other families had evidently banded together and hired a horse and cart to carry their old and their baggage. Only the poorest of the poor lived in the Podol district, but they all had more possessions than could be carried. The crowds up ahead were massed so thick that Lisa knew she would be lucky to get seats on the train for the two of them; to save a compartment for Liuba and her brood would be out of the question.

The suitcase was very heavy — too heavy for Kolya, when he pleased her by his politeness in offering to change burdens for a while — and she was quite glad at first that there were long pauses when the crowds ahead seemed to have come to a dead halt. She was able to rest the case on the road. It was so much better than all the cases being carried by others that she felt ashamed of it. Then, during one of the involuntary halts, a terrible thing happened: an old woman in a dirty headscarf darted out from a courtyard, snatched up the case and ran with it back into the yard. Screaming at her, Lisa and Kolya pushed their way to the yard gate; but two muscular men stepped out from behind the wall and barred the entrance. There was a whole pile of goods behind the men. Lisa pleaded, cried; but the men were unmoved. The crowd was moving onwards slowly, with eyes averted. There were no police or soldiers around to whom Lisa could appeal. She turned away from the gate, tears streaming down her face. Kolya timidly put his hand in hers, and they were carried on in the crowd. She stopped crying, and dried her eyes; but felt overcome with hopelessness when she thought of the irreplaceable treasures — the clothes, letters, photograph album, the drawing by Leonid Pasternak and other precious items, so carefully packed last night.

Faces were pressed to the windows of houses, looking down on the dense mass of migrants. Some looked sorry for them, but others laughed and jeered. Soldiers lounged in gateways now, studying the passers keenly. One group of them called out, to a young woman in front of Kolya: "Komm waschen!" They pointed to the yard behind them, as if to say, "It needs cleaning out." The girl turned her head in their direction, and in so doing saw Lisa but gave no sign of recognizing her. Lisa knew her at once: she was the daughter of the first cellist at the Kiev Opera. She spoke her name — Sonia — and the girl looked round again at the elderly woman, searching her memory. At last she remembered her, though she was much changed. Lisa was afraid she would reject her approach, and would not have blamed her had she done so. It was fairly clear that, to save his family, Victor had bartered the freedom, and even lives, of several of the musicians at the Opera — including the girl's father. But Sonia seemed glad to fall in with someone she knew, however distantly, and she paused to let them draw abreast of her.

She asked Lisa if she knew what time the train was due to leave. She was worried they might be left behind. They had almost stopped moving again, and the young woman was standing on the toes of her high-heeled shoes to try and see over the crowd. It was impossible to see anything except a grey mass of heads and vehicles piled with junk. She sighed in exasperation. Her suitcase was heavy and she was weary. "You're wise to travel light," she said, nodding at Kolya's parcel.

Lisa poured out her woe over their stolen suitcase. They had nothing. "Well, try not to worry," the young woman said. "I heard a rumour they're going to send the luggage on separately and divide it up in equal shares when we reach Palestine."

Rumours — there had been nothing but rumours since Kolya and Pavel had dashed in yesterday shouting that there was a notice up on the fence and crowds of people were gathered round it. Lisa and Liuba, who had been doing some sewing together, had run out and pushed their way through the excited crowd to read the notice. As usual it was on cheap grey wrapping paper, and printed in Russian, Ukrainian and German. The order said that all Yids living in the city of Kiev and its vicinity were to report by eight o'clock on the morning of Monday, 29 September, 1941, at the corner of Melnikovsky and Dokhturov

Streets (near the cemetery). They were to take with them documents, money, valuables, as well as warm clothes, underwear, etc. Any Yid not carrying out the instruction and who was found elsewhere would be shot.

The homely, commonplace words (warm clothes, underwear, etc.) were strangely more chilling than the cold and contemptuous word "Yid". People were whispering the decree aloud, as if not understanding it. "A ghetto, a ghetto," someone whispered; and an old woman started to moan. "They're blaming us for the fires," said a white-bearded old man. The people near him instinctively glanced towards the centre of the city, where the air was still scorched from the fires that went on burning.

The Germans had entered the city a week ago as triumphant deliverers from the Russian yoke, and had been welcomed with bread and salt. Ukrainian and Jewish barbers clipped the hair of affable German officers. No one mourned the fact that German generals — rather than Communist Party bosses and privileged actors and musicians — occupied the luxurious flats of the Kreshchatik. Then, when the new occupants had nicely settled in with the paintings and grand pianos, the Kreshchatik was turned into an inferno. Germans and Ukrainians alike were blown to bits. Lisa, like everybody else, had gone to look at the immense fire burning the historic city centre, where she had once lived.

Clearly the Red Army — who were blaming the Nazi barbarians, as though they would have been likely to blow themselves up! — were responsible for the explosions. A few soldiers had stayed behind to detonate the bombs. But then the rumour went about that the Jews were to blame. That was why this decree had been posted: the Germans were blaming the Jews, and were sending them to a ghetto, probably in Poland. Yet, even if the Jews *were* responsible, why punish everybody for the work of a few?

It was while the two women stood in front of the grey wrapping paper that Liuba Shchadenko had made a saintly offer. She led Lisa out of the crowd and whispered, "*You* don't have to go. You're not a Jew. I can look after Kolya for you. I'll hardly notice one more." Lisa flared in anger: that Liuba could imagine she would send her son off to a ghetto without her! But immediately she was overcome by the grandeur of her friend's generosity. Tears sprang to her eyes. How much she owed to this woman already. When Victor had been taken, and she and Kolya had to leave their apartment, Liuba Shchadenko, a poor widow who did sewing for the company, stepped in to offer her a room in her tiny tumbledown house. A woman she hardly knew! She said it was because Victor had given her work, when she was left without a breadwinner, carrying Nadia, and she was only repaying a debt. But her repayment had not stopped at the rent-free room. She had kept putting bits of sewing in Lisa's way, to keep them from starving. And now this offer! She was more than a saint — an angel. Lisa pressed her hands, and said, "No, but thank you! We'll all go together."

Mercifully, better news was arriving. There was no question of their being sent to a ghetto. Were not the Germans a decent, civilized race? Lisa knew that well, having lived half her life among friendly German voices. Even the Communists had had nothing but good to say about the Germans, in the last couple of years before the war. Why, when the Kreshchatik had blown up, the Germans had risked their own lives, sending squads of men around the city, warning people to leave their homes! They had rescued old people, children, invalids — the very people whom they were now supposed to be sending to a ghetto! No, they were being evacuated further behind the lines, to safety. But why, somebody asked, evacuate the Jews first? The answer came swiftly, confidently: "Because the Jews are related to the Germans."

And yet — how to explain the callous, brutal tone of the proclamation? "All Yids. . . Any Yids. . ." But that only sounded brutal to the Jews themselves; for the Germans, it was just a neutral description, like "warm clothes, underwear, etc.". And look — a young woman pointed out — they had written Melnikovsky Street and Dokhturov Street, which did not exist; they meant Melnikov and Degtyarev; so the order had gone through the hands of a bad translator. He or she had given it the unpleasant tone.

Lisa knew the German version carried exactly the same tone; but kept quiet about it. She did not know what to think. Her gift of intuition had vanished like the flesh on her bones. She could only hope and pray that the prophets of doom were wrong. Then, only an hour later, when they had begun to pack, the good news had spread like lightning through the Podol: they were being sent to Palestine.

Hours dragged past, and still the end was not in sight. The bottleneck ahead of them, whatever it was, refused to ease, yet they were being pushed forward by the mass of people behind them. It was quite frightening for the mothers with small children, and Lisa started to worry about how Liuba Shchadenko would manage. She and Kolya ought to have waited for them and helped; she felt guilty. Yet at the time it had seemed sensible to set off and claim seats. She helped a harassed woman close to her, who had four children to cope with, the oldest no more than ten or eleven, and the youngest about eighteen months. Lisa took this child, a little girl, from the mother, to give her arms a rest. The baby was screaming, and Lisa tried talking baby-talk to her, which had no effect, and then hummed a melody, which turned her screams to whimpers. She was rather an ugly baby, disfigured by a hare lip, and she smelled. She needed changing. But how could you change a baby in this crowd? Probably the mother hadn't even noticed, because the people of the Podol were used to smells, and vermin of all descriptions. Lisa had never felt at home among them, and she had mixed with few of them other than Liuba. Now the baby she was holding began screaming again, and her mother wanted her back. Lisa gave her up with relief. But how angry she felt that poor little children and old people were being made to suffer like this, no doubt through someone's inefficiency.

Kolya was bored and irritable — and who could blame him? She tried to think of word games to play with him, but he wasn't interested. When they had been standing in one place for at least twenty minutes she persuaded him to show Sonia his card tricks, and reluctantly he agreed: using the young woman's suitcase as a table. Sonia smiled pleasantly at the tricks, while her eyes darted over the heads of the people in front.

She told Lisa how unhappy she was at having to leave her father's cello behind. It had been her one friend in dark days. Lisa avoided her eyes. She wanted to say she was sorry, but could not find the words.

They were inching forward for two minutes, then stopping for five. By the time they reached the long wall of the Jewish cemetery, the sun was high overhead and fierce. Lisa was stifling in her moth-eaten winter coat, but was afraid someone would snatch it if she took it off. She let Kolya remove his, telling him to hold on to it tightly; and promised him a drink of water when they were settled in the train. The Lukyanovka goods yard was quite close to the cemetery, so they did not have far to go. Surely the crowds would move forward soon ? They should have organized it better than this.

Sure enough, they surged forward a little way. Now they could actually see a barbed-wire barrier, and ranks of German soldiers and Ukrainian police, each side of the street. As at all railway stations, the noise and confusion were extreme; for, apart from the travellers, there were a great many people, Russians and Ukrainians, who had come to see relatives, friends or neighbours off, and to help with the luggage and the invalids. Some of these were trying to push their way back through the crowds, others were as determinedly pushing forward, to see their loved ones safely aboard. There were even husbands and wives saying goodbye to each other: no wonder it was taking an age to move a few yards.

Kolya breathed a huge sigh of exasperation, and his mother roughed his hair consolingly. She would not be able to do that much longer, for he was already almost as tall as she and still growing like a fern. The cellist's daughter, Sonia, passed on a message from up front that a train had just pulled out, full, and another was about to come from a siding. The people in the train, it was said, were crushed shoulder to shoulder in the corridors. For them, it would be a most unpleasant journey.

They found themselves having to press back against the cemetery wall in order to let a cab get past. The driver waved his whip furiously to clear a passage. Having delivered his load at the station barrier, he was eager to collect some more passengers. Through the gap momentarily opened up, they could see all the baggage being put into a pile on the left. It looked as if Sonia was right: their luggage was going to be sent on separately, in another train, then divided equally when they reached their destination. Unless they were supposed to have attached name tags ? That problem no longer concerned Lisa, but many around her were panicking, and some were making impromptu labels out of bits of string and torn-off paper from their parcels.

It was too late, because there was a sudden surge forward. The man in charge of the difficult operation of stacking the luggage swiftly and efficiently was a tall, handsome Cossack with a long black moustache. It was hard not to admire his striking looks and air of authority; and equally hard not to feel, now, a grain of sympathy for the soldiers and police who were having to control the swearing, bad-tempered crowd. Lisa and her son were through the barrier at last. The expected train was nowhere in sight: simply, the same crowds waiting around, in a slightly different place, but, nevertheless, giving the impression of knowing they were a stage nearer the goal. Like waiting in a cinema queue, in the old days, moving at last from the street into the crowded foyer. As if to confirm the comparison, people were having their "warm clothes" taken from them. A soldier came up and, politely, peeled Lisa's coat from her back, and took also the coat Kolya was carrying over his arm.

No one had done that for her since the days when she had arrived at a theatre for gala performances.

She shivered; not at all because she was cold. Even without her coat she felt stifled still. What was odd was the occasional sound of machine-gun fire near by. It could not be anything to worry about, but the sound was troubling, all the same, and there was an undercurrent of panic around that expressed itself in a concentration upon trivial tasks. Sonia, for example, was reapplying her lipstick. It could not be that people were being shot — perhaps people who had tried to evade the deportation order and had been rounded up. Children were crying, which was a relief, for it was a human understandable sound. It was a clear day, of course, when sounds would carry from the Germans' firing practice, or even the front lines. Lisa put her arm round Kolya and asked him if he would like a drink. He looked pale and unwell. He nodded.

She unwrapped their parcel and gave him a cup and the bottle of water. She exchanged with Sonia some onions and potatoes for some of her mouldy bread and two small pieces of cheese. Others too, sitting on bundles, were eating. The scene had somehow split in two: heightened alarm and even panic; yet also the postures of picnic parties on a country excursion. A plane was circling low overhead; the machine-gun fire could still be heard at intervals, but the people either did not hear it, or put it out of their minds while they ate their food.

The soldiers were moving people through a few at a time. They counted out a group, sent them off, waited, sent off another group. When Lisa tried to swallow a small piece of cheese but found it would not go down her throat, her mind accepted what she had known ever since they came through the barrier — that they were to be shot. She sprang to her feet, like a young woman of twenty, pulled Kolya up too, and rushed back to the barrier with him. Many were still struggling to get out, as the mass of people continued to press in. Dragging her son by the hand, she pushed through to where the tall Cossack was giving orders. "Excuse me, I'm not Jewish," she said, panting.

He asked to see her identity card. She fumbled in her bag and by God's grace came out with an out-of-date identity card, one she had been issued with on her arrival in Russia, saying that her name was Erdman and her nationality Ukrainian. He told her she could go. "What about him?" he demanded, pointing at the boy.

"He's my son. He's Ukrainian too!"

But he insisted on seeing his papers, and when she pretended they were lost he seized her handbag and found a ration card. "Berenstein!" he exclaimed. "Jew-boy! Get back in!" He pushed Kolya away, and he was lost in the struggling throng. Lisa tried to push past the Cossack, but he barred her way with his arm. "You're not a Yid, you don't have to go through, old lady," he said. "But I *must*!" she told him in a choking voice. "Please!" The Cossack shook his head. "Yids only."

"I *am* a Yid!" she cried, struggling to get past his arm. "I *am*! My father was a Yid. Please believe me!" He smiled grimly, still barring her way.

"Mayim rabbim lo yukhelu lekhabbot et-ha-ahavah u-neharot lo yishtefuha!" she screamed. The Cossack shrugged contemptuously, dropped his arm and nodded her through. She glimpsed Kolya's white face and tore her way through to him. He flung himself into her arms. "What's happening, Mama?" he said.

"I don't know, dear." She stood rocking him in her arms. An enormous soldier came up to a girl standing near them and said, "Come and sleep with me and I'll let you out." The girl's face did not change its dazed expression, and after a moment the soldier wandered away. Lisa rushed after him and tugged his sleeve. He turned. "I heard what you asked that girl," she said. "I'll do it. Only let me and my son out." He looked down expressionlessly at the crazy old woman, and turned away again.

They found themselves in a group that was being prodded to form a queue. Kolya asked if they were going to the train now, and she pulled herself together and told him, Yes, probably; and in any case she would be right behind him, and not to be afraid. Their group started to move forward. Everyone had fallen silent. They marched for some time in silence, between rows of Germans. Up in front could be seen more soldiers with dogs on leads.

Now they were in that long narrow corridor formed by two ranks of soldiers and dogs. The soldiers had their sleeves rolled up, and each of them brandished a rubber club or a big stick. Blows rained down, from both sides, on heads, backs, shoulders. Blood was running into her mouth but she hardly felt any of the blows, for she was trying somehow to protect Kolya's head. She felt the savage blows that landed on him — including the crunch of a club to his groin — but hardly at all those that landed on her own body. His scream was only one strand in a universal scream, mixed with the happy shouts of the soldiers and the barking of dogs, but it was the one that stood out, even above her own. He stumbled; she gripped his arms and kept him from falling. They were trampling straight over fallen bodies that had been set upon by the dogs. "Schnell, schnell!" laughed the soldiers.

They tumbled out into a space cordoned off by troops, a grassy square, scattered with articles of clothing. The Ukrainian police grabbed hold of people, hitting them and shouting: "Get your clothes off! Quickly! Schnell!" Kolya was doubled up with pain, and sobbing, but she started fumbling at his shirt collar. "Quickly, dear! Do as they say." For she saw that anyone who hesitated was being kicked, or struck with a knuckleduster or club. She pulled off her dress and her slip, then took off her shoes and stockings in between helping her son, because his hands were shaking and he couldn't deal with shirt buttons and shoe laces. A policeman started hitting her with his club, on her back and shoulders, and in her panic she couldn't unhook her corset fast enough, and the policeman, growing more and more angry with the slow-witted, flabby-breasted old woman, ripped the corset from her body.

There was a moment's peace, now that they were undressed. One group of naked people was being herded off somewhere. Fumbling among discarded clothes for her handbag, Lisa took a handkerchief from it and gently wiped some of the blood and tears from Kolya's face.

She saw her identity card in her bag, and came to a quick decision. Among the white shapes of dazed demented people she saw a German officer who looked as if he might be in charge. She walked determinedly up to him, thrust the identity card in his face and said in German that she and her son were there by mistake. They had come to see someone off, and become trapped in the crowd. "Look!" she said. "I'm a Ukrainian woman married to a German." The officer, frowning, muttered that too many mistakes of this kind were being made. "Put on your clothes and go and sit on that hillock." He pointed to where a handful of people were sitting. She rushed back and told Kolya to dress quickly and come with her.

Everyone on the hillock was silent, crazed with fright. Lisa found she could not take her eyes off the scene which was being enacted in front of them. One group of people after another came staggering out of the corridor, screaming, bleeding, each of them to be seized by a policeman, beaten again and stripped of clothes. The scene was repeated over and over again. Some were laughing hysterically. Some became old in minutes. When Lisa's gift or curse of second sight had failed her so miserably and her husband was snatched away in the dark, her hair had gone grey overnight — the old saying was true. But now she saw it happen in front of her eyes. In the next group but one after theirs she saw Sonia; and her raven hair turned grey in the time it took for her to be stripped and sent away to be shot. Lisa saw it happen again and again.

There was a steep wall of sand, behind which the firing could be heard. They made the people form up into short lines and led them through the gap which had been hurriedly dug in the sandstone wall. The wall hid everything from view, but of course the people knew where they were. The right bank of the Dnieper is cut by deep ravines, and this particular ravine was enormous, majestic, deep and wide like a mountain gorge. If you stood on one side of it and shouted you would scarcely be heard on the other. The sides were steep, even overhanging in places; at the bottom ran a little stream of clear water. Round about were cemeteries, woods and allotments. The local people knew the ravine as Babi Yar. Kolya and his friends had played in it often.

She saw that, as the men and women were led through the gap, they all without exception clasped their hands over their genitals. Most of the children did so too. Some of the men and boys were in agony from blows there, but it was mostly an instinctive shame, of the kind that made Kolya not want her to see him undressed. He too, on stripping, had put his hands there, partly because of pain, but also out of natural modesty. It was the way Jesus had been buried. The women were trying to cover their breasts too, with their arms. It was terrible and strange to see them concerned for their modesty, while they were being taken away to be shot.

Kolya still had his hands clasped between his thighs. He was hunched forward, and could not stop shivering. He could not stop, even though she hugged him and warmed him and tried to whisper comforting words. And he said nothing. Speech had been shocked out of him.

She knew she herself must keep from breaking down altogether, even when Liuba Shchadenko staggered out of the corridor, clasping hold of her youngest, Nadia. The mouth of the three-year-old was open wide in a soundless howl. Liuba's face was covered in blood, as were the faces of Olga and Pavel, who staggered out after her. There was no sign of old Mrs Shchadenko. For an instant, just after she had pulled her dress over her head, Liuba seemed to look straight at her friend on the hillock, accusingly. But she could have seen nothing at that moment. When she had stripped, she started fussing with the buttons of Nadia's frock, but too slowly. A policeman grabbed the child angrily, carried her like a sack of potatoes to the sandstone wall and flung her over.

"Hail Mary full of grace. . ." "Ora pro nobis. . ." Lisa mumbled the prayers of her childhood as the tears pressed out between her eyelids.

No one could have imagined the scene, because it was happening. In suite of the shouts, the screams, and the patter of machine guns, Lisa heard nothing. As in a silent film, with the white cumulus drifting across the blue sky. She even started to believe that nothing terrible was happening beyond the wall of sand. For nothing could be worse than this, or as bad. She did not know where the people were being taken, but they were not being killed. She said as much to Kolya. "We're just being frightened. You'll see, we'll go home and then Pavel and the others will turn up safe and sound." She had always found it difficult to kill even a cockroach; and there was simply no reason to kill all these people. The Germans were lining the people up, firing over their heads at the ravine side, laughing at the joke, and telling them to get dressed in fresh clothes and go and sit in the train. It was mad, but not so mad as the alternative. She went on half believing it even after she heard a Ukrainian officer say the words: "We'll shoot the Jews first and then let you out."

Those words were spoken to a young woman she had known slightly in the old days — Dina Pronicheva, an actress at the Kiev puppet theatre. Lisa recognized her as she staggered out of the corridor. Two old people, perhaps her parents, waved to Dina from another group, probably telling her to try to get away. Instead of taking off her clothes, Dina marched up to the Ukrainian officer who was standing in front of the hillock, and Lisa heard her demand to be let out. She showed him the contents of her bag. She certainly did not look Jewish — less so even than Lisa, with her rather long nose. Dina's surname was Russian and she spoke Ukrainian. The commander was convinced, and spoke the words about letting her out later. Dina now sat a few places away, lower down the hillock. Like most there, she kept her head buried in her arms: from shock, grief, and perhaps also from fear lest someone recognize her and shout, "She's a dirty Yid!", hoping to save their own skin.

Lisa remembered a prayer her nurse had taught her, to protect her from nightmares: "You who are Saviour. . ." There are things so far beyond belief that it ought to be possible to awake from them. But, although the prayer helped her a little, the nightmare continued. The world was a world of little children being hurled over a wall like sacks of grain being thrown on to a waggon; of white soft flesh being flailed as peasant women flailed drying clothes; the shiny black boot tapped by the black whip of the bored officer standing in front of the knoll. "You who are Saviour. . ."

She felt helpless to help Kolya. There was nothing to do but to pray selfishly that all the others might be killed, with merciful speed, and those on the hillock allowed to go home. She prayed this selfish prayer continuously. But she did not once regret she had not accepted Liuba's offer and stayed behind. Now she knew why she ought never to have had children. And yet the thought of Kolya, her son, being here with strangers, perhaps in that group of children from the orphanage, was a hundred times worse than the terror of death.

She passed into a trance, in which everything that was being enacted before her happened slowly and without sound. Perhaps she had literally become deaf. It was quieter than the quietest night. And the clouds drifted across the sky with the same terrible, icy, inhuman slowness. Also there were changes of colour. The scene became tinted with mauve. She watched cumulus gather on the horizon; saw it break into three, and with continuous changes of shape and colour the clouds started their journey across the sky. They were not aware of what was happening. They thought it was an ordinary day. They would have been astonished. The tiny spider running up the blade of grass thought it was a simple, ordinary blade of grass in a field.

The afternoon, that was no conceivable part of time, wore on, and it started to get dark.

Suddenly an open car drew up and in it was a tall, well-built, smartly turned-out officer with a riding crop in his hand. At his side was a Russian prisoner.

"Who are these?" the officer asked the policeman, through the interpreter: pointing to the hillock, where there were about fifty people sitting by this time.

"They are our people, Ukrainians. They were seeing people off; they ought to be let out."

Lisa heard the officer shout: "Shoot the lot at once! If even one of them gets out of here and starts talking in the city, not a single Jew will turn up tomorrow."

She caught hold of Kolya's hand and gripped it tight, while the interpreter translated the officer's order, word for word. The boy started to pant for breath, and his hand shook violently but she tightened her grip. She whispered: "God will take care of us, darling -- you'll see." A sudden sharp unpleasant smell told her he had lost control of his bowels. She hugged him tightly and kissed him; now the tears she had bottled up for most of the day rolled down her cheeks. He had neither cried nor spoken all the time they had been sitting on the knoll.

"Come on then! Let's go! Get yourselves up!" the policeman shouted. The people stood up as if they were drunk. They were quiet and well behaved, as if they were being told to go and have some supper. Maybe because it was already late the Germans did not bother to undress this group, but led them through the gap in their clothes.

Lisa and Kolya were among the last. They went through the gap and came out into a sand quarry with sides practically overhanging. It was already half dark, and she could not see the quarry properly. One after the other, they were hurried on to the left, along a very narrow ledge.

On their left was the side of the quarry, to the right a deep drop; the ledge had apparently been specially cut out for the purposes of the execution, and it was so narrow that as they went along it people instinctively leaned towards the wall of sandstone, so as not to fall in. Kolya sagged at the knees and would have fallen, but for his mother's grip on his arm.

They were halted, and turned to face the ravine. Lisa looked down and her head swam, she seemed so high up. Beneath her was a sea of bodies covered in blood. On the other side of the quarry she could just see the machine guns and a few soldiers. The German soldiers had lit a bonfire and it looked as though they were making coffee on it.

She gripped Kolya's hand and told him to close his eyes. He would not feel any pain and when they were in heaven she would be with him still. She saw his eyes close. She thought of telling him that his daddy and his real mummy were already there to meet him; but decided it was the wrong thing to do. A German finished his coffee and strolled to a machine gun. She started to whisper the Lord's Prayer, and heard her son's faint voice beside her saying it too. She did not see as much as feel the bodies falling from the ledge and the stream of bullets coming closer to them. Just before it reached them she pulled Kolya's hand, crying "Jump!", and jumped with him off the ledge.

It seemed to her that she fell for ages — it was probably a very deep drop. When she struck the bottom she lost consciousness. She was at home, at night, lying on her right side, half dreaming, and the cockroaches were rustling on the walls and underneath the bed. The rustle of the cockroaches filled her mind. Then she started to understand that the sound came from the mass of people moving slightly as they settled down and were pressed tighter by the movements of the ones who were still living.

She had fallen into a bath of blood. She lay on her right side, and her right arm lay under her, at an unnatural angle. It did not hurt. She could not move or turn, because something else, presumably another body (perhaps Kolya), was trapping her right hand. She felt no pain anywhere. Apart from the rustling, there were other strange subterranean sounds, a dull chorus of groaning, choking and sobbing. She tried to call her son's name, but no voice would come.

When it got dark, she would find Kolya and they would crawl up out of the ravine, slip into the woods, and make their escape.

Some soldiers came out on to the ledge and flashed their torches down on the bodies, firing bullets from their revolvers into any which appeared to be still living. But someone not far from Lisa went on groaning as loud as before.

Then she heard people walking near her, actually on the bodies. They were Germans who had climbed down and were bending over and taking things from the dead and occasionally firing at those who showed signs of life.

An SS man bent over an old woman lying on her side, having

seen a glint of something bright. His hand brushed her breast when he reached for the crucifix to pull it free, and he must have sensed a flicker of life. Letting go the crucifix he stood up. He drew his leg back and sent his jackboot crashing into her left breast. She moved position from the force of the blow, but uttered no sound. Still not satisfied, he swung his boot again and sent it cracking into her pelvis. Again the only sound was the clean snap of the bone. Satisfied at last, he jerked the crucifix free. He went off, picking his way across the corpses.

The woman, whose screams had not been able to force a way through her throat, went on screaming; and the screams turned to moans, and still no one heard her. In the stillness of the ravine a voice shouted from above: "Demidenko! Come on, start shovelling!"

There was a clatter of spades and then heavy thuds as the earth and sand landed on the bodies, coming closer and closer to the old woman who still lived. Earth started to fall on her. The unbearable thing was to be buried alive. She cried with a terrible and powerful voice: "I'm alive. Shoot me, please!" It came out only as a choking whisper, but Demidenko heard it. He scraped some of the earth off her face. "Hey, Semashko!" he shouted. "This one's still alive!" Semashko, moving lightly for a man of his bulk, came across. He looked down and recognized the old woman who had tried to bribe her way out. "Then give her a fuck!" he chuckled. Demidenko grinned, and started unbuckling his belt. Semashko rested his rifle, and yanked the old woman into a flatter position. Her head lolled to the left and looked straight into a boy's open eyes. Then Demidenko yanked her legs apart.

After a while Semashko jeered at him, and Demidenko grumbled that it was too cold, and the old woman was too ugly. He adjusted his clothing and picked up his rifle. With Semashko's assistance he found the opening, and they joked together as he inserted the bayonet, carefully, almost delicately. The old woman was not making any sound though they could see she was still breathing. Still very gently, Demidenko imitated the thrusts of intercourse; and Semashko let out a guffaw, which echoed from the ravine walls, as the woman's body jerked back and relaxed, jerked and relaxed. But after those spasms there was no sign of a reaction and she seemed to have stopped breathing. Semashko grumbled at their wasting time. Demidenko twisted the blade and thrust it in deep.

During the night, the bodies settled. A hand would adjust, by a fraction, causing another's head to turn slightly. Features imperceptibly altered. "The trembling of the sleeping night," Pushkin called it; only he was referring to the settling of a house.

The soul of man is a far country, which cannot be approached or explored. Most of the dead were poor and illiterate. But every single one of them had dreamed dreams, seen visions and had amazing experiences, even the babes in arms (perhaps especially the babes in arms). Though most of them had never lived outside the Podol slum, their lives and histories were as rich and complex as Lisa Erdman-Berenstein's. If a Sigmund Freud had been listening and taking notes from the time of Adam, he would still not fully have explored even a single group, even a single person.

And this was only the first day.

A woman *did* scramble up the ravine side, after dark. It was Dina Pronicheva. And when she grasped hold of a bush to pull herself over, she *did* come face to face with a boy, clothed in vest and pants, who also had inched his way up. He scared Dina with his whisper: "Don't be scared, lady! I'm alive too."

Lisa had once dreamt those words, when she was taking the thermal springs at Gastein with Aunt Magda. But it is not really surprising, for she had clairvoyant gifts and naturally a part of her went on living with these survivors: Dina, and the little boy who trembled and shivered all over. His name was Motya.

Motya was shot by the Germans while shouting a warning to the lady, whom he now looked upon and loved as his mother, because she was kind to him. Dina survived to be the only witness, the sole authority for what Lisa saw and felt. Yet it had happened thirty thousand times; always in the same way and always differently. Nor can the living ever speak for the dead.

The thirty thousand became a quarter of a million. A quarter of a million white hotels in Babi Yar. (Each of them had a Vogel, a Madame Cottin, a priest, a prostitute, a honeymoon couple, a soldier poet, a baker, a chef, a gypsy band.) The bottom layers became compressed into a solid mass. When the Germans wished to bury their massacres the bulldozers did not find it easy to separate the bodies: which were now grey-blue in colour. The bottom layers had to be dynamited, and sometimes axes had to be used. These lower strata were, with few exceptions, naked; but further up they were in their underwear, and higher still they were fully dressed: like the different formations of rocks. The Jews were at the bottom, then came Ukrainians, gypsies, Russians, etc.

A great building site of manifold tasks was created. Diggers dug the earth; hookers hauled the bodies out; prospectors (*goldsuchern*) collected valuables. It was strange and touching that almost all of the victims, including the naked, had managed to secrete something of sentimental value to take with them into the ravine. There were even tradesmen's tools. Many of the valuables had to be extricated from the bodies. The fillings Lisa had had done soon after her return from Milan were mixed with fillings from elsewhere — including some from the mouths of Freud's four aged sisters — and turned into a consignment of gold bars.

The cloakroom attendants pulled off any clothing of good quality; the builders constructed giant pyres; the stokers set the fire going by igniting the people's hair; the crushers sifted the ashes for any gold that had escaped the prospectors; and the gardeners took the ashes in wheelbarrows to spread over the allotments near the ravine.

It was a frightful task. The guards could only endure the stench by swigging vodka all day long. The Russian prisoners were given no food (but woe betide them if they weakened); and now and again one of them, driven crazy by the delicious aroma of roast flesh, would be caught thrusting his hand into the flames to pull out a piece of meat; and for such barbarism would himself add to the tempting aroma, cooked alive like a lobster. In the end, the prisoners knew, they too would feed the flames, when the last corpse had been burnt; those who lived that long. The guards knew that they knew: it was a subject of banter between the two groups. One day an extermination van arrived, full of women. When the gas was turned on, the usual banging and shouting started; but it was not long before silence fell and the doors could be opened. More than a hundred naked girls were pulled out. The drunken guards hooted with laughter. "Go on! Have a go at them! Give their cunts a christening!" They almost choked on their vodka bottles: the joke being that the girls were waitresses from the Kiev night clubs, and therefore probably not vestal virgins. Even one or two of the prisoners cracked their bony faces into grins, as they piled the girls — the dead and the still living — on to the pyre.

When the war was over, the effort to annihilate the dead went on, in other hands. After a while Dina Pronicheva stopped admitting she had escaped from Babi Yar. Engineers constructed a dam across the mouth of the ravine, and pumped water and mud in from neighbouring quarries, creating a green, stagnant and putrid lake. The dam burst; a huge area of Kiev was buried in mud. Frozen in their last postures, as at Pompeii, people were still being dug out two years later.

No one, however, saw fit to placate the ravine with a memorial. It was filled in with concrete, and above it were built a main road, a television centre, and a high-rise block of flats. The corpses had been buried, burned, drowned, and reburied under concrete and steel.

But all this had nothing to do with the guest, the soul, the lovesick bride, the daughter of Jerusalem.

VI

The Camp

AFTER THE CHAOS and overcrowding of the nightmarish journey, they spilled out on to the small, dusty platform in the middle of nowhere. They struggled over a little bridge; then it was good to breathe the sweet air, and to be ushered through without bullying or formalities. Outside, there was a line of buses waiting.

The young lieutenant in charge of Lisa's bus had a diffident stammer which relaxed the atmosphere as he read out the roll. He smiled shyly when the passengers' chuckles told him he had got one of the difficult names wrong. He had particular trouble with Lisa's. Under a film of sweat — the day was very hot — a white scar ran up his cheek and across his forehead, and a sleeve rested uselessly in his uniform pocket.

As the bus moved off in a cloud of dust, he swung himself into the empty seat in front of Lisa. "Sorry about that!" He smiled. "Don't worry!" She smiled back. "It's Polish, I take it?" he inquired; and she confirmed it was so. Actually, she was embarrassed by her error. Having decided not to use her Jewish name, Berenstein, nor her German name, Erdman — because of all the harassment she had been through when asked to produce her documents — she had wished to give her maiden name, Morozova. But for some strange reason she had given her mother's maiden name instead: Konopnicka. It was too late now to do anything about it. The young lieutenant was asking her how the train journey had been. "Terrible! Terrible!" said Lisa.

He nodded sympathetically, and added that at least they would be able to rest at the camp. It wasn't a palace, but it was fairly comfortable. Then later they would be sent on further. Lisa said he would never know how much it meant, to hear a friendly voice. She looked out at the monotonous desert, under the burning sky, and missed his next question, about what she did in her previous life. He had to repeat it. He was pleased to hear she was a singer. Though he didn't know much about music, he enjoyed it, and one of his tasks was to arrange concerts at the camp. Perhaps she would be willing to take part? Lisa said she would be glad to, if her voice should be thought good enough.

"I'm Richard Lyons," he said, offering her his left hand over the back of the seat. Awkwardly she shook it with her own wrong hand. The name stirred a memory; and astonishingly it turned out she had known his uncle. She had met him while on holiday in the Austrian Alps. "He thought you were dead," she said; and Lieutenant Lyons said, with a wry grin, "Not quite!" and patted his empty sleeve. Of course he knew the hotel where she had stayed, for he had skied there often.

"It's a beautiful place," he said.

"Yes, but so is this," she replied, glancing out again at the sand dunes. "It's a beautiful world."

She took the opportunity to ask him how one should set about trying to trace relatives. He took a notebook and a pencil from his breast pocket and, using his left hand adroitly, both to grip the notebook and to write in it, wrote the name Berenstein. He promised to make some inquiries. "You can be sure your relatives will be scanning the new lists too," he said. She thanked him for his kindness and he said it was nothing, he was happy to help.

He excused himself to move back through the bus, and exchange friendly words with some of the other passengers. Kolya, tired out, was asleep, his head lolling on her shoulder. She changed her position to make him more comfortable. Her breast was very tender. Soon, anyway, she had to wake him, because the bus drew to a halt. Despite their weariness the passengers exclaimed with pleasure, seeing an oasis — green grass, palm trees, sparkling water. And the building itself looked more like a hotel than a transit camp. Lisa and her son had a room all to themselves. It smelled sweetly of wood. The beams were of cedar and the rafters were of fir.

Kolya was soon out exploring with Pavel Shchadenko, but Lisa was so tired that she flopped into bed straight away. She was awakened, in the half-light of dusk, by a timid knock on the door. She thought it was Kolya, not quite sure if this was their room. Naked as she was, not having unpacked, she went to open the door. It was the lieutenant. He apologized, flushing to see her naked, for disturbing her rest; he ought to have realized she would have gone to bed early. His stammer was embarrassing. He simply wanted to tell her he could not find a Victor Berenstein on the lists; there was, however, a Vera Berenstein. Was that any help? It was marvellous, she said: "Thank you." He blushed again, and said he would keep trying to find her husband's name. And he thought she might like to know there was someone else with her unusual surname — a woman called Marya Konopnicka. "But that's my mother!" she exclaimed in delight. He was glad, and promised to make more inquiries.

The days flashed by. She was forever glancing round the tables at mealtimes and seeing a face she thought she recognized. Once, she even thought she caught sight of Sigmund Freud: an old man with a heavily bandaged jaw, eating — or attempting to eat — alone. She was too much in awe of him to go up and speak. Besides, it might not be he; for the old man was said to have come from England. Yet could she mistake that noble expression? When she saw him painfully take a few puffs of a cigar, through a mouth that was no more than a tiny hole, she was almost certain. She had an impish urge to write him a postcard (with a picture of the transit camp, the only one available) saying: "Frau Anna G. presents her compliments and would you do her the honour of taking a glass of milk with her?" It might make him smile, remembering the chef at the white hotel. As she toyed with the postcard, wondering whether to buy it, she suddenly realized that the old, drying-out, kindly priest in her journal had been Freud; and she wondered how she could have failed to see it at the time. It was so obvious. Then she went hot and cold, because he himself, so profoundly wise, must have been aware of it, and probably thought she was laughing at him. It would hardly be tactful, therefore, to send him a postcard which would recall it to his mind.

She passed him one day, when he was being wheeled to the medical unit. His head was drooping, and he did not see her. He looked dreadfully ill and unhappy. If she made herself known to him, she would have to cast even more serious doubts on the accuracy of his diagnosis, and that might add to his gloom. It was best to keep away, and just pray that the doctors could help him. They certainly seemed to know what they were doing. The young, overworked doctor who had seen her had been efficient but gentle. Even so, she had flinched from his examination of the painful parts. "What do you think is wrong?" he asked, as she drew back from his touch. "Anagnorisis," she sighed. The drugs he had prescribed had eased the pain.

She felt well enough to start going to language classes — in the very next classroom to Kolya's! She wanted to learn Hebrew properly. All she knew was a quotation Madame Kedrova had taught her, the Hebrew for "Many waters cannot quench love, neither can the floods drown it". She had always found languages easy, and her instructors were pleased with her progress.

Yet it seemed you did not have to be Jewish to be here; for her mother was on the lists.

On the second evening — she thought it was the second — the young lieutenant came up to her table and asked her, shyly, for a dance. Since there were plenty of musicians among the immigrants, including some members of the Kiev orchestra, they had quickly formed a dance band. There was a happy communal spirit at mealtimes; married couples did not stick selfishly together but made sure the many widows and widowers were brought into the fun. Lisa did not think she could manage to dance, because of her painful hip; but she did not want to offend the shy young officer who had been so kind. They got through the waltz somehow: he with one arm and she, more or less, with one leg! They laughed about it. She went out for a stroll with him in the cool evening. By the oasis, he showed her a beautiful bed of lilies of the valley. He did not mind that she was bleeding.

What was really amazing — what everyone agreed was a miracle — was the 'illegal immigrant' who turned up a few weeks after the first train from Kiev. She limped through the vineyard, and the grape-pickers stopped their work and stared at her amazed. Liuba Shchadenko was in her room that morning, together with her children and mother-in-law; and she heard a scraping noise at the door. She opened it and saw a little black cat at her feet, mewing up at her pathetically. It was their cat Vaska — skeletally thin, and its paws a red pulp; but unmistakably Vaska. And soon it was curled up purring in Nadia's arms, and lapping milk from a saucer. Somehow, by that amazing instinct cats possess, it had crawled through streets, deserts, and over mountains, to find them again. Soon it had flesh on its bones, was scampering around the camp, and became everyone's pet and mascot.

The black cat took its proper place in the uproarious celebration of the vine harvest. It was a bountiful crop, and the grapes were tender. For the first time, Lisa tried out her voice: only quietly, and in the chorus of a drinking song. Her voice was husky and unsure of itself, but she was not displeased; and a few people even turned their heads, as if they wondered who was singing the pleasant descant.

Everywhere you went — there was Vaska! It even interrupted the camp film show one evening. Lisa usually went to these shows because, although the films were often uninteresting — badly made documentaries — they helped her with learning the language. On the evening of Vaska's appearance she and Liuba were watching a documentary about the settlement at Emmaus. They were showing the prison hospital, which claimed a lot of success in curing hardened prisoners. Among the patients seen and interviewed was a man whom Lisa thought she recognized, a pleasant-looking man in glasses. Armed guards flanked him as he was led between buildings. He was seen playing with children in the recreation hall, and even there the armed guards watched him closely. The commentator spoke his name, Kürten, as though the audience would know it well; and Lisa *did* think she had heard the name, and possibly seen his photograph in the newspapers, but she couldn't place him. She was on the point of whispering to Liuba, when the screen was suddenly full of Vaska. . . Vaska in silhouette! The audience woke up, and roared with laughter. Somehow the cat had got into the projection room; and now she was peacefully cleaning her face on the screen! The audience clapped for more — it was much more entertaining than the film!

And one morning there were four black and white kittens, mewling and wet, tugging at Vaska's tits. Liuba said it was a miracle, as she had had her neutered. . . . But the kittens were unmistakably real, and of course Vaska became more of a heroine than ever. All the children in the camp lined up to come and fuss over the newest immigrants, and tried to bribe Nadia into letting them have one of them to keep.

But the greatest miracle of all was — as Liuba said, laughing — where was the father?

Rise up, my love, my fair one, and come away. For, lo, the winter is past, the rain is over and gone; the flowers appear on the earth; the time of the singing of birds is come, and the voice of the turtle is heard in our land. O my dove, that art in the clefts of the rock, in the secret places of the stairs, let me see thy countenance, let me hear thy voice; for sweet is thy voice, and thy countenance is comely.

The quotation came in a letter from a totally unexpected source. She was in the fields when a man came round with mail, and when she saw the familiar, forgotten handwriting she had to leave the long line of gleaners and rush to the only secret place available to her, the latrines. So many emotions of the dead past swept over her that she really did need to go. During her years in

Kiev she had seen Alexei's name often in newspapers, and seen his picture, standing to attention in rows of uniformed men. Then she had read of his arrest and his sensational confessions. It rejoiced her heart that he had not been shot but allowed to partake in the diaspora.

He wrote that he had been imprisoned for a short while at Emmaus, and was now a changed man. Now he was at a settlement in the mountains of Bether. Conditions were tough, but they were working to create a better life. When he had seen Lisa's name on the lists, he had known at once that he still loved her, and he wished her to come and share his life with him.

Liuba, because she did not want her friend to go, pressed upon her the advantages of going to Alexei. He had not, of course, mentioned marriage, but the laws of the new land discouraged formal ties.

But Lisa wrote back that it was too late. She still loved him, too. But if she went to live with him they would always be haunted by the figure of a child. They both had too much on their consciences.

One day she was thrilled to hear Vera Berenstein's silver voice over the wireless. Unusually for Vera, she was singing a religious song, a setting of the Twenty-third Psalm. Her voice seemed more lovely than ever. Then, thanks to her friendship with Richard Lyons, Lisa was able to hear the silvery voice over a crackly telephone. Vera confirmed that her husband was not over here — just yet. She was excited, full of questions about her son. Lisa was, in fact, preparing him to meet his real mother: mentioning her name often, as if casually; reminiscing about her.

This was hard for her; much harder than the gentle work she had started to do in the fields. She shed tears privately over it. It was hard because she felt she was Kolya's mother, and *he* felt she was his mother; and yet she had to prepare the way for him to return to the woman who had given him birth. It would be much less hard to let Victor go, if and when he arrived. She was inwardly glad he was not yet here; and felt remorseful about it.

Much though she loved him, her soul did not see him as her true and eternal husband. As if in penance for her guilt, she tried to help people as much as possible.

She tried to help the old man she believed to be Freud Richard let her browse through the records of people who had moved on to settlements. The problem was that she could not remember the married name of Freud's daughter. But when she found the name Sophie Halberstadt, with a small son called Heinz, she thought these must be the right persons, and she wrote a brief letter to Frau Halberstadt. As though in reward for her good deed, she stumbled on the record card of her old friend in Petersburg, Ludmila Kedrova. And when she returned to her room, by one of those strange coincidences she found a letter waiting for her on her bed. It was from Ludmila, saying she had read Lisa's name on the lists, and was overjoyed that she was safe. She, Ludmila, was not well enough yet to travel far, but hoped to see her soon. They were treating her breast with radium; which was painful and made her sick. This was strange, because Lisa thought she remembered that her breast had been removed, in an effort to save her life. She worried about this, hoping it didn't mean that her other breast was infected.

On a roasting, windless day, Richard Lyons drove her in an army jeep further down the lake shore. Her mother wanted to meet her somewhere where it was quiet. He stopped the jeep under the shade of some fig trees, and told her to walk over the dune. On the crest of the dune she looked towards the lake, with the hills of Judaea beyond, and saw a woman standing. The woman's face was turned away, as if engrossed by the cloud of red dust over her shoulder on the horizon. Not even the hem of her dress was stirring. When she turned her face towards Lisa, Lisa saw that all the left side consisted of dead skin.

They walked along the shore together. They did not know what to say. Finally Lisa broke the silence by saying that she was sorry about the burns on her face.

"Yes, but I deserve it; and wonderful healing goes on over

here." Her daughter recognized that voice from half a century ago, and her breast churned.

The woman looked intently into Lisa's face and began to recognize features of her child. Noticing the cross, she said, "It's mine, isn't it? I'm glad you've kept it."

Still there was embarrassment and shyness between them.

Lisa, to break the painful silence, asked her what conditions were like in her settlement, which was the one at Cana.

Her mother gave a sad smile. "Well, it's not the lowest circle, by any means."

Lisa smiled too, politely, but was puzzled; she remembered her mother's irritating habit of never answering your questions directly.

"Your aunt is coming over," said her mother.

"Oh! When?"

"Soon."

A raven flew across the water, a morsel of bread in its mouth.

"Yury too, quite soon." Her mother's wistful, beautiful hazel eyes glanced sideways at Lisa. "You should get to know your brother. Of course I'm sure he was jealous when you came along. You're very different; he takes after his father, that's plain."

Lisa took her mother's hand. Their hands were fumbling and awkward. "Your father's here, did you know that?" her mother asked. "He's in isolation."

"He always was!" said Lisa; and the quip made them both chuckle, and broke the ice finally.

Lisa said: "Are you in touch with him?"

"Oh yes."

"Will you give him my love?"

"Yes, of course. Oh, and his folk — and mine — send their love, and they're very anxious to meet you."

The young woman nodded, pleased. They had fallen into step, walking quietly over the sand. Lisa opened her mouth to ask a question; but thought better of it. It was much too early. Besides, it was really just curiosity; it wasn't important to know. The only important, terrible thing had been the *death*; and now she knew that didn't apply, for her mother had not died, she had emigrated.

But as if by intuition her mother sighed, and said, "I expect you know what happened?"

"I know the bare facts. Not the circumstances. But you don't have to talk about it if you don't want to. It's really not that important. I'd have been just as shocked if you'd been attending a conference of nuns "

Her mother laughed. "That wouldn't have been likely! No, I don't mind talking about it. Your uncle's a nice man. He didn't have an easy time with Magda. He was healthy and normal, but her desires ran in an entirely different direction. She could do very little for him. She's not to be blamed for that; she didn't find out until it was too late. We were both terribly innocent when we got married. And young. As ignorant as mayflies. Do you understand?"

"Yes," said Lisa. "Yes, it's beginning to make sense."

"She knew what was happening between us — at least in the beginning — and I had the feeling she was even quite relieved." She looked anxiously at her daughter.

"So in *fact*," said Lisa, as the mistiness began to clear, "when all three of you . . . she really wanted — ?" She looked at her mother, blushed, and looked away again.

"Yes, probably. It was her suggestion. Franz and I found it very embarrassing. But later on she wanted *all* of it to stop — I suppose because she was lonely and jealous — so your uncle and I had to meet in secret. That was the unforgivable sin."

"Did Father know?"

"He knew, but it was never mentioned. We hadn't been sleeping together since — practically since Yury was born. Well, that's not quite true — of course! Once in a blue moon. He was very busy. He had his work, his espionage, his mistress. He didn't care what I did, so long as appearances were kept up."

The sun was at its fiercest, and Lisa started to feel unwell. It was a draining experience, hearing her mother's confession. She asked if they might sit down; there was a rock which provided a

little shade. They sat, resting their backs against the burning
rock. Her mother asked anxiously if she felt all right, and Lisa
said she just felt a bit faint, because of walking in the hot sun.
Her mother asked her if she would like a drink, and when Lisa
said yes she unbuttoned her dress and put her arm round her
daughter to draw her to her breast. The first refreshing drops
cooled Lisa's blood and her head stopped spinning. She took her
lips away, and rested her hand reverently on her mother's ample
white breast, tipped with the orange nipple. "I remember it!"
she said with a smile. Her mother returned her smile, saying,
"Drink as much as you like. I've always been blessed with plenty
of milk."

"But how — ?" said Lisa; and her mother said, with a sigh,
"There are so many orphans being sent over. There are never
enough wet-nurses. It's a way of making myself useful."

Lisa sucked contentedly, first at one nipple and then the
other. Her hand, embracing her mother inside her dress, felt the
stiff bones, and she smiled to herself to think that her mother still
wore the old-fashioned corselet. When she had finished drinking
and her mother had fastened her dress, she undid her blouse and
let her mother suck. She felt very happy with the lips sucking her
nipple, and remarked, stroking her mother's still thick, blond
hair, that she envied her the experience of suckling babies. Fas-
tening her blouse, blushing at her mother's question, she
explained that she had milk because of the young English lieutenant. She said how much she liked him, and he seemed to need
feeding and comforting, he brought out her maternal feelings.

Feeling fresh and strong again, they stood up and resumed
their walk along the lake shore. Marya Konopnicka said, "I felt I
was being kind to your uncle, in much the same way. Without, I
thought, hurting anyone unduly. Consoling him. Of course we
partly deceive ourselves."

"Yes, I *saw* you consoling him!" the young woman said, with a
sly sidelong grin.

"I know! Oh, that was terrible! It almost gave us heart
failure! We could only pray you were too young to understand,

but obviously you weren't. I'm sorry, Lisa darling. You see, we had no idea you were still on the yacht. Sonia had strict instructions to —"

"I didn't mean that time: I meant, in the summer-house!" She smiled teasingly, but her mother was serious, puzzled. "We *never* did anything in the summer-house; or anywhere where we might be seen. It was nearly always on the yacht; if your father was at work and your aunt preferred to stay behind. We were always very careful."

She coloured as light dawned. "Wait! Oh yes, I remember now! Yes, just once! Oh, that was very foolish of us! Did *you* see us? I didn't think you were even walking then! Yes, of course I remember! I was painting, wasn't I, on the beach? My thoughts were straying. . . . It must have been a dreadful picture! It was a very warm day, wasn't it? Almost like this. Then your uncle and aunt strolled down, and Magda wanted to lie in the sun, so Franz and I went for a walk in the grounds. Oh yes, heavens!" She smiled, and the flush, on the unburned side of her face, deepened. "We were only kissing, weren't we?"

Lisa shook her head vigorously, mischievously. "You were only half *naked*!"

"*Was* I? Oh my God! It's true! I remember! We must have been mad!" She let out a sudden, rich laugh, and Lisa saw the pearly, even teeth she knew so well. "There was a very strong sexual attraction, I have to admit that. Of course I tried to persuade myself I was in love. And, you know, I'd quote Pushkin: 'When we meet again / In the shade of olive trees / Beneath a sky that's always blue, / My dearest, we will share love's kiss. . .' — that sort of thing, by the ream! It's always hard for us women to admit it's mainly sexual desire. You'd probably find it more forgivable if it *had* been an immortal love; but I honestly can't say it was."

"No, you've got me wrong," said Lisa. "I've nothing to forgive. I just find it *interesting*." She took her mother's hand again. "In fact I can understand it. The excitement of travelling in a train to meet your lover, knowing he was travelling, just as excitedly, towards *you*. I used to think quite a lot about that."

"Yes!" admitted her mother, smiling sadly.

"Converging lines moving across the map! Sick with desire —
hardly able to wait! And the pleasure of its being *forbidden*."

Her mother inclined her head. "Yes, that too! It was a great
sin."

"Well, even if it was, it's the future that counts, not the past. I
know that sounds banal, but it's true."

Her mother stopped, put her head in her hands, and stood
shuddering. "The fire! That was awful, awful!" She went on
shuddering for a long time. Then she lowered her hands and
said, in a shaky voice: "It was the second night, I think. We
hadn't seen each other for three months, and we were engrossed
in each other. You must know how it is, when you're lying in bed
with someone, your senses are less acute, everything outside you
is shut out. We didn't hear or smell anything. Then, when we
had finished, we smelt smoke and started coughing. We heard a
roaring sound outside our door. Franz went to open the door,
and outside it was simply an inferno." She writhed, as if caught
by a flame again; herself like a flame.

"Well, it's over," said Lisa, taking her mother's hand.
Gradually the woman became calm.

"Anyway," continued Lisa, "I think wherever there is love, of
any kind, there is hope of salvation." She had an image of a
bayonet flashing over spread thighs, and corrected herself
hastily: "Wherever there is love in the heart."

"Tenderness."

"Yes, exactly!"

They strolled further along the shore. The sun was lower in
the sky and the day cooler. The raven came skimming back, and
a shiver ran up Lisa's spine. She stopped. "Is this the Dead Sea?"
she asked.

"Oh, no!" said her mother, with a silvery laugh; and
explained that it was fed by the Jordan River, and that river, in
turn, was fed by the brook Cherith. "So you can see the water is
always pure and fresh." Her daughter nodded, greatly relieved,

and the two women walked on.

White was the wind that came off the hills. The sun set on the desert, and its light through a distant dust storm streaked into circles and formed the likeness of a rose.

Their walk along the lake brought them to a small village, and they went into a tavern to have something to eat. The two women felt strange, as there were only men in the tavern — fishermen discussing their day's catch, over a glass of wine. The men politely ignored the strangers. The landlord, who welcomed them courteously, was very old, quavery, and slow in his reactions. When he shuffled across to refill their glasses, he paused when Lisa's glass was two-thirds full, and she put her hand over it to indicate that she didn't want any more. But the landlord resumed his hospitable act, and the wine flowed on to the woman's hand, and from there streamed steadily on to the table. She did not move her hand away, and the landlord carried on pouring. Lisa thanked him, with a grave face, but as he shuffled away with the empty bottle, the two women shook with silent laughter. Lisa's mother didn't know what to do with herself, she clasped her arms over her stomach, twisted in her chair, put her head in her hand to hide the tears that sprang from her eyes, bit her lip, pointed at Lisa's wet hand and went into another spasm.

There was a telephone booth in the tavern. Lisa was still choking with mirth when she went into it and picked up the phone. She asked for the number her mother had given her. When her father answered, it was hardly any different from the old days:

"How are you, Father?"

"Quite well. How are you?"

"Oh, I'm fine."

"Do you need any money?"

"No, I'm all right."

"Well, let me know if you need anything. Take care of yourself."

"Yes. And you."

But at least she had spoken to him, over the bad line, and some day they might even have a conversation.

By the time Lisa had returned to the camp, a full moon was shining, in a sky of tranquil stars. But there was nothing tranquil about the scene that met her. In the camp grounds, and stretching far out into the desert, there were tents, standing, or in the process of being erected. They stretched away to the horizon on every side. Young officers were directing the huge operation. Lisa caught sight of Richard Lyons, his thin face gleaming with sweat in the moonlight, and the scar livid. He was darting about here and there, his one good arm directing his toiling helpers in their tasks, his baton flickering like a shaman's stick. He caught sight of Lisa, ordered his sergeant to "carry on", and came over to her. "Why, it's the r-rose of Sharon!" he said, smiling. It was the teasing, affectionate nickname he had given her. He explained that more than a dozen trainloads had come in today. Each day there were more. The faster extra huts were built, the sooner they were filled and more were needed. But no one could, or would, be turned away; for they had nowhere else to go. Sticking his baton in his belt, he fished a packet of cigarettes from his pocket, opened it, took out a cigarette, put it in his mouth, fished out a box of matches, opened it, struck the match, lit his cigarette, put match box and cigarette packet back in his pocket — all with the one adroit left hand. He puffed the cigarette and watched with her the silently frenzied moonlit scene.

"Where Israel's tents do shine by night!" he quoted.

Many thousands of immigrants were waiting, standing by their pathetic wooden suitcases and holding their bundles of rags tied up in string. They looked, not sad — listless; not thin — skeletal; not angry — patient. Lisa sighed. "Why is it like this, Richard? We were made to be happy and to enjoy life. What's happened?" He shook his head in bafflement, and breathed out smoke. "*Were* we made to be happy? You're an incurable optimist, old girl!" He stubbed the cigarette, and took the baton from his belt. "We're desperately short of nurses," he said. "Can you help?" He pointed his baton towards the casualty unit. Camp beds had spilled out on to the grounds. White figures were scurrying among them. "Yes, of course!" she said. She hurried towards the unit, breaking into a run; and only then did she realize that all day her pelvis had not hurt, nor her breast.

She smelt the scent of a pine tree. She couldn't place it. . . . It troubled her in some mysterious way, yet also made her happy.